W9-BDX-543

Duke would have to tell Carol the truth.

And when he did, she would hate him for what he'd done. Not that he could blame her. She had made no secret of how she felt about the man who'd been her late husband's partner. To discover that the man with whom she'd made such passionate love was the same man she'd despised, the man she blamed for everything, would just about destroy her.

If only he had more time. Maybe if she had time to fall in love with the person he was now, she would realize that the man she'd once known no longer existed. . . .

Dear Reader,

The hits just keep on coming here at Intimate Moments, so why not curl up on a chilly winter's night with any one of the terrific novels we're publishing this month? American Hero Duke Winters, for example, will walk right off the pages of Doreen Roberts's *In a Stranger's Eyes* and into your heart. This is a man with secrets, with a dark past and a dangerous future. In short—this is a man to love.

The rest of the month is just as wonderful. In *Diamond Willow* one of your favorite authors, Kathleen Eagle, brings back one of your favorite characters. John Tiger first appeared in *To Each His Own* as a troubled teenager. Now he's back, a man this time, and still fighting the inner demons that only Teri Nordstrom, his first love, can tame. Terese Ramin's *Winter Beach* is also a sequel, in this case to her first book, *Water From the Moon*. Readers were moved by the power of that earlier novel, and I predict equal success for this one. Two more of your favorites, Sibylle Garrett and Marilyn Tracy, check in with, respectively, *Desperate Choices* and *The Fundamental Things Apply*. Sibylle's book is a compelling look at an all-too-common situation: a woman on the run from her abusive ex-husband seeks only safety. In this case, though, she is also lucky enough to find love. Marilyn's book is something altogether different. A merger of past and present when a scientific experiment goes wrong introduces two people who never should have met, then cruelly limits the time they will have together, unless . . . You'll have to read the book to see how this one turns out. Finally, welcome new author Elley Crain, whose *Deep in the Heart* is a roller-coaster ride of a story featuring a divorced couple who still have an emotional tie they would like to deny, but can't.

In coming months look for more great reading here at Silhouette Intimate Moments, with books by Paula Detmer Riggs, Rachel Lee (the next of her Conard County series), Marilyn Pappano and Ann Williams coming up in the next two months alone. When it comes to romance, it just doesn't get any better than this!

Leslie Wainger
Senior Editor and Editorial Coordinator

AMERICAN HERO

IN A STRANGER'S EYES

Doreen Roberts

Silhouette ™
INTIMATE MOMENTS®

Published by Silhouette Books New York

America's Publisher of Contemporary Romance

If you purchased this book without a cover you should be aware
that this book is stolen property. It was reported as "unsold and
destroyed" to the publisher, and neither the author nor the
publisher has received any payment for this "stripped book."

SILHOUETTE BOOKS
300 East 42nd St., New York, N.Y. 10017

IN A STRANGER'S EYES

Copyright © 1993 by Doreen Roberts

All rights reserved. Except for use in any review, the reproduction
or utilization of this work in whole or in part in any form by any
electronic, mechanical or other means, now known or hereafter
invented, including xerography, photocopying and recording, or in
any information storage or retrieval system, is forbidden without
the permission of the publisher, Silhouette Books, 300 E. 42nd St.,
New York, N.Y. 10017

ISBN: 0-373-07475-1

First Silhouette Books printing February 1993

All the characters in this book have no existence outside the
imagination of the author and have no relation whatsoever to
anyone bearing the same name or names. They are not even
distantly inspired by any individual known or unknown to the
author, and all incidents are pure invention.

®: Trademark used under license and registered in the United
States Patent and Trademark Office and in other countries.

Printed in the U.S.A.

Books by Doreen Roberts

Silhouette Intimate Moments

Gambler's Gold #215
Willing Accomplice #239
Forbidden Jade #266
Threat of Exposure #295
Desert Heat #319
In the Line of Duty #379
Broken Wings #422
In a Stranger's Eyes #475

Silhouette Romance

Home for the Holidays #765

DOREEN ROBERTS

was hooked from the moment she opened the first page of a Mary Stewart novel. It took her twenty years to write her own romantic suspense novel, which was subsequently published, much to her surprise. She and her husband left their native England more than twenty years ago and have since lived in Oregon, where their son was born. Doreen hopes to go on mixing romance and danger in her novels for at least another two decades.

To my sister, Vanda, and my nieces, Donna and Missy. My research for this book was all the more enjoyable for their company, and I would never have made it through the tunnel beneath the Thames without them. Thanks for being there.

Prologue

The sound came out of the black night, startling and deadly. He recognized it instantly. He'd heard that crack and the menacing whine that followed so many times in the past. Even before the car bucked into its fatal slide, he knew what the explosive vibrations beneath him signified. Someone had shot out a tire.

At three-thirty a.m. the freeway was clear of traffic, except for taillights disappearing around the bend up front and the twin pinpoints of light behind him. He'd been doing close to ninety. Cursing softly, he fought the wheel. He knew what the odds were.

It had been raining—the first heavy shower since late August. Washington had basked in an Indian summer for the past two months. Now the locked wheels of the Mercedes slid across the damp, oily lanes like a tank on skis.

The man at his side swore viciously in the darkness, just once, then sat tense and waiting. It seemed like a dream, or more likely a nightmare, played out in slow motion. The wheel seemed so light in his hands, yet he couldn't get a grasp on it.

He saw the guardrail coming at him and knew it was all over. How had they known? Someone must have tipped them off. Who? Damn it, who? At the very last moment he folded his arms around his head and closed his eyes.

He lay on a bed. A hospital bed. He tried to lift his head to look around, but soon discovered that the slightest movement had an interesting effect. Something like slamming into the heart of a raging volcano.

He had been in pain before. But never like this. Dear God, never like this. He squeezed his eyes shut and ground his teeth to stop from screaming while he waited for the murderous wave of agony to cease.

Something pricked his arm. He barely felt it above the sickening sensation that threatened to overwhelm him. He heard a soft, feminine voice, but couldn't make out the words.

Gradually the pain started to subside. He made himself relax, knowing that soon he would drift into the blessed relief of sleep.

There was something bothering him. Something he had to know. He struggled to stay awake. To think. To remember. All he could remember were flames. Hot, burning, excruciating heat. The memory was so horrifying he shut down his mind and let the darkness take him.

He seemed to have tubes sticking into every spare inch of his body. He frowned at the bottle swinging hazily above his head. The frown didn't feel right. He lifted a hand to touch his forehead and found his fingers encased in thick, white bandages.

"I'm glad you're awake," a man's voice said. A voice he knew well. Remembering the agony of movement, he very carefully turned his head. He had to squint to see clearly. Again his face felt odd, tight, as if the skin didn't want to move.

The man seated on a chair leaned forward. His silver hair looked striking against his deep tan. Piercing blue eyes looked at him with concern, and something else—a kind of apprehension that made him go cold.

"Hello, Charles." At least, that's what he'd tried to say. The words came out in a horrible growl.

"Don't try to speak. Just listen, okay?" Charles Findley shifted his chair and lowered his voice. "I haven't got long, the doctor will be back at any minute. Do you remember what happened?"

Unwilling to test his endurance against the pain again, he moved his head slowly, first right and then left. Then he fixed his gaze on the first familiar sight he'd seen since the nightmare had begun.

Charles looked agitated as he passed a hand across his damp forehead. "You had an accident. Car wreck on the way to the airport. There was a fire, you—"

He heard the door open. A brisk voice said, "Your time is up, Mr. Findley." The voice sounded irritated.

Charles gave him a quick nod that he knew was meant to be reassuring. For a moment the piercing blue gaze fastened on his face. He clearly read the warning in that look. "I'll be back," Charles promised, and hurried out the door.

"Well, it's good to see you alert at last, Mr. Winters." The doctor moved to the bottom of the bed and picked up the chart.

Mr. Winters. That was a new one. Obviously one that Charles had dreamed up. Personally he would have been much more inventive. He wondered what Charles had come up with for his first name. Probably something equally as unimaginative.

The doctor went on talking, but he wasn't listening. He was remembering what it was that had eluded him so far. Car wreck, Charles had said. He remembered nothing about that except the flames. And one intense question that had burned into his brain as fiercely as the heat had burned into his flesh.

Someone had betrayed him. Who? It could have been only one of three people. He weighed the choices as carefully as his scrambled thoughts allowed. And he didn't like the answers he came up with. He didn't like them at all.

Chapter 1

"What I want to know," Duke Winters said, as he lowered his lean frame into a chair, "is why Charles felt it necessary to name me after a damn dog."

The man behind the desk lifted his head and smiled in apology. "I guess it was the first name that came to mind. In all the confusion Charles didn't have much time to think."

"Well, I guess it could have been worse. It could have been Rover. Or Spot."

"It could at that." Royce Westcott's dark eyes sparkled with guarded amusement behind the thick lenses of his glasses. "So how're you doing, Duke? You look real good. Real good."

Duke sat on his rising resentment. Royce meant well. Even so, he couldn't help the dry question that slipped out anyway. "Compared to what?"

Royce's smile vanished, and he lowered his chin. Duke studied the ever-increasing bald patch on his ex-commander's head before adding, "I feel good. Considering."

Royce nodded, still unable to meet Duke's gaze. "I guess...it will take some getting used to. Though it has been almost a year."

It was amazing, Duke thought wryly, how he could have known this man for so long and never have noticed how obtuse he could be. "Not quite. I didn't get a good look at myself for six months."

"Okay, six months. But they did a hell of a job. A hell of a job. If you could have seen—" Mercifully, he broke off the rest of the sentence.

"Don't think I'm not grateful," Duke said quietly. "But it's not easy to look in the mirror every day and see the face of a stranger."

This time Royce did look up. "I can understand that. But bear in mind, Duke, that without your new face, you would be a walking target for the rest of your life. It was vital that we convince everyone that both you and Mack died in that wreck.

"I can't imagine the hell you must have been through this past year, but at least now you'll be able to live a normal life, without having to look over your shoulder every second. There are few men, if any, that could walk away from your kind of work with that guarantee."

"I imagine there are few men, if any, who could walk away from the organization, period."

"Now you're being melodramatic."

Duke saw Royce's lips tighten and knew he'd hit a button. If there was one man who was loyal to the agency, it was Royce Westcott. Deciding to change the subject, he leaned back in the chair and folded his arms across his chest.

It still gave him a feeling of triumph to manage that small feat. For months he hadn't been able to move as much as an eyelid. Probably because he hadn't had much eyelid left to move.

His therapy had been brutal, agonizing and frustrating as hell. But with one purpose in mind, he'd fought with every ounce of strength he could muster to get back on his feet, then to walk, and finally, to begin the long road back to normal health.

Normal, he thought, running a finger across his new eyebrow. Would he ever feel normal again? He had a new name. His hair, once a sun-bleached dark blond, had grown back much darker and now had a coarse texture to it. It was longer than he was used to, in order to hide the hairline scars.

His face had been reshaped and rebuilt, even his voice had been drastically altered by the intolerable heat of the flames. The contacts changed his amber eyes to dark brown. No one would recognize him now. No one. Which reminded him of why he was there.

"So where's Charles?" he asked abruptly. "I've seen him only once since the accident. And when I called the office they gave me the runaround. Even though I gave them the code."

"The code's been changed." Again Royce's gaze slid away.

"Oh?" Duke narrowed his eyes. "Since when?"

"Since . . . some months ago. We felt it necessary."

"We?"

"Charles and I."

He knew why they'd changed it. The agency never took chances. His cover had been blown. In spite of his altered looks, he was still a risk. Duke unfolded his arms and leaned forward. "So where is Charles?"

"Vacation."

Several moments passed while Duke digested this interesting piece of information. In the ten years since Charles had been divorced, Duke had never known him to take a vacation. "When's he coming back?"

Royce fidgeted with some papers on his desk. "I'm not sure. He needed a break. A long break."

"So what's his problem?"

Royce's chin came up, and his eyes had lost all trace of amusement. "You seem to forget, Duke, that you are no longer a member of this establishment. Don't get out of line, or I'll have to ask you to leave."

Okay. So now he was mad. But he was damned if he was going to let this pompous ass know that. Taking a slow breath, Duke deliberately relaxed his muscles. It was a trick he'd become very adept at performing. He waited, counting off five seconds in his head, then said calmly, "I just wanted to talk to him, that's all."

"About what?"

He barely waited another second before saying clearly, "I want to know where to find Carol."

He'd never noticed until then how loud the clock ticked in the quiet office. He flicked his gaze upward, above Royce's head. It was a large, round clock, with Roman numerals and thick gold hands. He watched the sweep of the second hand complete a full circle before Royce said, "Are you out of your mind?"

"I don't think so." Duke let his gaze wander back to Royce's incredulous face.

"But...why? Why? For God's sake, Duke, *why?*" Royce's habit of repeating words and phrases seemed to have run away with him.

Duke shrugged. "I want to talk to her."

"You know how dangerous that could be, for both of you. To all intents and purposes, Brandon Pierce is dead. I thought we agreed that you would have no further contact with her, under the circumstances. Why would you want to see her now, after all this time?''

"I think that's my business."

He watched Royce's face turn an interesting shade of red. "You're still a young man, Duke. Only forty-two years old. You have your whole life ahead of you. If you want to enjoy it, I suggest you put this ridiculous idea out of your head. Right now. *Right now.*"

Duke scratched his chin with his thumbnail. Shaving still gave him problems at times. The plastic surgeon had told him it was a miracle his hair had grown back. There were times when he'd wished it hadn't. But the alternative was to grow a beard. He'd tried it. It had driven him nuts.

"I'm not going to forget it, Royce, so you might as well give me the information. I'll find her sooner or later. You could make it a lot easier."

"No." Royce rose half out of his chair, then sat down again with a thump. "I forbid it. I absolutely forbid it."

Duke smiled. At least the slight movement of facial muscles didn't hurt anymore. "You seem to forget, I'm no longer a member of this establishment. You can't forbid me to do anything."

"I can make things very uncomfortable for you."

His control disintegrated. Before he'd fully realized his intention to move, he was leaning across the desk, one hand gripping Royce's shirtfront. "Now you listen. And you get this straight. Someone shot out my tires that night. It was a miracle I survived. Mack wasn't so lucky.

"In less than twenty seconds I lost my best friend. In less than twenty seconds my life literally blew up in my face. I spent a year of hell clawing my way back to sanity. A whole year. And I can never get it back, Royce. It's all gone. What I did, what I looked like, who I was, my entire identity has been ripped away from me. I don't know who I am any-more. And a man I loved like a brother is dead.''

He paused for breath, regaining some of his control. "But I tell you one thing. I am going to find the bastard who did this to us. And I'm going to destroy him. Period.''

He still shook. He hadn't let the rage get to him like that in quite a while. Slowly he released his hold on Royce's shirt and straightened his back. "So you had better tell me where I can find Carol before my temper gets the better of me and I beat it out of you.''

Royce stared back at him, white-faced, genuine puzzle-ment in his eyes. "What has Carol got to do with this? Even we don't know who did it. We don't even know if they were after both of you or one of you. It could have been any one of a dozen groups. With your reputation it was bound to happen sooner or later. You can't go around the world wip-ing out key operatives without someone getting mad at you.''

"Yeah, well, we didn't exactly make those decisions. The top brass in Washington were responsible for that. We were just following orders.''

"You were the ones pulling the triggers and setting the explosives. That's all they care about.''

"Okay. I know all that.'' Duke slumped down on his chair and smoothed his fingers across his forehead. "The point is, only three people knew where we would be that night at that precise time. Only three. You, Charles and Carol. Some-one had to tip them off.''

"I hope you're not suggesting—''

Duke dismissed the question with a sharp movement of his hand. "You know better than that. For one thing, nei-ther you nor Charles had a motive. In fact, at the risk of blowing my own horn, the loss of both your top agents must have put quite a hole in your resources.''

"You're right. It did."

"So that leaves Carol."

"That," Royce said, quietly, "is the most ridiculous thing I've ever heard."

"I agree. But she knew about the mission. She could have given the information away without realizing it. She was never questioned after the crash, was she?"

"Of course not. There was no reason to question her."

"Then again, it's no secret how badly she wanted that divorce. She wanted out. She might have wanted out just bad enough to—"

"Nonsense." Royce pounded the desk with his hand. "Nonsense!"

"Maybe," Duke said softly. "But I'm sure as hell going to find out. And she's my only lead." He watched Royce's Adam's apple move slowly up and down again.

"Even if she were involved," Royce said a little hoarsely, "she's not likely to tell you anything."

"She might," Duke said, getting slowly to his feet, "if she doesn't know who I am."

"Good grief."

Duke smiled, though he'd never felt less like smiling in his entire life. "Carol thinks I'm dead. Even she won't recognize me now. Thanks to a very skillful plastic surgeon, I'm not exactly ugly. And I don't think I've lost my touch."

"That's low, even for you."

"That, my friend, is determination. Someone destroyed my identity. And my best friend. I'm going to find that someone, and I'm going to wipe him out. And no one, *no one* is going to stop me."

"Duke, listen to me." Royce held up his pudgy hands in appeal. "You could be putting yourself in serious danger just by contacting Carol. These people never give up. True, we've put out the word that both of you were killed—it was the safest way to go. But they are clever. They could have found out there was only one body, not two. They could still be looking for one of you."

"And if they find me, so much the better." Duke set his mouth in a grim line. "This time I have a slight advantage. This time I'll be ready for them."

"But have you thought about Carol? You could be putting an innocent woman in danger—"

"Don't you think I've asked myself all these questions over and over again?" He gripped the edge of the desk, still fighting the unpredictable anger. "I know what I'm doing. You should know me well enough to know that by now. I'm not going to walk away from this, Royce, you might as well give me the address. I have other ways of finding it that could be a lot more dangerous for Carol."

Sighing audibly, Royce unlocked a desk drawer and withdrew a small notebook. Quickly he scribbled something on a scratch pad and tore it off. "If anything happens to her, anything at all," he said fiercely, "I will hold you personally responsible. And you know what that means."

"I know. But hell, Royce, what have I got to lose?" He grabbed the note Royce held out, and transferred it to the inside pocket of his jacket. "Now," he said, twisting on his heel, "you'll have to excuse me. I have a plane to catch." The last thing he heard just before he slammed the door behind him was Royce's profane cursing.

Rain spattered the dull red steps as Carol stepped from the door of the town house into the gray October morning. A London summer apparently was much briefer than the ones she was accustomed to, she thought, wistfully remembering the comfortably warm days of a New England fall. No wonder the British had such soft skin. They had so little sun to dry it out.

She winced as the cool wind found the back of her neck, and dragged up the collar of her raincoat. Even at this early hour people dashed by, their umbrellas looking like huge black mushrooms bobbing in a tide of flapping coats and flying scarves.

The majority of them were heading for the subway. Carol picked her way across the wet sidewalk, wondering how they possibly survived the journey into the city. The very thought of it gave her nightmares. She couldn't go down into those underground caverns to save her life.

By the time she'd walked the block to the garages that housed her car, her blond hair had already begun to frizz. That was the problem with natural curls, her mother had told her many times. One hint of a shower and they froth up.

The attendant in the glass booth waved at her as she approached and flicked the switch that would allow her to enter the main gate. A gust of wind tossed her hair across her face and she snatched it back, vowing once more to have it cut short. In this unpredictable English climate it would be so much easier to manage.

Once inside the garage, the warmth enveloped her in a toxic cloak of gas and exhaust fumes. Holding her breath, she crossed to her car, her high heels tapping out a staccato beat on the cement floor. The smell pervaded the interior of the compact. It overpowered the smell of new leather.

The Volvo had been an extravagance, a moment of weakness after one memorable trip on a crowded bus had reduced her almost to tears. If it hadn't been for her claustrophobia, Carol thought as she fitted the ignition key into the slot and turned it, she wouldn't have to pay exorbitant amounts of money for parking and upkeep, not to mention the hassles of driving in and out of the city five days a week.

She frowned as the engine coughed, then died. Usually it sang like a boiling kettle the second she turned on the ignition. Praying she didn't have a problem, she flicked the key again.

It never failed to amaze her how much more inconvenient everything was in England. Something as simple as driving a car became a major operation, fraught with hidden perils. Not only was it almost impossible to park, unless she used the underground parking lot, which charged an outrageous fee, but she also had to deal with a city full of suicidal drivers who seemed bent on destroying everything in their path.

Again the engine coughed an apology, then subsided into silence. Carol muttered a low curse and opened the car door. It swung back and hit something with a sharp thud.

A curse, deeper and much more coarse than hers, erupted from somewhere beside her.

Twisting her head sharply around, Carol met the injured gaze of a tall man dressed in dark green overalls. He peered at her over the top of the door, and said succinctly, "Don't worry, I have another one."

His voice sounded hoarse, as if he had a touch of laryngitis. Poking her head out, Carol looked down to where he was massaging his knee. "I'm so sorry," she said, disturbed by the flinch of pain that had crossed the man's face. It seemed out of proportion to the force of the blow.

"That's okay. I guess I shouldn't have crept up on you like that." He gave her a tight smile. A smile that didn't reach his dark brown eyes.

Staring at his face, Carol felt an odd sensation, a sense of déjà vu. He looked familiar, and yet she was perfectly sure she'd never seen him before. Something about the way he'd tilted his head reminded her...

A voice spoke her name, interrupting her uneasy thoughts. She swung around, relieved to see the burly man who smiled down at her. Jim Bedford was the owner of the garage. He was a big man with a big voice, and had taken a fatherly interest in her that she'd found reassuring in the midst of strangers.

"Something's wrong with my car, Jim. Can you take a look at it for me?" He couldn't have arrived at a better time, she thought, glancing at her watch.

"Well, why don't we let my new mechanic take a look at it." Jim looked from one to the other. "I see you two have met?"

"Not formally," the mechanic answered.

In that instant, Carol realized something she'd missed. "You're American," she said, holding out her hand. "I'm sorry. I would hate even more to have crippled a fellow countryman. I'm Carol Everett, and I hope I didn't do too much damage?"

"Duke Winters."

His grasp felt every bit as strong as he looked. Powerful, she amended silently. Yet it wasn't really his size. Although he was tall, his lean, hard build revealed less muscle than the beefy giants that some women seemed to prefer.

Something in the way he held her hand sent a warning tingle up her arm. Withdrawing her fingers from his grasp, she said lightly, "You've just started work here?"

"Yes, ma'am. That's why I was on my way over. I heard your engine stall and thought I'd better take a look." He glanced at Jim, then his gaze came back to rest on her face, and once more she felt a small jolt of familiarity. She knew now who he reminded her of. She didn't know why, but it was there, elusive, haunting and painful.

She pulled her thoughts back. She hadn't allowed herself to think about Mack in almost a year, and she wasn't about to start now. Besides, she was already late for the office. And very late for her first appointment.

"I'll let you get on with it," Jim said, moving off. "I've got a couple of jobs to take care of. Cheerio, Carol." He lifted a hand in farewell and disappeared through a doorway.

Carol looked back at Duke Winters, her pulse skipping when she met his shrewd gaze. "Well, if you wouldn't mind..." She leaned inside the car and pulled the lever to open the hood. "I can't think what's the matter with it," she added, as she watched the mechanic peer into the engine. "It was running fine yesterday."

He had long, strong fingers. Well-shaped and confident. Not the kind of hands she would have expected of someone who earned his living with them. Now that she thought about it, his palm had been smooth against hers, as smooth as...

A tiny shiver touched her spine. She dragged her gaze away from his hand and asked, "How long have you been in England?"

"Not long." He lifted his head again. "Try it now."

She climbed back in and twisted the key. This time the engine fired, then purred like a contented lion. "That's wonderful," she said in delight. "How much do I owe you?"

"Nothing, it's only temporary." Duke Winters closed the hood with a bang. "Looks like you got a problem with the fuel pump. It should hold for a while, but I can't guarantee how long. Do you have far to go?"

"Cheapside." Dismayed, she looked at her watch again. "And I'm late now. I have a nine-thirty appointment I'm never going to make."

"Tell you what." He pulled a rag from his back pocket and wiped his hands. "How about I ride with you, then bring the car back here to fix it? That way you won't be stuck in traffic with a dead engine. If you want, I could even pick you up in it this evening. Save you fighting the crowds on the subway.''

She shivered in earnest this time. ''I never go on the subway,'' she said shortly. Noticing his raised eyebrows, she gave him a small smile. ''I have claustrophobia. Tunnels are my biggest problem.''

''Ah.'' He nodded as if he really understood.

No one understood, Carol thought, unless they shared the same predicament. That's what made it such an inconvenient problem.

''Look,'' Duke Winters said, reaching into the breast pocket of his overalls. ''I'll give you my home address. You can check with the records here. You'll know where to find me if anything goes wrong.''

Embarrassed, Carol shook her head. ''Oh, no, that won't be necessary. . . .''

Her voice trailed off as he tore the scribbled message from his notebook and held it out to her. Staring at the address, she made up her mind. He was obviously making an effort to reassure her. And anything was better than dealing with public transport.

''That would be great,'' she said, leaning over to unlock the other door. ''I really appreciate this.'' Though it was probably going to cost her, she thought ruefully.

He climbed in and settled down next to her, seeming to take up more room than was necessary. His arm brushed hers, and she inched away from him. Unsettled by her reaction to his presence, she concentrated on steering the car out into the narrow street. ''You don't mind if I drive?'' she asked, in a belated afterthought.

''Not at all.''

She frowned, staring past the swishing wipers and the drops they left behind. She couldn't shake that vague feeling of familiarity. Maybe it was just the accent. Except for the television, it had been a while since she'd heard an American voice.

The solid rear of a London taxi blocked her way, and she stepped on the brake. Glancing at her passenger, she found his expression bland and unemotional. "This could take a while," she said, feeling the need to make some kind of conversation.

He turned his head, and again the expression in his eyes unnerved her. "Don't worry. Jim will understand." His mouth curved in that tight smile.

"I'm sure he will." She made herself meet the scrutiny in his dark brown eyes. He had a hard mouth, she decided. It made him look a little...ruthless. Disturbed by the thought, she switched her gaze back to the windshield. The cab still sat there.

"How long have you known him?" Duke Winters asked, easing his knee into a more comfortable position.

Carol wondered if she'd hurt him more than she'd realized. "Since I moved here three months ago. I was lucky to find a lockup garage with a guard two blocks from where I live. Most people have to park on the sidewalk."

A loud honk behind her made her jump. Snatching her gaze back to the road, she saw the taxi had moved on. She drove for some time without speaking, while Duke Winters seemed quite content to sit back and gaze out the window.

She wondered if he'd just arrived in the country. If so, had he brought his family with him? Wife? Children? Somehow he didn't strike her as the fatherly type. In fact, she was having a great deal of trouble thinking of him as a mechanic. He seemed too sophisticated, and much too imposing. If she'd had to guess, she would have placed him in a position of authority, something out of the ordinary.

Startled by her observations, she tensed when he asked, "So what brought you to England?"

She took a moment before answering. "The cosmetics company I work for is setting up a branch in London. I was sent over to set up the operational system, since they wanted to apply the same methods they use in New York."

"So you come from the East Coast?"

Why did she have the feeling his questions were more than just natural curiosity? she wondered. Dismissing her uneasiness, she answered, "Connecticut, originally. Though I moved to New York after my husband died."

Surprised that she'd told him, she gripped the wheel harder as memories nudged the wall she'd built against them.

"I'm sorry."

"Thank you." Desperate to change the subject, she forgot about his reluctance to answer questions. "So where do you come from in the States?"

"I'm East Coast, too. How do you like working in London?"

"It's interesting. I meet a lot of fascinating people." She negotiated the tricky corner onto Cheapside and pulled up at the curb. The tall drab buildings loomed on either side like disapproving sentinels watching over the scurrying mass of people. "And this is my office," she added. "I'm on the third floor."

Leaving the keys hanging from the ignition she opened the door, letting in the roar and fumes of traffic. "Thanks again, Mr. Winters. I really appreciate this. Can you find your way back all right?"

"Duke." Again he attempted that tight smile. "Don't worry. I'll find it. What time do you want me to pick you up?"

Her pulse fluttered. For a moment the question had seemed disturbingly personal. "I should be through by five-thirty. I'll wait for you in the lobby, where I can see you pull up."

He touched his forehead in a mocking salute. "I'll be here."

Unnerved, she scrambled out of the car. Again his gesture had been uncannily familiar. She really had to stop doing this, she thought irritably. It was becoming a fixation, and thoroughly irrational. She was so intent on her escape she almost bumped into the petite brunette who paused on the step ahead of her.

Anna Gurlaine was an astute, sharp-eyed woman in her late twenties. She'd racked up an impressive amount of sales in the two months she'd been with the company, and Carol envied her seemingly boundless energy.

Anna's smile flashed across her face. She said something, but Carol couldn't hear her above the roar of traffic, though she did notice the curious glance the younger woman sent the car still parked at the curb.

Carol resisted the urge to look back at the car. She couldn't wait to escape the gaze of the man behind the wheel. Though she had no idea why she should imagine he still watched her.

Taking hold of the saleswoman's arm, Carol steered her through the glass doors.

Anna's grin widened. "Nice. New boyfriend?"

Feeling warmth creep over her cheeks, Carol shook her head. "He's the mechanic from my garage. He's going to fix my car."

"I wish my mechanic looked like that." Anna's husky laugh expressed her enjoyment of Carol's obvious discomfort.

Carol paused at the foot of the escalator. "I just hope he knows what he's doing. I would hate to go home on the bus. It takes forever, and all that lurching about ruins my appetite for dinner."

To her relief, Anna rushed off, putting an end to the teasing.

Carol stepped onto the escalator, wondering if she had made a mistake. She couldn't escape the fact that Duke Winters disturbed her. Far too much for comfort. The thought brought back an uneasiness that seemed all too familiar.

Chapter 2

Duke slid across to the driver's seat and restarted the engine. So far so good. Though if he wanted to pull this off, he'd have to relax a hell of a lot more. It had been tough. Tougher than he'd imagined.

He pulled out into the stream of traffic amid a blast of horns. He ignored them. His mind concentrated on his next move. He couldn't tell how she was reacting to him yet. Not that he'd given her much reason to react to him so far. But he'd been afraid of rushing it. Carol never did like pushy men.

He wasn't too sure how she felt about dating a mechanic, either, but this had seemed the best way to arrange a meeting. He was fairly sure he could overcome that particular barrier, if it arose. His other options left too much to chance, and he couldn't afford to take chances.

He pulled up at the light with a screech of brakes. It rained in earnest now, washing down the window in a steady stream to be swept away by the wipers. How he hated driving in the rain.

It had been raining that night. The night he couldn't remember. Nothing except the flames. The heat of them still tortured him in his nightmares. He'd read the police report. He'd insisted on knowing every detail, although it tore him apart to know exactly what had happened to Mack.

Shaking off the memories, he brought his mind back to his present problem. He would have to be careful. He'd had a bad moment when she'd first looked at him. He'd wondered if the change in his appearance had been drastic enough to fool the one woman most likely to know him. Apparently he'd passed the test. As far as Carol Everett was concerned, he was a mechanic named Duke Winters.

It had been easy enough to get the job at Bedford's, with the credentials he'd requested from headquarters. And it had taken no more than a few seconds to loosen the fuel pump.

It surprised him that he could feel such repugnance over what he'd had to do. At one time he wouldn't have thought twice about it. But then, he was no longer the man he was. In many more ways than one.

Duke swore when a red double-decker bus hurtled in front of him, its towering body swaying as the driver hauled on the wheel. He still hadn't got his nerve back completely when it came to driving. The narrow London streets and the apparent reckless driving habits of the British population made the entire process a nightmare.

He forced himself to relax and took a firmer grip on the wheel. This wouldn't be easy. He knew that. He'd known that since he'd first made up his mind that this was something he had to do.

He didn't want to believe that Carol had been involved, whether intentionally or not. But who else could have given that information away? Who else knew where Mack Everett and Brandon Pierce were going to be that night, at that hour?

He had even considered, for one wild, crazy moment, that it could have been Charles, or even Royce. He was not that naive to think there couldn't be some kind of corruption going on at the top level. But if either one had wanted him dead they could have easily arranged it while he was recovering.

Besides, as he'd told Royce, they had no motive. Neither one of them could possibly want the deaths of their top agents. Just the opposite. Without them, the organization had lost its most valuable assets as far as world affairs went. No, they had no motive.

Whereas Carol had made no secret of the fact that she detested both men. It was a toss-up who she disliked more, her husband or his best friend.

Duke slowed for the turn into Carol's street. The guard in front of the garage peered at him, then smiled and waved him on. The gates opened up and he drove through, then parked the car in its usual spot.

He removed the keys from the ignition and studied them thoughtfully. He'd overlooked one point when he'd planned this whole thing. And it was an important point. Under the circumstances, a totally unexpected point.

He'd been attracted to Carol long before she married Mack. If he hadn't owed his friend his loyalty, Duke thought, watching the keys swinging in his fingers, he would have told her she was making the mistake of her life.

He and Mack had spent some hair-raising moments during their tours of duty. At times like that, people tend to spill their guts. Mack had grown up in a series of foster homes. He'd never known a real family and desperately wanted a child, someone of his own flesh and blood. That's why he'd married Carol. He hadn't loved her. He'd used her, taking advantage of her love for him, and marrying her to have his son.

Duke swore under his breath. Despite his suspicions, his feelings for Carol hadn't changed. He thought he'd lost that unreasonable yen for her when he'd lost everything else. Apparently he hadn't.

He'd discovered that fact the second he'd sat next to her in the car and smelled that familiar perfume. That exotic, flowery fragrance with a hint of citrus. Sweet and tangy, and incredibly seductive.

"Damn." He shoved the door open and swung out his legs. It was the one thing he hadn't bargained for. And the one thing that could bring about his downfall. He would have to find some way to deal with it. If he didn't, he could very easily be a dead man.

Carol tapped the end of her pencil against the surface of her desk, barely aware of the nervous staccato in the quiet office. All day her concentration had been disrupted by memories she thought she'd successfully buried. To find them surfacing again bothered her.

Now that the afternoon was drawing to a close, she wished she had simply made arrangements to pick up the car at the garage. She wasn't sure she wanted to be closeted in close quarters again with Duke Winters.

Yet part of her had to admit she had enjoyed talking to him that morning. She was homesick for New York. Although the differences between the two countries were subtle, they were a constant reminder that she was in a strange country and far from everything that was familiar to her. It could be a very lonely feeling at times.

Talking to a fellow American helped to alleviate that. They had shared something in common. The problem was, he made her uncomfortable. He stirred up too many forgotten emotions. And something about him, something she couldn't pin down, reminded her of someone she'd rather forget. A man who had been dead for more than a year.

Try as she might, she couldn't understand why. Although they were roughly the same height and build, that's where the similarity ended.

Carol propped her chin on her hand and gazed out the office window. No, it wasn't looks, she decided. It was more intangible than that. His attitude, perhaps? His way of speaking, a familiar gesture, his walk—maybe the way she held himself—

"Where are you, Carol?"

Carol blinked, and swung her head around to look at Anna's smiling face. She'd almost forgotten the saleswoman's presence in the office.

"I swear, Carol," Anna said, shaking her head in mock concern, "I do believe you were daydreaming about that handsome mechanic."

The words, spoken in Anna's soft, musical accent, had hit a little too close to home. Carol's laugh sounded false even to her as she gathered up the scattered papers on her desk. "I'm more worried about my car than the mechanic."

"Well, if he doesn't arrive, I'll be happy to give you a lift home."

Carol smiled. "Thanks, but if he doesn't turn up, I'm going to be on the phone to Jim Bedford, demanding to know why."

Anna glanced up at the clock on the wall above Carol's head. "Then I'm going to run. I've got a hot date tonight, and it will take two hours to make me look beautiful."

Carol looked at the perfect oval face, the smooth cheeks glowing like the rose pink scarf Anna wore around her neck. "You," she said with sincerity, "look wonderful all the time."

"Thank you." Anna's pleased smile seemed to light up the office. She reached the door and looked back. "So do you. So watch your step with that mechanic." Before Carol could answer, she'd disappeared.

Carol flipped her gaze up to the ceiling and sighed. Either she was being particularly transparent, or Anna was sharper than she'd given her credit for.

Stepping into the chilly darkness a few minutes later, she couldn't prevent a shiver of anticipation. The lamplight wore a misty halo and cast a hazy orange glow over the car waiting at the curb.

The engine hummed expectantly as she approached. The window rolled down and Duke Winters looked out at her. "Want me to drive?"

"If you like." She slid onto the seat next to him, feeling almost a sense of anticlimax. There was no similarity at all. She'd let her imagination run away with her as usual.

Even so, she couldn't shake her awareness of him. His well-shaped hands rested lightly on the wheel, the skin smooth and lightly tanned. They looked as if they belonged to a musician instead of a mechanic.

With a jolt she realized he wasn't wearing overalls. Instead, he had on a leather jacket and jeans. He looked more rugged dressed that way, and dangerously attractive.

"Had a good day?"

Caught staring at his thighs, she jerked her gaze up. He was concentrating on the road ahead, though she saw an infuriating twitch of his firm lips.

"Yes, thank you." Casting about for something else to say, she decided to be practical. "How much do I owe you for the repairs?"

"Nothing. I fixed it during my coffee break this afternoon. It wasn't that big a problem."

He must have felt her surprised stare. Giving her a quick sideways glance he added, "But it could have been if left unchecked."

Only partly satisfied, Carol said, "Well, I insist on paying you. There must have been parts involved, as well as the labor."

He was silent so long she thought he was ignoring her. Then he surprised her by saying. "Tell you what. I haven't had a decent meal since I got here. If you really want to repay me, how about cooking me dinner? Something real American, like fried chicken."

She didn't know quite what to say. Her first reaction was to refuse. But that would sound tacky after all the trouble he'd gone to. And she did enjoy talking to him. It would be nice to chat about issues only another American would understand. Yet something about him touched a raw nerve, and she wasn't at all sure she wanted to deal with that for an entire evening.

Aware that she was hesitating a little too long, she blurted out, "Sure. Though I can't guarantee my fried chicken is up to your standards."

His slight smile sparked a rush of pleasure. She pulled her gaze from his mouth and the unbidden thought that took her unawares. She hadn't thought about kissing a man since...

"I'll take my chances. Tomorrow night?"

Flustered, she said quickly. "Fine. Around seven."

"Anything I can bring?"

"Do you like wine?"

"I enjoy a glass or two with dinner. A good German Riesling?"

"Sounds wonderful." She looked out the window in surprise as he pulled to a stop. She hadn't realized they had arrived back at the garage.

"I'll walk you to your apartment," Duke offered, as she climbed out of the car.

"Oh, thanks, but that isn't necessary. It's just up the street."

"I insist. Then I'll know where to come tomorrow night."

She had to concede to that. The traffic had thinned out in the quiet suburb, and their footsteps echoed eerily behind them as they walked side by side in the misty rain.

They passed the huge double doors of a warehouse, locked and bolted for the night. Here the lampposts were farther apart, and the space in between seemed dark and chilly. Carol gathered the collar of her raincoat closer around her neck, hunching her shoulders against the keen wind.

"You walk up here alone every night?"

She glanced up at him, feeling a tiny pang of something she couldn't define. "Yes. It's not far, and I like to walk."

He didn't answer, and she felt compelled to add something. Anything to break the awkward silence. "Have you always been a mechanic?" Surprised at her own question, she waited long seconds for his answer.

"I've been a lot of things."

Realizing he didn't intend to enlarge on that, she gave up. Duke Winters was obviously a person who didn't like talking about himself. Which would limit the conversation during dinner, she thought uneasily.

They reached the apartment building and she paused on the step, hoping he wouldn't insist on coming inside. "Thank you for the escort, Mr. Winters. I appreciate it."

His dark eyes looked down at her, and once again she felt a shiver of apprehension, like a warning whisper in her mind.

"It's my pleasure. I'll see you tomorrow, at seven."

"I'll look forward to it." Not exactly the truth, she silently amended. Already she wished she'd found some other way to repay him.

"And the name's Duke."

"Good night...Duke." She couldn't imagine why she had so much trouble calling him that.

"Good night, Carol."

Her name on his lips unsettled her. His gravelly voice somehow managed to make it sound different, even sensual. Disturbed by the thought, she turned and hurried into the building.

Duke watched her go, inwardly cursing himself. He would never make any headway with her if he didn't relax. That business about being a mechanic had taken him by surprise. He had to be slipping. In the old days he would have been prepared and rehearsed for such a question.

Jamming his hands in the pockets of his jacket he strode briskly along the wet pavement. This wasn't the old days, he reminded himself. He'd been out of it for more than a year. Half of it spent flat on his back, wondering if he'd ever walk again, let alone work.

He'd lost a lot in that year. It wasn't just the reflexes, the sixth sense that had saved his life more than once. He'd lost something far more important than that.

Scowling, he turned the corner and continued on, past the darkened shop fronts, the barber's striped pole and the post office with its red mailboxes. He might have gained it all back in time if he'd concentrated his energy on it, he reflected. But something vital was missing. He knew it, and Royce had known it. The decision for him to retire permanently had been mutual.

He could hear the thump of a bass guitar as he approached the neon lights of a café. The noisy warmth and the pleasant aroma of fresh-brewed coffee almost tempted him, but he kept going. He needed the fresh air and the quiet solitude of the rainy evening to clear his head.

He'd had time to think during those long, painful months. He'd weighed all the possibilities, analyzed them to death, and he'd finally acknowledged the truth. He didn't have the stomach for it anymore. Maybe he never had. Maybe it had taken Mack's death to make him realize that.

He paused at the traffic light, waiting for the signal to cross the road. He still felt the pain of losing his friend. He still missed him. He had to remember that when he was dealing with Carol. It would be too easy to be distracted by those dark blue eyes that had always made him think of a starlit sky on a warm summer night.

It had been a night like that when he'd first met Carol. It was a Fourth of July barbecue in the park. He was at a loose end and Mack had talked him into going. He'd agreed more out of curiosity than anything. He'd wanted to see what kind of woman would get the attention of a hard-nose like Mack.

He'd been captivated by that first sight of her. She'd worn a white dress that had dipped low in front and left her tanned shoulders bare. He'd watched her hair brush her shoulders in a gleaming curtain of gold, and his mouth had gone dry when he'd looked into the depths of her navy blue eyes. If it had been anyone but Mack involved with her, he would have made a persistent and determined play for her that night.

A deep sigh shook Duke's body. It hadn't taken him long to realize that Mack's interest in Carol wasn't fueled by the emotions of a man in love. He doubted if his friend was capable of such sentiment.

But the adoration in Carol's eyes every time she'd looked at Mack had been unmistakable. It had been more difficult than he'd expected to watch the radiant bride walk down the aisle to marry his best friend.

With a start he realized the light had changed. He barely made it to the other side before the traffic began to surge forward. Irritated by his lack of concentration, he tried to clear his mind of the memories. But they crept back, in spite of his best efforts to prevent them.

As the months had gone by, he'd been at first surprised, then disappointed by the incidents Mack had described. According to Mack, Carol had quickly become disillusioned with her marriage, driving her husband insane with her whining and complaining, always on his back, always demanding more of his time.

In the end, Duke had tuned out Mack's complaints, sick at heart that the woman he'd admired so much had turned out to be so different from the person he'd imagined her to be.

She'd made it very obvious that she disliked him, though he'd never been sure why. Gradually, he'd come to resent her. He'd watched Mack become irritable and withdrawn, until he became seriously worried about his friend.

Mack took chances he would never have considered before his marriage. He'd become almost reckless, and Duke had cursed Carol more than once for the dangerous change in Mack's temperament.

Duke turned into the steps that led down to his basement apartment. And now Mack was dead. Had Carol hated him enough to arrange his death? That was tough to believe. She had already started proceedings for a divorce.

Unless she'd decided she stood to gain more from his death. The organization had been extremely generous to her, according to Royce.

Duke let himself into the cramped quarters he'd rented, and slumped down on the couch. He just couldn't visualize the woman he'd just left as a cold-blooded killer. But then, who would have thought that the fascinating, warm, intelligent woman he'd met that Fourth of July night could turn out to be such a harridan?

Duke swore, his harsh voice filling the room with repressed anger. True, he had no stomach for this anymore. But he owed it to Mack, and to himself, to find out who was responsible and make them pay. Only then could he finally put that part of his life behind him and go on with his new one.

He just hoped that if and when it came down to it, he'd have the guts to do what he had to do. Even if his suspicions about Carol were correct, God help him.

"Have you got a minute, Carol?"

Carol looked up as Anna approached her desk. "If it is only a minute. I was just getting ready to finish up for the day."

Anna's dark eyes flicked up to the clock. "A half hour early? It must be something very important. You're meeting the good-looking mechanic, perhaps?"

Carol closed her logbook with a loud snap. "Perhaps."

"Aha! So he made the most of your trip home last night, and captured your heart."

Carol rolled her eyes. "He didn't capture anything. I'm simply paying him back for repairs on my car."

"He doesn't take money?"

"He prefers a home-cooked meal."

"This is good news. It means he must be a bachelor."

"It could mean his wife is waiting for him back in the States."

Anna looked surprised. "He is American?"

"Yes, he's American." Carol sighed. "Now I guess you're going to tell me that makes everything just perfect."

"Well, it does make a difference, doesn't it? You have so much more in common with an American."

"The only difference it makes," Carol said, getting to her feet, "is that we can discuss the American economy, politics or the crime rate, as opposed to British issues, which I find confusing."

Anna's impish grin darted across her face. "Carol, your mechanic didn't look like the kind of man who would want to discuss politics with you."

"Maybe not," Carol said firmly. "But that's the direction I intend to direct my comments. Now, if you'll excuse me, I have to go shop for a chicken."

She had forgotten just how good fried chicken could smell, Carol decided, as she stood in the narrow kitchen checking over her menu. Green salad and rice, French bread and one of her favorite recipes, a delicious concoction of cooked peas and bacon. That should hold his attention.

The sharp ring of her doorbell interrupted her thoughts, and she glanced at her watch. He was five minutes early. She ignored the ridiculous fluttering of her pulse and hurried to open the door.

"I hope you remembered the wine. . . ." Her voice trailed off as she stared into the dark gaze of the giant who stood in her doorway. "Mr. Golding! I'm sorry, I thought you were my dinner guest."

The burly man lifted his nose and sniffed the air. "I'm sorry I am not. Something smells delightfully delectable."

Carol grinned. Her landlord's West Indian lingo never failed to entertain her. "It's fried chicken."

"Really." Jasper Golding loudly smacked his lips. "I do not remember fried chicken *evah* emitting such an utterly exquisite aroma."

"That," Carol said solemnly, "is because it's not home cooked."

"Ah." The landlord rubbed a hand slowly over his protruding belly. "That would explain it, indeed."

Carol glanced down the hallway. She didn't really want to ask the man in. Duke could be arriving any minute. "Is there something I can do for you?"

"Ah, yes. Well, I won't keep you. I just needed to inform you that much to my profound regret, I am in the unfortunate position of having to raise your rent."

"Oh." Carol tried to look concerned. Since the company paid her rent, the hike didn't affect her personally, but Jasper Golding looked so stricken, she felt obliged to show some kind of reaction. "Is it a big raise?"

"Oh, no, no, dear lady. Just ten pounds a month. Unfortunately, these ancient buildings are always in dire need of repair and—"

Carol's pulse leapt as she saw the lean figure of Duke turn the corner down the hallway. "Well, I appreciate you coming to tell me personally," she said, smiling up at Jasper. "Now, if you'll excuse me, my guest has arrived."

Jasper turned his head slowly, his stare almost insolent as he watched Duke approach. "You are entertaining a man for the night?"

Carol flushed. "For the evening. There are no rules against that, I take it?"

"Oh, goodness, no." Jasper returned Duke's nod of greeting with a thin smile.

Carol introduced the two men, irritated by the landlord's attitude. He stood blocking the doorway, as if reluctant to let Duke in.

"I'm not too early, am I?" Duke asked, raising his eyebrows at Carol.

"No, as a matter of fact, you're right on time. Mr. Golding was just leaving."

"Yes, I was. Just leaving." Jasper shifted sideways, and Duke stepped past him, his eyes signaling a question at Carol.

"I'm right upstairs if you need me," Jasper said, giving Duke one more hard look.

"Thank you, but I'm sure that won't be necessary." Carol closed the door on him. "I'm sorry," she said, giving Duke a rueful smile. "He's only been here a couple of months, but he takes his job very seriously. He's appointed himself guardian to all the helpless females in the building. He finds it intolerable that women should live alone and unprotected in this den of iniquity, as he calls it."

Duke grinned. It was the first time she'd seen him really smiling. It did wonders for his face. "How well does that sit with an American woman's sense of independence?"

"Not well with any woman's independence. I have a friend who lives upstairs, and she bitterly resents Jasper's constant vigilance." She took the bottle of wine Duke handed her. "Though I must admit, it's reassuring to know he's close by if I should have any problems."

"I hope you're not anticipating any tonight?"

Embarrassed, she waited while he shrugged out of his jacket, then held out her hand for it. "Of course not. I expect you to be the perfect gentleman."

She'd said the words lightly, but she was conscious of his gaze on her as she headed for the door to the bedroom. "I'll hang this up for you."

"Want me to put the wine in the fridge?"

She turned back to hand him the bottle and found him disturbingly close. He had to be very light on his feet. She hadn't heard him move. "If you can find room for it. The appliances in these places were designed for dollhouses."

"I know what you mean." His eyes appraised her as he took the bottle. "You look very nice tonight."

"Thank you." He looked good, too, in dark blue slacks and maroon sweater worn over a white shirt. Feeling a little breathless, she decided not to tell him that. "I'll be right back."

Hurrying into the bedroom with his jacket, she was glad she'd chosen to wear the pale blue beaded sweater with her black pants. Dressy casual, she'd decided, when pondering the age-old question of what to wear. She'd considered pinning up her hair, but had opted to leave it loose. If the approval in Duke's eyes was anything to go by, she'd made the right choice.

Carol felt ridiculously pleased about that as she drifted back to the kitchen, where she found Duke rearranging her fridge.

"Organization," he said, straightening. "It works wonders. I made space for the wine."

"Wonderful. Dinner should be ready soon. Would you like a drink while you're waiting? I have a fairly good Scotch, or beer?"

"Beer sounds good." He helped himself to a bottle from the fridge and twisted off the cap. "And a glass?"

She reached into the cupboard for one, pleased that he didn't drink it out of the bottle. Pouring herself a mineral water, she followed him into the living room, where he settled himself on her comfortable couch. She chose an armchair opposite him, trying to remember the list of topics she'd rehearsed in her mind.

"So how long will you be in London?"

His question threw her for a moment. "About another three months," she said. "Things should be running pretty smoothly by then. What about you? Do you plan on living here permanently?"

She hadn't really expected him to answer, so she was surprised when he said easily, "Just for the time being. I like to travel a lot, so I'm never in one place too long."

"Working your way around the world?"

"Something like that."

She'd meant it more as a joke than anything. She was still trying to analyze his answer when he added, "Tell me what it's like living in London on your own. Have you managed to make friends?"

Once again he'd turned the tables on her. Shrugging, Carol leaned back in her chair. "I've been too busy to make many friends. Except for Win upstairs, and Anna."

"Anna? That's a nice name."

Carol smiled. "She's a nice woman. She's very tiny, looks as if a strong wind could blow her away, but inside she has the determination and persistence of a drill sergeant. She's well on her way to becoming our top salesperson."

"Sounds formidable."

"You wouldn't think so, to hear her on the phone. She had some kind of throat surgery, and it's left her with a husky voice. Little more than a whisper, actually. It amazes me she does so well, since most of her work is on the phone. I guess the men like it, though. They think it's sexy."

"And Win, I take it, is the friend upstairs?"

"Yes." Carol sipped thoughtfully from her glass. "I'm not sure what to make of Win. She's been a tremendous help to me, showing me around the neighborhood, pointing out the best places to shop, that kind of thing. She's very friendly and yet..."

"And yet what?"

She felt uncomfortable discussing her friend with this man who was, after all, a complete stranger. Yet he didn't seem like a stranger. She felt at ease with him, as if she'd known him for a long time....

She pulled herself together. "Oh, it's nothing. Win comes from one of the eastern European countries. I think she must have been through some great trauma in her life, as she never talks about her past, or her homeland. She changes the subject if I bring it up."

Duke nodded, and Carol realized uneasily that he did the same thing. Maybe he had some great trauma he was trying to forget. It seemed to be endemic.

"No men friends? Or is that too personal a question?"

She did her best to look as if it didn't bother her. "No, no men friends." She made an attempt to laugh. "Though there is this window cleaner who comes by now and again. He's an outrageous flirt with loads of British charm that would be hard to resist if I didn't know better."

"Better watch the British. They're notorious for their persistence."

Carol shook her head. "I'm careful not to encourage him. I have no intention of getting involved with a man again. Any man."

"You might change your mind after a while. You're too young and attractive to be alone for long."

She stood up quickly, narrowly missing her glass on the table beside her. "I don't think so. Dinner should be about ready, if you'll take a seat at the table."

She hurried into the kitchen, before he noticed how much his remark had flustered her. She didn't need this, she told herself as she spooned rice into a dish. Somehow he managed to get past the reserve she'd built up over the past year. A reserve she was determined to hang on to. Never again would she be vulnerable with a man. Never again.

Dinner turned out to be thoroughly enjoyable, much to her surprise. Duke's vivid descriptions and fascinating anecdotes about some of the places he'd traveled to intrigued her. Though he never mentioned anything about the jobs that had taken him there.

He was lavish in his praise of the fried chicken. "Best I've ever tasted," he proclaimed, after clearing his plate of his second helping.

Carol couldn't help a little rush of pleasure. "That's because you haven't tasted it lately. As a matter of fact, that's the first fried chicken I've cooked in a while. I used to cook it all the time for Mack—"

She broke off, shaken by her mention of her dead husband. It was the first time she'd spoken of him to anyone. What had possessed her...?

"Was Mack your husband?"

Slowly she nodded. Her heart thumped faster as she stared at his dark eyes. What was it about him...?

"Can you talk about it? Was he sick?"

She moistened her lips with her tongue. "No. It was an accident. A car wreck, on his way to... He was on his way to work." She twisted a fold of the white tablecloth in her fingers.

"I'm sorry. That must have been a terrible shock."

"I... Yes, it was... I..." She was floundering. For some reason she found it impossible to look in this man's eyes and lie. But how could she tell him the truth? That her husband's death was a release, a miraculous escape from a life that had been filled with terror, uncertainty and unpleasant surprises?

She had cried when they'd told her. She had loved him once, and no one deserved to die that way. But when the first bout of grief had subsided, she'd been thankful that the danger, the hidden menace, was finally over. She was free.

To her immense relief, the phone rang loudly in the silent room. "I'm sorry," she said jerkily. "Will you excuse me a minute?"

He nodded, but just before she turned away she saw a look in his eyes that chilled her. For a moment he'd looked as if he resented her.

Shaken, she reached for the phone in the kitchen. It was her imagination, she told herself. The result of reliving the memory of that night, and the guilt she still suffered because she couldn't feel sorry that Mack was dead. Drawing a deep breath, she kept her voice steady as she spoke into the phone.

Duke sat at the table, a frown creasing his brow. There had been no mistaking her reaction. He'd shaken her pretty badly when he'd asked her about Mack.

She was hiding something, something more than the obvious need to keep silent about what Mack did for a living. He was too familiar with that kind of secrecy to confuse it with the emotional response he'd sensed in Carol.

He had to find out what she knew. Whatever she hid under that uneasy smile and wary eyes, he had to uncover it. Straining his ears, he tried to hear the conversation from the kitchen.

Carol relaxed her grip on the phone as Win's brittle voice spoke in her ear. "Would you care to join me for a glass of wine and a movie tonight?"

"Oh, thanks, Win. I'm sorry, but I have company. Give me a rain check?"

"Of course." Carol heard the barest of hesitations. "Ah . . . would you want to call me back later?"

Carol sighed. Win was unabashedly curious, and thrived on local gossip about the residents of the apartment building. The fact that until now Carol had never before entertained a guest in the two months she'd known Win would drive her crazy until she knew all the details.

Carol wasn't at all sure she wanted to tell Win anything, but the very fact that she didn't want to talk about Duke would only make Win more persistent. Reluctantly she promised to call and then hung up.

Duke sat back in his chair as Carol returned from the kitchen. The conversation had been short and sweet. She obviously hadn't wanted to talk. Too conscious of being overheard, no doubt.

God, how he hated these suspicions. Yet he couldn't deny the fact that Carol had been visibly agitated when he'd mentioned Mack. And it wasn't because she was overcome with grief. He had to get to the bottom of it. And the more he thought about it, the less he liked it.

"Sorry," Carol said, with a smile of apology. "That was Win. She's a great friend, but one of those people who has to know everything that's going on in your life. If I didn't like her so much I might resent it."

She had incredible eyes. So vivid, so clear, so warm, it didn't seem possible that they could hide anything, let alone something as hideous as murder. He pulled himself together. He couldn't do this. Damn it, he had to stay detached.

"She probably knows everything about everyone in the building," he said casually.

Carol nodded. "I'm afraid so. I think she's lonely. She's a free-lance writer, so she works at home. She doesn't get to see too many people—maybe that's why she's so interested in everybody's lives."

She picked up her plate and reached across for his. "Can I get you some coffee?"

He wanted to stay for coffee. The way he was feeling right then, he wanted to stay the night. What was it about her that stirred his blood every time he looked at her? Why was it that despite his suspicions, he only had to look in her eyes, watch her mouth curve in a smile, see her hips sway when she walked across the room and he ached to grab her in his arms and—

"Is something wrong?"

He blinked, aware that he'd been gazing at her for the last ten seconds. She stared back at him, wariness plain on her face and in the set of her shoulders.

Inwardly cursing, he rushed to make amends. "I'm sorry, I just remembered something I was supposed to take care of. Guess I'll have to forget the coffee for now."

He had to get out of there now, before he blew the whole thing. He couldn't seem to think straight. He needed time to sort things out in his mind and decide on his next move.

"Of course." She looked at him for a second longer, a tiny frown of puzzlement on her face, as if she were still trying to figure him out. Then she turned her back on him and carried the plates to the kitchen.

He rubbed furiously at his forehead with his thumb and forefinger. He had to do better than this. He couldn't afford to be careless. Damn it, why did it have to be Carol?

Chapter 3

Duke pushed back his chair and stood. He didn't know that Carol had been involved, he reminded himself, trying to calm his erratic thoughts. Even if she had been, that didn't mean she had deliberately betrayed her husband and his partner. She could have connections no one knew about, someone she trusted, someone she'd told about that last mission, unsuspecting...

He jerked himself away from the table and headed for the door through which Carol had taken his jacket. Whoever she had told, for whatever reason, she knew better. She knew the danger of talking to anyone about her husband's movements. If it hadn't been deliberate, it had at the very least been criminally careless. She was still responsible for Mack's death.

He found the bedroom lit by a simple bedside lamp and opened the closet. His jacket hung inside and he snatched it off the hanger. One thing he could be sure of, she was his only lead.

No matter the circumstances, she could give him the answers he needed. The answers that would lead him to Mack's killer, and the person who had destroyed his own identity. And nothing, *nothing*, was going to get in his way of finding that person.

He turned to leave, and his gaze fell on the bed. The satin quilt gleamed in the light from the lamp. Creamy lace edged the pale blue fabric, sweeping to the floor at the foot. Two huge lace-trimmed pillows sat propped against the headboard, soft and inviting.

Duke swallowed. He found the feminine bed appealing—enticing, seductive . . .

"Oh, you found your jacket."

He jumped, as if he'd been caught doing something outrageous. Maybe he had, he thought guiltily. For a moment he'd let himself imagine . . . "Uh . . . yeah. I found it. I'd better get going."

He started forward to brush by her. She sidestepped at the same time and he barely managed to pull up to avoid colliding with her. He stood so close to her he could hear her breathing. Her perfume filled his head, his mind, his senses . . .

He saw a faint flush stain her cheeks. "I'm sorry," she muttered, and stepped out of his way. He felt sorry, too. Sorry he had to go through with this mess. Sorry he had to hound her until he knew what she knew.

"Thanks for dinner. I enjoyed it very much. You're a good cook."

She smiled at that. "And you're an entertaining guest. I enjoyed your company."

"Good." He managed a fairly normal smile. "Then we'll have to do it again."

For a moment she hesitated, then said quietly, "I'd like that."

She walked with him to the door, opening it for him as they reached it. "Where did you leave your car? At the garage?"

"I don't have a car. I prefer to walk. It's not far."

He had his back to her, and by the time he turned to face her, he had the mask under control. "Thanks again."

She looked up at him. "You're welcome."

He hesitated, then said good-night and left before he could change his mind about staying for coffee. For a moment there he'd been sorely tempted to tell her his true identity. To ask her what she knew, to beg her to tell him so he could finish this, get out of her life and put an end to his misery.

Luckily for him, his common sense had held strong. If she had the slightest notion of his true identity, she'd scream bloody murder. He hadn't needed Mack's recounting of her scathing comments to know how she felt about him. She'd tell him to go to hell.

And then there was always the possibility that she had planned Mack's death. Which would mean she'd planned his, too. She undoubtedly knew they would be together that night.

He paused on the step outside, pulling the cold, damp air into his lungs. He couldn't believe that. All his instincts screamed at him not to believe that. But then he couldn't trust his instincts anymore.

He was on shaky ground, and unless he pulled himself together, he could blow this whole thing. For no matter how vehemently he denied it, Carol Everett was still firmly under his skin. And if he couldn't ignore that and concentrate on what he needed to know, he was in deep, deep trouble.

Carol walked slowly back to the kitchen, wishing she could shake the nagging feeling of unrest. Or, better still, understand why she felt that way about a man whom she found charming, friendly, entertaining and, much to her gratification, intelligent.

She liked him. Even if he did unsettle her poise every now and again, making her feel more like a high-school graduate than an accomplished businesswoman.

She sighed as she lifted the phone from the hook. It might be better if she didn't tell Win that he disturbed her pulse when he said her name and made her insides flutter every time he gave her his slow smile.

In fact, she cautioned herself, it might be better if she didn't take him up on his suggestion to have dinner together again. The last thing she needed, or wanted, was to become interested in someone who reminded her so much...

She stabbed out Win's number, smothering the thought before it could surface. A voice answered in mid ring.

"It's me," she said, hoping Win wouldn't get too persistent.

"Your friend has left?"

"Five minutes ago."

"He looks very nice."

Carol frowned. "Where did you see him?"

"We came up in the elevator together. I saw him get off on your floor, carrying a bottle of wine. So, when you said you had a guest, I thought it would be him."

"You were right." She had to change the subject, Carol thought, and now. "So, when shall we get together?"

"Tomorrow night?"

"Sounds fine."

"Good. Then you can tell me more about your new friend. What is his name? Are you going to see him again?"

She didn't want to tell Win his name, but there didn't seem to be any way around it. "It's Duke. And I'll tell you about him tomorrow." She hung up, uncomfortable with the knowledge that if he asked to see her again, she'd have a hard time turning him down.

Duke kept up a brisk pace, conscious of his footsteps echoing behind him. He'd turned his collar up against the rain, which had begun again in earnest. Splashing through the puddles he watched his distorted shadow stretch and shrink as he passed under the lampposts, then disappear altogether in the darkness between.

He paused on the curb to let a car turn down the narrow street, and as he did so, he thought he heard another pair of footsteps behind him. Looking back over his shoulder, he could see nothing but the silent buildings and the empty sidewalk.

He jammed his hands in his pockets and crossed to the next curb, aware of a prickly sensation on the back of his neck. In the old days he would never have ignored such a feeling. And he wasn't about to now.

He waited until he was level with the entrance to an alleyway. At the last minute he sidestepped into it and flattened himself against the wall.

He could feel his heart pounding as the seconds ticked by. A car engine growled in the distance, then sped by, sending up a spray of muddy water.

His shoulders ached with tension. Raindrops crept down his ear and fell into his upturned collar. A shiver shook him, rattling his teeth.

Nothing. Only the steady dripping of rain from the overhang above his head and the ripples in the puddles beneath. Just to be sure, he edged to the corner of the building and stuck his nose out just far enough to see.

The lights of an approaching car sliced through the slanting rain, lighting up the sidewalk on either side. The street was empty. He'd let his nerves get the better of him.

Cursing himself for behaving like an idiot, he quickened his pace, anxious now to get home and into some dry clothes. Even so, he couldn't resist one last scrutiny behind him when he reached the steps to his apartment. As he did so, he saw a figure in a dark overcoat wheel around and start walking briskly in the opposite direction.

Swearing, Duke began chasing after him, knowing as he did so that he didn't have a chance of catching up. Already the sprinting figure drew rapidly away from him. The accident had slowed him down more than he'd realized, Duke thought, gazing furiously after the retreating figure.

He retraced his steps, his mind turning over the possibilities. It could have been a potential mugger, losing his nerve when Duke turned and confronted him. On the other hand, it could have been someone following him, and once he'd reached his destination, had achieved what he wanted.

Wishing fervently he knew which it was, Duke moved quickly down the steps. He saw the light flashing on his answering machine the moment he opened the door. First things first, he decided. He was wet, chilled to the bone, and ready now for the Scotch he'd turned down at Carol's place.

It took him several minutes to get his circulation back under a hot shower. He toweled himself dry, enjoying the brisk rubdown as his blood warmed. Then, fastening the towel around his waist, he padded to the kitchen where he kept his Scotch. The liquid burned his throat as he crossed the carpet to the phone. Feeling a whole lot better, he dismissed his apprehension about the figure on the street and pressed the button with his thumb.

The voice that filled the room gave him a start of surprise. He'd expected to hear Royce's voice. But the somewhat breathless tone was unmistakably that of Charles.

"Duke. I have to talk to you. Urgent. Don't call me back. I'll call you later." The silence that followed the click seemed particularly dense.

Frowning, Duke set his glass on the table. He'd left his watch in the bathroom and he went back to retrieve it. Ten-thirty. It would be five-thirty on the east coast. He might just catch him. Dialing the number, he prayed Royce would still be there.

The phone rang in an empty office, seven times before he replaced the receiver. He hesitated only a second or two. This couldn't wait. He took another swig of Scotch, then picked up the phone and dialed again.

He'd memorized the special code Royce had given him. The operator answered the call and asked the specified questions. Duke answered without hesitation. Seconds later, he heard the phone ringing in Royce's Washington apartment.

Royce's murmur sharpened as soon as he heard Duke's voice. "What is it? What's wrong?"

"I don't know. I was hoping you'd tell me."

"If you're being deliberately ambiguous," Royce said irritably, "let me assure you I do not appreciate it. I do not appreciate it at all. Not at all. Is everything all right there?"

A tiny warning sounded in the back of Duke's head. "Sure," he said, adopting a light tone, "everything is fine here. Moving along according to plan. I was just wondering if Charles is back from vacation."

His senses tingled as the pause on the end of the line went on a little too long. "What do you want to say to Charles you can't say to me?" Royce said finally.

"Charles told me where I could buy my favorite brand of bourbon. I can't remember the name of the street it was on. I wanted to ask him where it is."

"Is that all? You took this risk for a bottle of bourbon?" Royce cleared his throat. "Well, you're out of luck. Charles is still on vacation. Won't be back for a while longer."

"You haven't seen him then, since I left?"

"No, I haven't. Of course I haven't. He's in the middle of the Pacific somewhere. I haven't talked to him. Don't know when I will. And you should know better than to call here unless it's important. You must call the office, where the conversation is scrambled. You should know that. What's the matter with you?"

"Sorry. Out of practice, I guess." Without saying goodbye, Duke replaced the receiver.

He sat down on the edge of the couch and reached for his Scotch. Something was definitely off base. He sipped the Scotch, no longer feeling the bite of it. The only person he'd given his phone number to was Royce. And Royce himself had insisted that Duke give it to no one else. It was one of the conditions he'd laid down before disclosing Carol's address. He was going to give her as much protection as possible.

It was safe to assume that Royce had not given the number to anyone else. And if Royce hadn't seen or talked to Charles, that raised a very interesting question.

How, Duke wondered, as he reached for the button on the answering machine, did Charles get his number from the middle of the Pacific ocean? And what was so desperately urgent that he'd broken the rules to call?

"I am glad to see you are unharmed, dear lady," Jasper Golding said, as Carol approached the main doors of the apartment building the next morning.

She hid her resentment with a smile. "I told you there was nothing to worry about."

"I think you young ladies are taking far too much of a risk, entertaining men alone in your flats."

Deciding it was time to change the subject, Carol peered up at Jasper's face. "Your voice sounds odd. Are you coming down with something?"

Jasper cleared his throat. "Possibly. This English weather is not good for your health. All this damp fog and rain. I was wringing wet last night when I arrived home. How I miss the warm nights and sunshine of Jamaica." This last sentence was delivered in a low, drawn-out mournful tone for effect.

Carol managed to look sympathetic. "Better wrap up warm. Drink lots of liquids." She left Jasper still muttering about the consequences of the weather on his health. Never in her life, she thought as she hurried down the street to the garage, had she seen anyone more robust than Jasper Golding. It would take a full dose of pneumonia to bring him to his knees.

The rain had stopped, leaving occasional patches of pastel blue sky in the gaps between the smoky clouds. There might even be a chance of sun, Carol thought, glad now that she'd left her umbrella behind. She hated carrying the thing anyway. She was always leaving it somewhere. Most of the time she left it at home and braved the rain.

Inside the garage the smell of oil and diesel almost overpowered her. Her heels clicked on the concrete floor as she crossed to her car. She fitted the key in the door, then froze as a voice said behind her, "Good morning."

Bracing herself, she turned to smile at Duke Winters. "It certainly looks like one. The rain has stopped."

"Yeah. I noticed."

He stood directly under the harsh neon lighting. She hadn't noticed until now, Carol thought, just how smooth

his skin looked. Even when he smiled, his eyes barely crin-
kled.

From things he'd told her, she'd put his age somewhere in
his late thirties, maybe three or four years older than herself. Yet he had the skin of a much younger man. She made
a mental note to find out his secret.

Maybe she could bottle it, she thought with a wry smile
to herself.

"Something wrong?"

She switched her gaze to his eyes, surprised by the wariness in his voice. The quickening of her pulse disturbed her,
and she twisted the key in the lock. "No, I was just wondering..." Deciding that the question would sound silly, she
let it go.

"Wondering what?"

She pulled the door open and climbed into the car. "Oh,
it's not important. By the way, the car runs beautifully.
Whatever you did seems to have worked."

"Glad to hear it." He leaned on the door, preventing her
from closing it. "And I'm not married, just in case that's
what you were wondering."

She felt a sharp thrill of excitement as he looked down at
her, his dark eyes intent on her face. "So," he added softly,
"what are you doing tonight?"

She was so tempted. It took an effort to say, with a light
note of regret in her voice, "I'm spending the evening with
a friend."

He said nothing for a moment or two, but stood there
looking down at her with a quizzical expression on his face,
almost as if he didn't believe her.

Her breath caught in her throat, and she forced a laugh.
"I don't want to be rude, but I'll be late if I don't leave
now."

He waited a couple of seconds longer before stepping back. She closed the door, aware of her heart beating rapidly. She concentrated on fitting the key in the ignition, then gunned the engine. Looking back, she found him still watching her. She tried for a casual smile, but her lips felt stiff as she raised her hand.

He nodded, his gaze still hard on her face. With her heart racing, she drove out of the garage and into the pale sunshine.

She found Anna waiting for her when she arrived at her office door, still feeling out of breath as if she'd just come off a brisk jog.

"By the look of those sparkly eyes, your dinner date must have been a huge success," Anna observed, as she walked into the office behind Carol.

"It was, and I'm not prepared to discuss it right now," Carol said firmly. She sat down at her desk and began sorting through the mail.

"Okay. Just one question." Anna perched a slim hip on the corner of the desk. "Are you going to see him again?"

Carol slit open an envelope with her thumbnail. "I'm amazed at the number of people who have an inordinate interest in my social life. I feel like taking out an ad in the personal column of the *Daily Mirror*. 'To whom it may concern. As of now, I have not made a decision as to whether or not I will be keeping company with Duke Winters again.'"

"Duke Winters? Is that his name? It sounds very dashing."

Carol put down the envelope. Anna's nose was positively twitching with curiosity. But her eyes, Carol noticed, were watching her with a shrewd, calculating expression that for some reason made Carol uncomfortable.

"I've got a lot of work to do," she said, waving a hand at the pile of mail. "Did you want something specific, or are you just here to bug me?"

To her relief, Anna slid off the desk. "I'm going. But I need the list of potentials you drew up yesterday. I can't find my copy of it."

Carol opened her desk drawer and took out a file. "Here. Make a copy of it and bring it back to me. I'll need it for the staff meeting this afternoon."

"Thanks." Anna tucked the file under her arm. "How about lunch?"

"Sounds good. On one condition. We don't talk about my love life."

"In that case," Anna said, backing away from the desk, "you're paying." She escaped through the door, missing the indignant look Carol sent her.

Duke stared down at the bowels of the station wagon's engine and frowned. He had more than the average motorist's knowledge of mechanics, thanks to a series of broken-down wrecks he'd bought cheap and attempted to fix up during his teenage years.

But his résumé had been padded. Considerably. It would be only a matter of time before Jim Bedford realized that his new mechanic's success so far with car repairs was due more to luck than judgment.

He'd better quit experimenting with the fuel line, he thought, while he still had some measure of credibility. The job had served its purpose. He'd achieved what he'd set out to do. Now that he'd contacted Carol it was up to him to continue the relationship. His job didn't matter anymore.

He went back to the car door, leaned in and twisted the ignition key. To his immense satisfaction, the engine caught and settled into an even purr. With a smirk he slammed down the hood, then went to find Jim to tell him he was quitting.

Carol was late leaving the office that evening. By the time she'd fought the traffic out of the city, she was feeling irritable, hungry, and not at all in the mood to face Win's avid questions.

Letting herself into her apartment, she toyed with the idea of calling her friend and begging off with a headache. But that, she thought dismally, would only prolong the inevitable. When Win got her nose into something, she didn't let up until she'd milked the subject dry.

The tall, too-thin woman who opened the door to her that evening seemed unusually preoccupied. Win had a habit of running her hand through her wiry brown hair when worried about something, and one look at the untidy tangle of short curls told Carol that Win had something on her mind.

She seemed reluctant to talk about it, answering Carol's concerned questions with her usual excuse of a tight deadline. "Now tell me all about Duke—is that his name?" she said, handing Carol a glass of pale yellow wine.

She had known the inquisition was coming, Carol thought, but even so, she was hardly prepared for the barrage of questions Win shot at her.

"Where did you meet him?" she wanted to know, watching Carol's face as she sipped the sweet-tasting wine.

"He fixed my car."

"How romantic! You broke down and he rescued you?"

"No, of course not. He's a mechanic at Bedford's down the road."

"A mechanic?" Win's face mirrored her surprise. "He doesn't look like a mechanic."

"No one looks like a mechanic when they're dressed up." But that wasn't it, Carol thought uneasily. It wasn't so much the way he looked as the way he acted, the way he held himself, that certain urbane attitude that could only come from knowledge and experience.

"Well, that is true. He lives close by here?"

"Not far. About a twenty-minute walk, I guess."

"Ah." Win nodded her head. "He doesn't drive?"

"He doesn't have a car. He's only here for a short time." She tried without success to change the subject. "This is good wine. What is it?"

Win answered with a German name impossible to recognize. "That's too bad your Duke is leaving. Where is he going?"

So much for her efforts to steer Win off course. Carol tipped her glass to catch the light in the crystal-clear liquid. Even for Win, these questions seemed excessive. Or maybe Carol was just being overly sensitive on the subject.

She sighed. "He's an American, and will probably be returning to the States before too long. So you can put away your hopes of a budding romance."

"How sad. He looks like such a nice man."

Something in her voice made Carol look up sharply, but Win's expression appeared to be sincere. Even so, she couldn't seem to forget that odd note she'd heard in the simple words, though she had no idea why it bothered her. The thought remained with her throughout the evening, and long after she should have been asleep.

Jim Bedford had reluctantly accepted Duke's notice to quit, especially after such a short time. Duke had felt bad about that and promised to work the next few days until Jim found a replacement. The next morning, Jim asked him to take out a customer's newly repaired Bentley on a test run.

Duke guided the sleek car out onto the street, listening intently to the engine for any telltale sounds that could indicate a problem.

He had driven only a hundred yards or so when he saw Carol on the steps of her building, apparently arguing with a short, muscular young man with a tangled mass of ginger curls.

As he drew closer, he could see Carol's expression. She looked mad, and a little scared. She was tugging at her arm, which her companion held tight in the crook of his elbow. Sensing trouble, Duke leaned on the horn.

Carol didn't know if she was relieved or embarrassed when Duke stuck his head out of the car window. She'd been flattered and somewhat comforted by Gordon's attention when she'd first met the friendly window cleaner. She'd just moved into the building, knew no one, and alone in a strange city, it had been pleasant to have someone chat and joke with her.

But lately he'd become a little too persistent, taking too much for granted and ignoring her attempts to fend off his propositions. Now he'd made her look inept and foolish in front of Duke Winters. The thought irritated her no end.

"Morning," Duke called out, giving Gordon a significant warning look. "I was hoping to catch you before you left. I'm just on my way out on a test run."

"Who's he?" Gordon muttered, still holding tight to Carol's arm.

"A friend of mine." Again Carol tugged, and this time the window cleaner let her go.

Duke appeared to ignore the man with her as he leaned farther out the door. "How about dinner tonight? I'll pick you up at seven?"

"Another bleeding Yank," Gordon said nastily. "Got a nerve, 'e has, butting in on our conversation."

Carol glanced at Gordon's belligerent face. When she looked back, Duke had climbed out of the car. Dismayed at the possibility of a confrontation, she said loudly, "Dinner would be fine, Duke. I'll be ready at seven."

Her heart thumping, she watched his gaze travel up and down Gordon's thickset frame. Duke's expression seethed with menace, sending a chill down her back. He looked tougher, somehow, and thoroughly dangerous. Beside her, Gordon took a small step backward.

"You need a ride to the garage?" Duke asked, without taking his gaze off Gordon.

Struggling to gain control of the situation, Carol shook her head. "No, thanks. I'll be fine. And I'd better get going." Moving off the steps, she sent a nervous glance at Gordon. His face was a mask of hostility.

Apparently satisfied, Duke slowly turned and climbed back into the car. "See you tonight, then," he said quietly.

Carol nodded. Then Duke raised his hand, and she felt as if a cold hand had clamped her stomach. His forefinger and thumb were curved into the military signal, A—OK.

It was all she could do to stop the gasp of horror from escaping. She had seen that signal so many times before. Mack had used it every time he'd said goodbye to her.

For a moment, she froze on the sidewalk. Duke withdrew his head, started the engine and pulled away from the curb. Carol glanced back at Gordon, still poised on the top step. He was watching the car move down the street, an odd, watchful expression on his face.

Unnerved, Carol sped down the sidewalk toward the garage. She was being ridiculous. A lot of people used that signal. He reminded her of Mack. But Mack was dead. It was just coincidence, that was all. *Mack was dead.*

Arriving at his apartment late that afternoon, Duke's breath hissed through his teeth when he saw the light flash-

ing on his answering machine. He crossed the floor in two
strides and punched the button. Charles's soft voice answered him.

"Where are you? I need to talk to you. No, for heaven's
sake don't call me. I'll call you back tomorrow. Fourteen
hundred hours. Be there."

Cursing, Duke lifted the receiver, his fingers hovering
over the buttons. Then, cursing again, he lowered his hand.
For heaven's sake, don't call me. There had been no mistaking the urgency in Charles's voice.

He knew that to call could put Duke in danger. Someone, somewhere could be monitoring the phone. The only
safe call was through the channels, where it was impossible
to monitor. Even then, there was a possibility that Duke's
phone could be tapped, though he doubted it.

But then Charles hadn't called through the channels.
Royce would have known if he had. Whatever Charles had
to tell him, it was something he didn't want Royce to know
about.

Duke headed for the bathroom, glancing at his watch.
Was it something about Carol? Did Charles know something Royce didn't? Or was there something Royce was reluctant to tell him?

Duke turned on the faucet of the shower full blast, then
began stripping. Damn it, surely Carol couldn't be directly
involved. Charles would have told him if he'd had evidence
of that.

He dropped his shirt on the floor and unfastened his belt.
But he hadn't seen Charles since that day in the hospital.
He'd been pretty fuzzy at the time, but he was damn sure
he'd have remembered if Charles had said anything then.

Pushing his jeans over his knees, he stepped out of them.
Why hadn't he seen Charles since then? Now that he
thought about it, it was as if Charles had been deliberately

avoiding him. Was it because he knew how Duke had felt about Carol and didn't want to tell him the truth?

Hands clenched, Duke stepped into the shower. No, he wasn't going to do this. He would wait until he talked to Charles before jumping to conclusions. Until then, he'd give Carol the benefit of the doubt.

Stepping under the water, he let it pour over his body. On the other hand, there was no sense in wasting an opportunity. He was spending the evening with her. And he'd do his darndest to find out what she knew. If he had to pull out all the stops to do it. With a grim smile, he poured shampoo on his head and began to lather.

The restaurant, much to Carol's surprise, glowed with flashing neon lights and was obviously very popular, judging by the number of people trying to make themselves heard above the background of rock music.

She wondered what Duke was trying to prove as they were led to a corner booth by the windows, which turned out to be quieter and more intimate than she'd expect in a place like that. Then the waitress handed her the menu, and she smiled when she saw the typical list of American hamburgers and steaks.

"Thought you'd appreciate a taste of home," Duke said, when she looked up to find him watching her.

A tiny smile played around his mouth, and once again she was reminded of how attractive he could be. And how familiar. She dropped her gaze back to the menu, wondering what had prompted that thought this time.

"Something wrong? You don't like the menu?"

"Oh, no, it's fine. I'm just trying to make up my mind which of these delicious-sounding hamburgers I can't live without." She studied the list, trying to shake the memory of his signal to her from the car that morning.

She had to stop doing this. He reminded her of Mack, true, in too many ways to be comfortable, but she was in control of the situation. Just because she was having dinner with him didn't mean she was creating a lasting relationship.

He was an attractive, entertaining man, and she enjoyed being with him. That was all. She would be in town for another three months at most. And it was pleasant to have someone to take her out. She'd missed that. So where was the harm? She would just have to accept that he made her think about Mack every now and again and try to ignore the anxiety pangs that gave her.

"You only have to eat it, you don't have to make a long-term commitment to it."

She jerked her chin up and met his amused gaze. "I'm sorry?"

"The hamburger. The amount of time you're taking to decide, I figured it was serious."

"Oh." She forced a laugh. "Sorry. It's been so long since I've had a really good hamburger, I'd hate to make the wrong choice."

"We can always come back and try again."

She didn't know what to say to that and was relieved when the waitress arrived to take their order.

The hamburger turned out to be every bit as delicious as it had sounded, and Carol enjoyed it immensely. Even if she was conscious of the fact that her pale blue dress and navy blazer were a little overdressed for the type of restaurant.

Although Duke was more casual in dark pants and a bomber jacket, he still managed to look more elegant than most of the men seated around her. It was his travels, she decided, that gave him that man-of-the-world attitude. Anyone who could pick up and go anywhere at the drop of a hat had to be a special kind of man. An exciting, fascinating kind of man.

He looked up at that moment, catching her studying him. To cover her discomfort, she launched into a discussion about the differences between American and British ways of doing business. They were still arguing over a point when Duke suggested an after-dinner drink.

Carol ordered a brandy and Babycham, a cocktail Win had introduced her to. After the waitress had left, Duke picked up his Scotch. "Whether it's the British or the American way, here's to a successful conclusion of your stay here."

Carol smiled. "Thanks, I'll drink to that. And here's to wherever and whenever you travel next."

"I'll drink to that." His eyes looked grave as he studied her over the top of his glass. "You'll find it hard to settle down once you get back to the States, after this."

"Probably." Carol put down her glass and wrapped her fingers around it. "But I'm sure I'll keep busy enough to keep my mind occupied."

"You live alone in New York?"

"Yes." Carol twisted the glass in her hands. "I have a small apartment in Manhattan."

"You must have a very good job."

"I had a generous settlement from my husband's company when he died."

"Oh? I thought you said he died in a car accident."

Mad at herself for the slip, Carol said casually, "He did. But he had some kind of insurance with the company, since he did a lot of driving for them." Weak, but it would have to do.

"I see." His voice had sounded odd, but when she looked up his expression was bland. "How long were you married?"

"Seven years." Had it really been that long? Looking back it seemed so much shorter. They had spent so little time together—

"You must miss him very much."

Again she heard that odd note. Puzzled, she said slowly, "I was on the point of divorcing him when he died." She saw his expression change. She was startled herself, not sure why she'd told him that.

In spite of her reservations, she seemed to be slipping into a comfortable, relaxed relationship with this man. And it wasn't what she wanted at all.

Chapter 4

"We met in New York," Carol said, before Duke had a chance to comment. "I had just started working there, and I'd been invited to my first party. Mack asked me to dance, then told me he'd gate-crashed and would I tell the hostess I'd invited him."

She smiled at the memory. Those had been the good days. Before all the secrecy and lies. Before all the unexplained accidents, the whispered threats on the phone, the long, lonely nights of terror.

"And did you?"

Startled, she looked up. "What?"

"Did you tell her you'd invited Mack?"

"Oh...no. I didn't even know the hostess. I'd been invited by a friend. Mack told her someone else had invited him. She believed him. She was so captivated by his charm she would have believed anything. Mack could charm a bone from a starving wolf."

"And what about you? Were you charmed by him?"

His eyes were uncomfortably intent on her face. Carol felt a tiny shiver touch her spine. Lifting her glass, she drank from it, then set it down carefully in front of her.

"I was fascinated by him. He was good-looking, and had a warm sense of humor that I couldn't resist. I was lonely. I grew up an only child, with the security of a close-knit family. New York can be frightening when you're out on your own. Mack was attentive, confident, and acted as if he wanted to take care of me. By the end of the evening, I think I was already halfway in love with him."

"So you married him."

"Yes. Though I don't know why he asked me to marry him."

"I imagine it was because he loved you."

Why, she wondered, was she telling him all this? What was it about him that made her feel as if she'd known him for years? She had known him for a few days, yet at times she felt as if she were talking to an old friend.

"I don't think he ever loved me," she said deliberately. She watched Duke slowly raise his glass and sip his Scotch.

"Then why would he marry you?"

"I don't know. I often asked myself that. I tried so hard to make it work. I wanted to make him happy, but something was driving him, something I couldn't understand. Something he wouldn't let me understand. And yet he fought so hard against the divorce. He didn't want it."

"But you did."

She hesitated, wary of saying too much, yet part of her finding a tremendous relief in just talking about it. "He wasn't the man I thought he was. It took me a long time to realize that it had all been a very clever, polished act. When I found out what . . . who Mack really was, I was terrified."

"Why? He was abusive?"

"No, not like that." She played with her glass for a moment, then took a sip of the champagne. It was time to change that line of thought. "Mack had always wanted a child. It's all he thought about, or talked about. It was an obsession with him."

"To have someone of his own. It's not unusual."

Carol frowned. "Anyway, we tried, but I could never get pregnant. I saw a specialist, who could find nothing wrong, but Mack refused to go. I think it would have killed him if he'd found out he was sterile."

"So he blamed you."

She looked up and saw something she hadn't seen before in his eyes. A deep, undeniable sympathy. She could feel warmth creeping over her, like a soft, comfortable blanket. "Yes," she said quietly. "He blamed me. I think if he could have had a child, things might have been different."

Duke's fingers curled around his glass. He seriously doubted it. He'd started the conversation in an attempt to find out more about the people Carol had been in contact with before Mack's death. Instead of that, he'd been given an entirely new insight into his friend's marriage. And he wasn't at all comfortable with what he'd learned.

He'd known from the start that Mack hadn't loved Carol the way a man should love the woman he marries. But he figured that Mack had done his best to make the marriage work. Now he wasn't so sure.

From what he could make out, it appeared that Mack hadn't been truthful with Carol about what he did for a living before he'd married her. That must have been a terrible shock for her to find out later.

He was beginning to get a very different picture from the one Mack had painted of his life with Carol. The woman seated opposite him was nothing like the complaining shrew that Mack had described. This was more like the fun-loving, warm-hearted, sensitive woman he'd always imagined her to be. Until Mack had poisoned his mind.

Duke lifted the glass and took a healthy swig of the liquor. Had Mack known how his partner had felt about his wife? Had he fabricated all those stories to cool Brandon's interest, because things were not going right in his marriage, and he was afraid that Brandon might step in?

One thing Duke was certain of. The reason Mack had held onto the marriage and fought for it, was for the baby he so desperately needed. He needed a son, and he needed a mother to take care of it. And Carol had been there, ready and willing, until she'd found out what kind of man she'd married.

Even the whiskey couldn't warm his heart as he looked at the misery on Carol's face. He wanted to reach across the table and cover her hand with his. Offer her whatever comfort he could. What a waste. What a damn waste. Maybe if he'd stepped in long ago, instead of considering Mack's feelings he might have—

Shock rippled through him as he realized where his thoughts were leading him. He couldn't afford these feelings, he warned himself. There were too many problems involved; it was just impossible. He'd never allowed himself to get personally involved with any woman and he wasn't about to start now. Not with Carol. Especially not with Carol.

Even as his mind formed the words, he knew the futility of fighting them. If he wasn't mistaken, it was already way too late. And he didn't have one single idea of how he was going to deal with it. Not one.

"My main problem," Carol said, picking up her drink, "wasn't another woman, like so many broken marriages. My problem was another man."

Seeing the shock on Duke's face, she hurried to explain. "Oh, no, I don't mean like that. It wasn't a sexual relationship. If you had known my husband, or his partner, Brandon Pierce, you would have no doubts about that."

Aware that the bitterness had sharpened her voice, Carol drained her glass before continuing. "My husband," she said carefully, "and Brandon Pierce were very much alike. They were ruthless men who played too hard and drank too much and used women for their own ends."

She pushed the glass away from her, unable to stop her hands from shaking. "Brandon Pierce was to blame for the breakup of my marriage. He was the leader, and Mack followed. My husband idolized Brandon, with a sick kind of worship like he was some kind of god. I begged Mack to give up what he was doing, to leave Brandon Pierce and everything he stood for behind, in order to save our marriage."

She took a steadying breath. "He refused. Brandon meant more to him than anyone. If it hadn't been for his friendship with that man, my husband might have been alive today."

"That," Duke said coldly, "is pure and utter nonsense."

Shocked more by his tone than his words, Carol looked up. The sympathy had vanished, to be replaced by a stark resentment that stunned her.

"Don't you think," Duke said more calmly, "that it's possible it was your unhappy marriage that drove your husband into that kind of friendship? He sounds like the kind of man who was quite capable of making his own decisions. Wasn't it possible that he preferred his friend's company to yours?"

Stunned by this unexpected attack, Carol could only stare at him, speechless and at a loss as to how to defend herself.

Apparently realizing he'd gone too far, Duke signaled to the waitress for the bill. By the time he'd settled it, Carol had recovered her composure enough to gather up her purse and make a dignified exit.

Standing on the curb outside, she waited while he hailed a cab. She wished now she'd insisted on bringing her car. Whatever had triggered that outburst, it was totally uncalled for, she thought, tapping her foot impatiently on the ground.

She was just glad she'd found out how unreasonable he was before she'd let herself get in too deep. Not that she'd intended to, anyway. At least now she had a good reason.

The bulky cab swung into the curb and jerked to a halt. Duke pulled the door open and she climbed in, sliding across the seat to get as far away from him as she could. Her heart was still thumping with suppressed resentment at his lack of understanding. She might have known he'd defend the male side of the issue. Men were all alike.

"I'm sorry," Duke said quietly, as the cab pulled away from the curb. "That was none of my business. I apologize."

"Forget it. It's not important." Why, she thought wearily, had she told him all that, anyway? How could she expect him, a complete stranger, to understand?

She leaned back in the seat and stared miserably out of the window. To make matters worse, drops of rain smeared the glass. God, how she longed to be back in the States. She'd had enough of this city, its unfamiliar streets teeming with people she didn't know. At least in New York she had her friends, and people she worked with who knew and understood her.

Here there wasn't one person she'd known longer than three months. They were all strangers, compared to the people back home.

So why was it, she wondered, that even now, sitting straight-backed and tense next to the silent man at her side, did she still feel that strange sense of familiarity?

Frowning, she cast her mind back over the conversation. Something he'd said still clung in her mind, something that had struck her as odd at the time, but then she'd dismissed it, caught up in the conversation. She worried at it, like a child with a loose tooth.

The cab was drawing up at the curb outside her building before she remembered. It was when she'd talked about Mack's obsession with having a child. What was it Duke had said? *To have someone of his own.* As if he'd known that Mack had been an orphan. But that was impossible. She hadn't mentioned that at all, she was positive. So how in the world, she asked herself with a growing sense of misgiving, could Duke Winters possibly know that?

Seated at her side, Duke fought his frustration. He'd blown it, he thought savagely. And what made it worse was the knowledge that his ego had been the cause of his reaction. Now he'd have to work twice as hard to make amends.

How could he have been so stupid, so damn sensitive, to have made such a mistake? True, he'd always known that Carol resented him. He hadn't known why, until now. The fact that she blamed him for Mack's death had been just too much to take.

However unjust her statement had been though, it convinced him of one thing. Carol had not planned her husband's death. Her sincerity when she'd accused Brandon Pierce of being the cause, however indirect, had been painfully clear.

He never had believed her capable of murder. But now he had to find out who had been clever enough to find out from her just where he and Mack would be that night. And why she had kept quiet about it. Was she protecting someone? Someone she trusted and couldn't believe was capable of murdering her husband. Someone who had a big enough stake in something to want the deaths of two men.

But who? He had to find out who were Carol's friends, Duke thought, as the cab pulled up at the curb in front of her building. And he'd be lucky now if she'd even speak to him again.

He thrust a handful of money into the cab driver's hand, knowing he was being overly generous with the tip. He was more concerned about catching Carol before she had a chance to shut the door on him.

He scrambled out of the cab with the driver's thanks ringing in his ears. Carol stood on the steps, looking more pensive than mad. Taking that as a good sign, he relaxed his face into a smile.

She didn't return it. Her eyes searched his face as she said quietly, "Thanks for dinner."

"You're welcome. I enjoyed it. In fact, I enjoyed it so much, I'd like to do it again. How about tomorrow night?"

Her face changed, becoming cool and distant. "Sorry, I'm busy."

She turned to go and he stepped forward, laying his hand on her arm. "Look," he said, putting all the warmth he could manage into his eyes, "I'm sorry about the stupid remark I made back there. Too much male egotism, I guess. I'd like the chance to make up for it."

She looked up at him, and he was dismayed to see real pain in her expression. "You should never make a judgment, Mr. Winters, without knowing all the facts. And there's no need to make up for anything. It's not that important to me."

He had no idea what prompted him to do what he did next. Something about the way she looked at him reminded him of that first night at the barbecue. He'd wanted to kiss her then, and only his friendship with Mack had stopped him.

But this time there was no Mack to prompt his conscience. There was only him and Carol, alone on a wet, deserted street, standing in the warm glow of the street lamp. He stared down at her upturned face and lost all sense of reasoning.

He tightened his grip on her arm. He felt her resistance but he was past worrying about it. All he could think about was covering that soft mouth with his until she gasped for breath.

Her eyes widened when he grabbed her other arm and pulled her against him. He didn't give her a chance to protest. Instead, he lowered his lips to hers, forcing her head back with the pressure of his mouth.

He wasn't sure what he'd expected. He really hadn't had time to think about that. He only knew that somewhere in the back of his subconscious mind, he'd wanted this since the moment he'd first set eyes on her seven years ago.

He might have come to his senses sooner, if Carol had gone on resisting. But the moment their bodies collided, she melted against him. Her unexpected surrender fired his blood as no amount of resistance could have.

He growled, low in his throat, and wrapped his arms around her, desperate to know the intimate touch of her body. Her mouth opened under his, and the blood roared in his ears. He deepened the kiss, grinding his hips against hers in an unconscious effort to release the pressure of his need. As he did so, he felt a spasm shudder through her.

It was enough to shake some sense into his reeling mind. Though it took a supreme effort to drop his arms and move away from her. "I'll call you," he said, his voice husky with the strain of his self-denial.

Her eyes looked huge in the light from the street lamp. She was breathing too fast. He watched her hand move up to her throat, as if she wanted to hide the fact from him. God, how he longed to bury his mouth in that soft, warm hollow.

The touch of her still heated his belly. He would carry that memory throughout the night, he thought, and probably long after that. The memory of her warm, firm body, the swell of her breasts, the curve of her back, and the sweet torture of her mouth under his would torment him for days.

"Good night, Duke," she said softly, and disappeared through the doors.

He felt an odd sense of loneliness after she'd gone. He was glad of the long walk home. It gave him time to get his thoughts straightened out. He hadn't planned to kiss her. It had just happened. And it had nothing to do with his need to stay in close contact with her. In fact, he could well have blown the entire thing if she'd taken offense.

But she hadn't. She'd responded in a way that had made his heart sing and his body crave more. He had to be crazy. Of all the stupid moves to make, this had to be the worst.

If she had the slightest inkling of who he really was, she would cut him up in little pieces and feed him to the sharks. She would never forgive him for taking advantage of her like that.

Cursing himself, he quickened his stride. If he had one ounce of sense left in his scrambled brain, he'd get out of here before things went too far. Yet he couldn't do that until he'd accomplished his goal. He had to find Mack's killer. Somehow. And to do that, he had to see Carol again. He had to gain her confidence and trust in order to find out who it was she trusted so completely that she had broken the golden rule and put her husband in danger.

And how, he thought in quiet desperation, was she going to feel when she found out that not only had she been responsible for Mack's death, however innocently, but the man she detested above all others had been the one to prove it?

He couldn't let that stop him, he reminded himself as he turned into his stairwell. He had sworn to find the man who had wrecked his life and killed his best friend. He couldn't let anything stand in the way of that, even if Carol stuck pins in his effigy.

He might as well face it. It just wasn't in the cards. She'd never been meant for him, and never would be. And he had better get damned used to the idea before he let his sexual urges get the better of his common sense.

He unlocked the door and flung it open. He was two steps into the room before he saw what was waiting for him. When he did, he could only stand and swear, loudly and profusely, using every curse he could think of.

Carol let herself into her apartment and closed the door gently behind her. Leaning up against it, she closed her eyes. Her heart still raced and her skin felt flushed when she pushed the damp curls back from her forehead.

She couldn't believe the force of her reaction to Duke's kiss. It had been a long time, if ever, since she had felt such a strong surge of sexual need. The second he'd touched her, she'd felt the primitive tug of desire. It had billowed in hot waves up her body until she'd felt dizzy with the sheer power of her hunger.

She'd felt an insane urge to tear the clothes from his body, desperate for the longing to feel his naked flesh pressed against hers. Where in heaven's name had all that passion come from?

She let out her breath in a loud sigh. She had always enjoyed the physical side of her marriage, at least until her fear had taken over all her senses. Her reaction to Duke's touch was a clear indication of how much she'd missed that part of it. She had never been quite that carried away before.

She moved into the room, slipping off her jacket before slumping down on the couch. And she had better not get that carried away again, she warned herself. This was crazy. Not only was this man a clone of Mack in every respect except looks, she had this weird feeling there was something very wrong somewhere.

She couldn't forget that odd remark he'd made during dinner, and then his very strange reaction to her statement about Brandon Pierce. Could Duke have known either man? she wondered. Was it possible he was connected to the organization somehow?

Frowning, she got up and walked into the kitchen. But if he was, what could he possibly want with her? She had nothing to do with them anymore. And why wouldn't he explain who he was? It just didn't make sense.

She reached for the coffee, aware of the flutter of apprehension that had once been so familiar. No, it couldn't be starting all over again. She couldn't stand to go through all that again. She'd escaped from all that terror and pain when Mack had died. It was over. It was time she put it all behind her and forgot it.

The hot liquid warmed her, calming her fears. She was overreacting, that was all. She wandered into the bedroom to hang up her jacket. She'd always had an active imagination. She'd been unnerved by Duke's move on her and her response to him. The remark had meant nothing, she was reading too much into it.

As for his reaction to her remark about Brandon Pierce, that was understandable. He was an attractive man, and it was hard to believe he hadn't been married at some time in his life. Maybe he'd been through a bitter divorce, with all kinds of accusations flung at him. She'd met men like that before who were oversensitive about who was to blame for a breakup.

She shed the rest of her clothes and climbed into bed, anxious to let sleep put an end to her chaotic thoughts. But as she drifted off, she couldn't help wondering uncomfortably if she wasn't finding excuses for Duke Winters because she found him attractive, seductive and wholly irresistible.

Duke stared at the chaos in his living room, his mind churning out fragments of thoughts in all directions. Someone had done a pretty good job. Cushions everywhere, drawers pulled out and ransacked, waste bin in the kitchen emptied out on the floor, and more of the same in the bedroom.

Duke kicked a shoe across the room and sank onto the stripped bed. As far as he could tell, nothing was missing. So it wasn't a burglary. Whoever had done this had been looking for something. Probably whoever was on his tail the night before. Perhaps someone who suspected he might not be who he claimed to be and wanted to find out more about him.

Duke got up from the bed and walked back into the living room, his mind grappling with the implications. If whoever had shot out the tires that night had found out that Brandon Pierce hadn't died, they would be very anxious to find him and finish the job before he caught up with them.

There were only two ways they could suspect Duke Winters of being the man they were looking for. There could be a leak in the head office. Somehow he couldn't believe that.

Only Royce and Charles knew his real identity. The hospital staff had known him only as Duke Winters.

That left only one connection. Carol. They could have figured that Brandon Pierce would be bound to contact her sooner or later. They could have had her watched ever since the crash, waiting for a likely subject to turn up.

Cursing, Duke picked up the cushions and threw them back onto the couch. It could be anyone. Someone in her apartment building. A friend, someone she worked with; there were a dozen possibilities, all of them dangerous. It was pretty safe to assume that once they got him, they would get Carol, too.

Duke sank onto the couch and reached for the phone. He couldn't tell her about the search of his apartment. But he had to track down who it was who knew her well enough back home to trust them with vital information, and who was their connection. And he had to do it now. He'd just run out of time.

He'd begun to dial the number when he remembered Charles. Urgent, he'd said. Urgent enough to have discovered his phone number and called without Royce's knowledge. Maybe Charles had information and could tell him what he needed to know.

He closed his eyes and concentrated. At one time he'd had the phone number memorized.

Lifting his chin, he struggled with the combination. After a minute or two he thought he had it. Sending up a silent prayer, he put the call through. The anxious leap of his pulse was followed by frustration when a recorder kicked on.

He'd remembered the number all right. But Charles's voice announced that he was out of the country and would be in touch when he returned, sometime at the end of the month. That was two weeks away.

With Charles's warning still ringing in his ears, Duke hung up without leaving a message. He would just have to wait until his friend called back tomorrow.

He dialed again, and waited while the distant phone rang once, twice, three times, four—

"Hello?"

Guiltily, Duke glanced at his watch, then winced. "Hi," he said carefully. "It's me."

After a long pause, Carol said, "You woke me up."

"Oh, I'm sorry." He closed his eyes as the impact of her sleepy voice hit him. He tried not to imagine her lying in bed, wearing nothing but—

He shifted the receiver to the other ear. "Well, the truth is, I couldn't sleep and—"

"So you decided I shouldn't, either?"

"I figured that since you don't have to go to work tomorrow, you might not have gone to bed yet." He knew that sounded lame, and added quickly, "I wanted to catch you before you made any plans for tomorrow."

"I see."

He could actually see the vibration of his heartbeat under his shirt. Rubbing his chest with his free hand, he said casually, "I've always wanted to see the Tower of London. But it's not the kind of place you want to go to alone. So, I thought—"

"Do you think we could discuss this in the morning?"

Encouraged by the faint note of warmth in her voice, he pressed his luck. "Tell you what, I'll pick you up around ten. If it's not raining we can walk from there, or get a cab if it is. You show me around the Tower and I'll take you to lunch. Now how's that for a great deal?"

"What makes you think I'm an authority on the Tower?"

There was no mistaking the warmth now. His pulse began to race, and it had nothing to do with his need to question her. What he felt was a much more basic need. "You mean you're not?"

"I've never been inside the walls. Though I do know there are several towers, not just one."

"Okay, then, we'll explore together. And I'll still take you to lunch. How's that?"

Her pause seemed to go on forever. "That sounds fine. On one condition."

"Anything."

"If you want to see dungeons, you're on your own."

"Oh, right. Claustrophobia. I'll skip the dungeons."

"I'll see you at ten, then."

He still smiled, long after the click had told him she'd put down the phone.

Carol lay back on her pillow and stared up at the ceiling. What was it about that man that turned her brain to mush? The minute she heard his voice all her doubts and reservations vanished and all she could think about was how much she wanted to see him again.

She groaned and turned onto her stomach, burying her face in the pillow. So he was charming, and entertaining, and had a take-charge attitude that appealed to her. Mack had been all those things, too. At least, that's what she'd thought, until the veneer had started to rub off his subterfuge.

How could she have fallen in love with him and not known what kind of man he was? How could she not have known that the respected diplomat she planned to marry was in fact a ruthless, cold-blooded killer for hire?

When she'd discovered the truth and confronted him with it, he had defended himself by saying that if what he did wasn't exactly ethical, it was, in the eyes of the law, legal.

Carol twisted onto her back, pushing her hair from her eyes with both hands. Legal. As if that made everything all right. He said he hadn't told her before because it was safer for her not to know. Yet he'd never believed her fears.

He'd been impatient with her, until she was afraid to tell him anything for fear of starting another violent argument. She had actually begun to think she was losing her mind, as he kept suggesting. That the accidents that happened far too frequently were due to her own carelessness, and the whispered threats on the phone were nothing more than hallucinations.

Only after his death had she known the truth. That he'd had enemies who had used threats against his wife to send warnings to him. He'd ignored them all. He and his demon partner, Brandon Pierce, had gone on slaughtering the enemy, bought by some underground organization "working for the security and peace of the country," as Royce Westcott had been careful to explain after the funeral.

Carol sat up in a fruitless attempt to obliterate the memories. She didn't know what had made her more sick, to find out how he'd died, or the reasons why. But after the initial reactions, she'd felt the first real peace she had known in years.

And now it was being threatened again, by a man with the same easy charm and confidence that had first attracted her to Mack, and who was every bit as irresistible.

She had to be crazy, Carol thought, sliding down in the bed again. It was the only explanation she could come up with for her deadly attraction to the wrong man. Some people never learned, no matter how badly they were burned.

At last she fell into an uneasy sleep, disturbed by the hazy dreams that hadn't plagued her in months.

Duke arrived early the next morning, enjoying the wintry sunshine that chased away the hint of frost in the air.

Carol answered the door, looking flushed and a little agitated.

"Come in," she said, heading back across the room before he'd stepped inside the door. "I'm on the phone, but I'll be with you in a minute."

He waited, trying not to look as if he was listening, while Carol stood just inside the kitchen. "Yes," she said, her voice sounding oddly strained, "I told you, I'm going to be busy all day."

She paused, then said loudly, "I don't think that's any of your business. I have to go now."

Duke winced as the receiver crashed into its cradle.

"I'm sorry," Carol said, her face pink, "I'll be with you in just a minute." She disappeared in the direction of the bedroom.

He unzipped his leather jacket and jammed his hands in the pockets of his jeans. He'd have given anything to know who she'd been talking to with such vehemence in her voice. Jasper Golding, with his penchant for being overprotective? Win, perhaps, with her insatiable curiosity? Maybe the smart mouth he'd seen her arguing with the day before.

He paced slowly across the room, his mind racing with possibilities. He'd meant to ask her about that guy when they were at dinner. Then he'd jumped all over her when she'd accused him of being responsible for Mack's death, and lost the opportunity to question her any more after that.

He glanced up as Carol came back into the room, dressed in a pale blue jacket and black pants. She'd tied her hair back with a blue ribbon, and in spite of the casual clothes, managed to look breathtakingly elegant. He felt his concentration slipping away as he looked at her.

She flashed him a smile that warmed his whole body. "Ready for the tour?"

"You bet." He followed her outside, glancing up at the sky as she closed the door behind them. "Want to walk? It looks like it's going to stay dry."

"I'd enjoy that. It's not that far, and we can always get a cab home if we get tired."

He resisted the urge to take her arm and fell into step beside her, shortening his stride to match hers. "I hope you didn't have any trouble after I left yesterday morning," he said casually.

She sent him a brief glance. "Oh, no. Gordon's harmless enough, just a little persistent, that's all."

"He's the window cleaner you mentioned?"

"Yes. As a matter of fact he was on the phone when you arrived."

So that answered another of his questions, Duke thought grimly. Apparently Gordon was a little too persistent for comfort. Something worth looking into. "Where does this guy live?" he asked, as they paused at the edge of the curb. "In the neighborhood?"

Carol frowned. "I don't know. I don't know him that well. He doesn't drive, at least I've never seen him in a car. Usually I just bump into him on the street."

And not by accident, Duke was willing to bet. Wary of pushing too hard, he said lightly, "Well, I'm sure glad I beat him to it today."

Her frown disappeared. He was pleased to see the faint flush on her cheeks when she answered, "So am I."

He reached for her hand as they crossed the street, his spirits lifting when she closed her fingers around his. He couldn't think of a reason why he couldn't enjoy it. He might not have much longer to be with her like this.

Pushing the depressing thought away he asked her, "What do you usually do with your weekends? When you're not escorting lonely Americans around historic buildings, that is?''

She laughed. "I must admit, I don't meet too many lonely Americans. I shop, catch up on my chores, or do the tourist bit. I've peered through the railings of Buckingham Palace, taken a boat ride down to Greenwich, listened to the speakers in Hyde Park, visited Windsor Castle, taken a walking tour of Westminster, got lost in the maze at Hampton Court..."

Taking advantage of her pause for breath, he cut in. "All that and you haven't been to the Tower?"

"No." He felt the sudden tension in her fingers, but before he could wonder about it, she added, "I guess it's the thought of the dungeons. I know it's silly but—"

"I don't think phobias are silly. They are very serious to people who suffer from them."

She rewarded him with a warm smile. "I guess you do understand."

He raised her fingers and bent his head to press his lips against them. "You bet I do. Promise not to tell a living soul, but I have a horror of rats. I saw a movie once when I was a kid about a man who was eaten alive by them, and had nightmares for years. I've been terrified of them ever since."

Her eyes searched his face and his pulse leapt. He wanted to pull her into his arms and kiss her again, the way he had last night. Only this time he wouldn't let her go until—

"Some people don't understand how debilitating a phobia can be." She twisted her head to look straight ahead as they reached the busy intersection of Great Tower Street.

They crossed the street in silence, jostled by the crowds on their way to the Tower. Reaching the sidewalk, Carol said quietly, "It can be embarrassing at times. Tunnels, elevators, anything enclosed can trigger it. I literally freeze. I just can't move."

He nodded. "Like when someone's afraid of heights. They can go up all right, but when they look down, they freeze."

"Exactly. I try to avoid places where I know I could have a problem. Especially anywhere underground."

He felt her shudder vibrate through her fingers and slipped his arm around her shoulders, giving her a slight squeeze before catching her hand again. "Don't worry, we won't go anywhere near the dungeons. I promise."

"I don't want to stop you from seeing them," she said quickly. "I'll just wait outside."

He smiled down at her. "I wouldn't think of it. Besides, it wouldn't be any fun without you to hold my hand."

Again her smile warmed her face. "That's nice."

He met her gaze and held it, noticing with a spasm of pleasure how her lips parted for breath before she quickly turned her head.

Then the guilt hit him squarely in his midsection. What would she say if she knew who he really was? He knew what she'd say, he thought, his pleasure evaporating. She'd call him every name under the sun for playing this low, underhanded game. And she'd be right.

Chapter 5

Reaching the entrance to the grounds, Duke dropped Carol's hand to pull out his wallet. Ignoring her protest, he paid for them both, then followed her through an archway and across the stone causeway above a wide, dry moat.

Now that he was sure she was innocent, he reflected, as they paused to listen to a friendly man in a bright red beef-eater coat, he might have taken a chance and told her who he was. But he still had to find out who she had talked to that night, and why. He would learn nothing if she refused to talk to him.

Whoever had ransacked his apartment obviously had strong suspicions about his identity. As long as Carol didn't know who he was, she couldn't give him away. As long as his adversary wasn't sure about him, it was unlikely they would make a move. All he had to do was find out the identity of that person, before they discovered the truth about him.

"I don't believe you heard a word he said."

Carol's voice penetrated his thoughts, and he looked down at her with a guilty start. "Sorry. I was wondering where they keep the crown jewels."

"If you'd listened to him, you would have heard him tell you all about it." She peered up at him, her concern evident in her expression. "Is something wrong?"

Yes, he wanted to say. Something is wrong. This whole damn situation is wrong. "The only thing wrong," he said, taking her hand, "is that you've let go of my hand."

"I was planning on grabbing it again, the minute I saw a sign for the dungeons."

He grinned. "Feel free to grab on to me anytime you want."

"I might just do that."

She sent him a look that started a chain reaction in his body he wasn't sure he could control. He started walking, trying to ignore the urges that plagued him.

She led him alongside a large lawn strewn with dying leaves. The sun cast shadows of the majestic trees across the lush, dark green turf, and birds chirped madly in the almost bare branches.

"That's Tower Green," Carol said, looking across the wide expanse of grass. "Anne Boleyn died on the scaffold there." He watched a shadow cross her face. "I can't believe that something so terrible happened in such a beautiful and peaceful spot."

Something stirred in his heart. The longer he was with her, the more she fascinated him. He could relax with her, laugh with her, and just enjoy watching the different expressions chase across her face.

She had a certain air of confidence that he admired, yet there was also a vulnerability about her that appealed to his protective instincts. He found her incredibly seductive at times, in the way she smiled, the certain way she looked at him, the unconscious body language that made him ache to take her in his arms and make love to her.

He liked her compassion, her eagerness to please, the inner strength that had enabled her to make a new life for herself after Mack's death. It was too bad he hadn't met her first, before Mack had staked his claim.

Carol paused in front of the entrance to the Bloody Tower. "Well, here goes," she said, a little too cheerfully.

He squeezed her fingers. "You okay?"

"I'm fine." To prove it, she moved forward, tugging him after her.

He and Mack had been alike in many ways, Duke thought as he stepped into the musty shadows inside the stone walls. Who knows what might have happened if he'd met Carol first. He might have been the one to marry her, instead of Mack. And if he had, he sure as hell wouldn't have messed things up the way his friend had done.

The morning passed quickly for Carol, absorbed so deeply in the history of the ancient buildings she forgot her apprehension about the dungeons. She enjoyed sharing the experience with Duke, who was attentive and appeared to be every bit as enthralled as she was by the momentous events from the past.

"Can you imagine wearing that all evening?" she said, as they paused in front of the crown jewels. "It must weigh a ton."

"It would sure give your neck muscles a workout." Duke leaned closer for a better look. "The Imperial Crown of State," he read out. "That's one hell of a ruby."

"It says here it belonged to the Black Prince. It was given to him by Don Pedro for his help in the Battle of Navaretto in 1367."

Duke whistled. "That sucker's been around."

"It's not as old as the sapphire. That was buried with Edward the Confessor in Westminster Abbey in 1066."

"Buried?" He peered over her arm at the guidebook. "They dug it up again?"

"The shrine was broken open in 1101, and the sapphire was used in the crown made for Henry the First." She felt a warm rush of pleasure when he lifted his head, his face very close to hers.

"Fascinating," he said softly, his gaze on her mouth.

Feeling suddenly self-conscious, she closed the book. "So where do you want to go next?"

He took her arm and led her out into the sunshine. "All those dates make me feel dry. How about we stop for lunch at that quaint little pub we passed on the way in? I could just go for an English beer right now."

She grinned. "Just like a man. Ask him what he wants to do and his thoughts go straight to his stomach."

"Oh, I don't know about that." He grabbed her hand and tucked it under his arm. "I can think of one or two other activities that could catch my interest."

She decided not to pursue that train of thought. Though she found it difficult to ignore the sudden fluttering of her pulse as she walked with him to the pub.

The stroll around the Tower grounds had been invigorating on such a beautiful, crisp autumn day, and Carol felt a wonderful sense of well-being as she sat in the smoky parlor waiting for the fish and chips she'd ordered.

It helped, she had to admit, to have an attractive man dancing attendance on her. She was even beginning to forget the uneasiness that had bothered her for so long. He was nothing like Mack. Not in any way. Except for an occasional gesture now and again that was pure coincidence. The whole thing had been a product of her imagination.

"You must miss your friends in the States," Duke remarked, after swallowing a mouthful of foaming beer from a pint mug.

Carol shrugged. "Not really. Since I moved back to New York, I haven't had much opportunity to make friends. The Big Apple isn't the easiest place to meet people."

"So I've heard. So you didn't live there when you were married?"

"No. I gave up my job, as Mack's headquarters were in Washington, but he was gone so often, I moved back to Connecticut to be near people and places I knew. Mack didn't want me living in New York." She sipped the cool lager in front of her, wishing she'd changed the subject.

"What did your husband do in Washington?"

She tightened her grip on the glass. The question had been innocent enough, but her reflexes still jumped like crazy when someone asked it. "He was a foreign diplomat."

"Ah, a government man. No wonder he was gone a lot."

"They kept him pretty busy."

She made herself relax when Duke said, "Then you moved back to New York after he died?"

"Yes. I didn't want to stay in Connecticut—not with so many memories . . ."

"I'm sorry, I guess you don't want to talk about it."

"No, it's all right." It was time, she thought, time to face the past and lay out all the ghosts. Maybe then she could finally put it all behind her.

"I got a job with my old company," she said, tracing the side of her glass with her finger. "I found an apartment and settled down into a new life. It was hard at first, but I'm gradually adapting to being on my own again. Now that I'm getting used to it, I even enjoy it, most of the time."

"But what about your friends in Connecticut? Don't they keep in touch with you? It isn't that far from New York."

"We never really had any close friends. People feel uncomfortable with a fifth wheel. I was on my own a lot, yet I wasn't single. It made things awkward."

"That must have been tough for you, when you were having problems, not to have someone you could talk to and confide in."

"Yes, it was." Not that she could have talked about anything. Mack's insistence on secrecy and his hints of the dire consequences of saying too much made her afraid to mention his name to anyone. That had been the real cause of her lack of friends. She hadn't been able to trust anyone. But she could hardly tell Duke Winters that.

Even now, she couldn't break the bonds that had held her. Maybe, she thought in quiet desperation, she never would. Maybe she would never have a normal life again.

"So how do you spend your free time in New York?" Duke asked, mercifully changing the subject. "I imagine you don't do much sightseeing there."

Carol laughed. "Not anymore. I go to the movies with a friend, a theater when I can get tickets. Or out for a meal somewhere."

"Ever go to a symphony concert?"

She looked at him in amazement. "You like the symphony?"

He shrugged. "When I'm in the mood. Is that strange?"

"No, it's just that... I don't know. I guess I figured you more as a jazz fan." She wasn't sure why she'd thought that. Mack had loved jazz. It had been his favorite way of unwinding, just to lie back and let the music wash over him.

"Oh, I like jazz, too. It's a great way to unwind."

Her stomach jerked. She took a hasty gulp of her beer. It had been a coincidence, nothing more. Almost as if he'd read her mind.

The fish and chips arrived then, steaming hot and smelling delicious. She was hungrier than she'd realized, Carol thought, separating the light batter with her fork to reach the creamy halibut underneath.

They ate in companionable silence, with only a comment or two about the meal, until they had cleaned their plates. "That was good," Duke commented, laying his fork down. "I could get used to that."

"You must be used to eating all kinds of different foods, considering all the traveling you do."

Again she saw a wary look cross his face, but he answered readily enough. "Sometimes it's more authentic in the States than it is in its native country. Take Thai food, for instance. The best Thai food I ever tasted was in a tiny little restaurant in San Francisco. I never had one meal I enjoyed while I was in Bangkok."

"My husband was in Bangkok," Carol said, dabbing her mouth with her napkin. "He brought me back a lovely jade necklace. Pale lilac. Up until then I thought all jade was green."

"I'd like to take a look at the Tower Bridge on the way back, if that's okay with you."

She looked up in surprise at the abrupt change of subject. He had his head twisted away from her, one hand raised to signal the waitress. Maybe she'd imagined the odd note in his voice.

His smile when he turned back seemed genuine, yet she couldn't help thinking she detected a certain tension in the set of his jaw as he pushed back his chair and stood.

"I guess I'll pay at the bar," he said, picking up the bill. "I won't be a moment."

She waited for him outside, still trying to decide what she'd said to provoke his strange reaction. But then he appeared in the doorway, just as an elderly couple was about to step inside.

He stood back to let them pass, and Carol spent the next few minutes trying to recover from the sudden rush of emotion she'd felt at the sight of his smile, even if it hadn't been directed at her.

He was an attractive man. And the longer she spent with him, the more she became aware of that. He appealed to her on a very basic level. She recognized the fact that it was purely physical at this stage, but nonetheless dynamic. She hated to think what would happen if she allowed herself to become emotionally involved.

She had better avoid that at all costs, she told herself as they strolled up the Approach to take a look at the bridge. Or she could be in big trouble.

Reaching the archway, she paused to stare up at the magnificent turrets that guarded each end of the bridge.

"Impressive," Duke said, following her gaze.

"Yes, it is. And fairly new compared to the Tower. It was opened at the end of the nineteenth century." Dropping her chin, Carol noticed a poster on the wall, announcing tours of the walkway in the upper level of the bridge.

"I didn't know there was a walkway up there," she said, when Duke suggested they take a look.

After submitting to a security search, it dismayed her to discover that in order to reach the walkway, she would have to go up in an elevator. Trying not to show her discomfort, she stepped inside the square metal room and pulled in a deep breath.

Several people followed Duke inside, cramming Carol into a corner. Already she could feel the first rise of panic. She clamped her teeth together, determined not to give in to the rush of fear she knew would follow.

For a few miserable seconds she fought the symptoms, barely aware of Duke squeezing into the small space behind her. His arms came around her, drawing her back against his chest. She couldn't control the trembling, but his grip tightened, offering her a small measure of security.

Closing her eyes, she leaned back against him, drawing strength from his solid form behind her. Then it was over. The doors slid open and the passengers surged out, giving her room to breathe and space to relax.

Out on the glass-enclosed walkway, she sent him a grateful smile. "Thanks."

He looked down at her, and his eyes burned with a message that sent her heart racing. "Are you all right?"

She nodded. "I'm fine. Just a little embarrassed, that's all."

He reached for her hand and squeezed it. "You don't ever have to feel embarrassed with me, okay?"

Her smile felt a little lopsided as she nodded. She tightened her fingers on his, enjoying the warm feel of his grasp. Ahead of her, the walkway stretched in a long narrow passageway, divided by a partition all the way down the middle.

Several people stood aiming cameras through the small, square windows in the walls, which had been placed there at intervals between the iron girders for viewing.

"Let's take a look," Duke suggested. She followed him to a vacant window and stepped up on the viewing blocks. Looking through the glass, she saw a panoramic view of the river. The Thames flowed directly underneath her, curling round to the left between the buildings that studded the banks, from the very old to the very new.

A half-dozen small boats chugged across the water, while a huge barge plodded slowly up the middle. Pointing them out to Duke, Carol said, "That's the quickest way to get downriver. It beats sitting in the traffic. You can get to Greenwich in half the time on a boat." She leaned back so that Duke could peer through the window.

"That must be the St. Katherine's Dock down there," he said, tapping the glass. "I've been reading about that. It used to warehouse cargos from Africa and the East. Spices from the Indies and teas from China."

"I know. Sounds so exotic, doesn't it?" Carol pushed her head close to his in order to see down. "They started remodeling it around 1970. Now look at it. Offices and flats, restaurants, shops and pubs, not to mention the World Trade Centre."

"Just goes to show that nothing is obsolete. Someone can always find a use for it. I'll have to remember that when I'm old and doddery."

She laughed. "Somehow it's a little difficult to imagine you old and doddery."

He turned his head to look at her, just inches away from her own. "I guess no one likes the thought of growing old," he said softly. "Especially if they're alone. It isn't natural to be alone."

She knew if she looked at him he'd be too close for comfort. Yet she wanted to be close to him, to feel his breath on her cheek. She wanted his kiss again, much as it unsettled her. Hoping he couldn't read her mind, she turned her head to meet his gaze.

"You have incredible eyes," Duke said, his voice low and infinitely disturbing. "Like blue velvet."

"Thank you." Her skin tingled when he looked down at her mouth. She forgot about the other tourists moving about behind her. She forgot about all her instincts warning her not to get too interested in this man. All she could think about was how he'd made her feel when he'd kissed her, and how much she wanted to feel that way again.

From close behind them came the strident wail of a baby, shattering the intimate bubble enclosing them. Drawing back, Carol said breathlessly, "Did you want to go down and explore the Dock?"

Duke's eyes seemed to glow with warmth when he looked at her. "Sure. You know the way?"

Nodding, she stepped off the blocks. Then, from out of nowhere, someone shoved her violently aside. Struggling to control her balance, Carol saw a thickset man push rudely between her and Duke.

She caught her breath when she saw the man's face. A zigzag scar sliced down one of his wine red cheeks in a startling blaze of white. Shaken by the unexpected disfigurement, she moved backward, out of his way.

Everything happened so quickly that she had trouble grasping it. One minute the man was poised between her and Duke, then he turned and raised his camera. Taking careful aim, he pressed the button, and with a blinding flash, the bulb went off.

White light drenched Duke's face, so close it must have temporarily blinded him. For a moment he stood transfixed, as if in shock, then he lunged forward with an explosive sound of rage and made a grab for the camera.

Astonished, Carol stared at him as the man easily evaded him and raced toward the elevators. Duke rubbed his eyes, then to Carol's dismay, charged down the walkway after the photographer.

People scattered left and right as the two men pounded along the stone floor. Unable to believe what she could see happening in front of her, Carol's heart hammered, as in stunned bewilderment she watched the man disappear through a door at the end of the walkway. Seconds later, Duke plunged through after him.

People stood and stared at the doorway, as if expecting someone to come dashing out again. Shaken, Carol walked to the end of the passageway and approached the door. All her qualms about Duke came rushing back as she tried to understand his irrational behavior.

It must have been irritating to have a flashbulb go off in his face, she conceded, but to react so violently that she worried for the photographer's safety was wholly inexplicable.

Reaching the doorway, she paused, wondering what she was going to find on the other side. Then, holding her breath, she stepped over the threshold.

The number of people jammed into the small room unnerved her. She realized she was in a gift shop, surrounded by shelves and glass cases stuffed with mementos of London and its famous tourist spots.

People rushed and squeezed by each other in an effort to examine the merchandise, while a long, patient line of customers at the counter waited for assistance. The air felt heavy and unbearably warm.

Looking wildly around, Carol searched the crowd for Duke's familiar dark head, but couldn't see him anywhere among the jostling shoppers.

She caught sight of another doorway in the corner of the room and fought her way toward it, trying to ignore the jolting heartbeat that signaled another attack of claustrophobia.

Dodging elbows, bulging shopping bags and an elderly man's walking cane, she finally came up against the doorway and dragged in a breath. A sign announced the entrance to the museum.

She was still trying to decide whether to go in or go back to the street when Duke appeared in the doorway.

"Hi," he said, his voice belying the anxiety in his eyes. "Sorry about that. Guess I lost my temper."

"I guess you did. What happened to him?"

"He must have gone down the emergency staircase. The guard stopped me from following him."

"I think that's probably a good thing for both of you."

Apparently hearing the reprimand in her voice, he appeared contrite. "Let's get out of here," he said quietly. "I'll take you home."

She let him lead her through the crowd of eager customers and back out onto the walkway, where they found an elevator waiting for them. This time Duke seemed preoccupied, and Carol was thankful that a handful of passengers traveled with them. Even so, she held her breath all the way down to the bottom.

Once outside on the street, she immediately felt better. She didn't have to put up with this, she decided, as she walked silently beside Duke, who didn't seem to notice her disapproval. It would be better for her peace of mind if she didn't see him again.

Things had been happening much too fast as far as her feelings were concerned. The last thing she needed was to get involved with someone who not only reminded her of her dead husband, but who at times mystified her with his behavior, just as Mack had done.

Carol lifted her face to catch the last of the sun's rays. High up on the battlements of the Tower the British flag rippled in the stiff breeze.

She had gone through a lot of pain and anxiety in rebuilding her life, she thought, watching a bright red double-decker bus rumbling by. She didn't need any more heartache. And something told her she could feel deeply enough about Duke Winters to risk getting hurt again.

And then there was the matter of the uneasy misgivings she felt at times. Something about the incident on the walkway scared her, though she wasn't quite sure why. No, if Duke asked her for a date again, she'd make it clear she wasn't interested. Wishing she felt happier about her decision, she waited with him at the crosswalk for the traffic to halt.

At her side, Duke's worried mind replayed the scene again and again. It couldn't have been a coincidence. The guy had deliberately pointed his camera right at his face. And he'd taken a considerable risk to get that close.

There could only be one reason why someone would want a close-up of his face. Although his features would be difficult to recognize, an expert would be able to compare bone structure, shape of his head, whatever, and identify him as Brandon Pierce.

The lights changed and the traffic squealed to a halt. Crossing in front of it, Duke concentrated on remembering the man's face. He'd only had a brief glimpse before the flash had blinded him for several seconds, but he knew he would recognize that scarred cheek again.

This proved one thing to him, Duke thought, dodging the oncoming pedestrians. Whoever was behind all this definitely suspected him. He and Carol had probably been followed from the moment they'd left her apartment. It wouldn't have been difficult, since they'd walked the entire way.

Once they had the proof they needed, his life would be on the line. Whoever had botched the job last year must be anxious to finish it this time. He had to get some answers fast. At this point, Charles was his only hope.

Duke glanced at his watch. Fourteen hundred hours on the East Coast meant seven p.m. in London. He had plenty of time to wait for Charles's call after he'd made sure Carol was safely home.

For the rest of the walk back he chatted with her about the sights they'd seen that morning, though his mind was only half on the subject. Carol seemed a little quiet, but he figured she was tired, and wondered guiltily if he should have caught a cab back.

It had been a long day for them both. A day he'd remember for a very long time. Thinking about the lunch they'd shared, he smiled at the memory of her quick smile. She had an expressive face, making it easy to guess her emotions.

Especially when she talked to him about Mack. Her feelings for her husband must have gone very deep at one time for him to have been able to hurt her so badly. Duke had seen traces of nostalgia in her eyes at times. Especially when she'd talked about the jade necklace. He'd wanted to lean across the table and kiss her.

He wondered what she would have said if she'd known he'd been there when Mack had bargained for the necklace on a crowded street in Bangkok. Watching the dealer wrap up the tiny box, Duke had found himself wishing he could see Carol's face when she opened it. And wishing he could have been the one who had bought it for her.

The feeling had grown stronger when Mack had made an offhand remark about keeping women happy, as if buying the gift for her gave him no pleasure.

That was before Mack had poisoned his mind against her, Duke thought wryly. Before he'd been disillusioned by Mack's lies. It made him wonder what Mack had told Carol about his partner, to make her resent him so much. Mack had done a pretty good number on both of them.

Reaching the apartment building, Duke paused on the step and smiled down at Carol. "How about making me a cup of coffee before I walk home?"

She looked a little uncomfortable. "I'm sorry, Duke, but I promised Win I'd proofread her article before she sends it in. I should have been up there an hour ago."

He didn't want to push it. He didn't want her to know he was worried about her and wanted to check out her apartment before she went in.

"I'll call you later, then," he told her, trying to reassure himself that they hadn't had time to develop the film yet, let alone make a positive ID. He still had time, and with luck Charles could put him on the right track.

Carol nodded and turned to go, but he caught her arm, turning her to face him. "Thanks for the tour," he said, pulling her into the circle of his arms. "I had a good time."

"So did I."

She looked up at him, her face serious in the fading light. Once more he felt himself drowning in the depths of her eyes. Slowly, he lowered his head and covered her mouth with his. The second his lips touched hers his body responded, urging him to take more.

He lifted his head, disappointed that Carol hadn't returned his kiss with the passion she'd given it the night before. But he had too much on his mind to worry about it now. He had to get home, to wait for Charles's call.

And once he knew who he was looking for, he would no longer need to put Carol in danger. The thought hit him hard, almost cutting off his breath. He would have to tell her, he decided. Before he walked out of her life, he had to tell her the truth. He didn't want her to hear it from anyone else.

But until then, he was going to use what time he had left with her to try to show her that he was a different person. That he was no longer the hard-living, ruthless man Brandon Pierce had been. Maybe if he could do that, just maybe, there might be a chance for them yet.

Feeling better already, Duke let her go and waited for a good ten minutes after she'd left before he figured that she was safe, and he could go back to his apartment to wait for the call from Charles.

The flashing light on his recorder when he opened the door sent his spirits down to his boots. Praying it wasn't what he thought it might be, he pressed the replay button.

Charles's voice jumped at him, demanding to know where he was, repeating again that what he had to tell him was extremely important and urgent. Two more calls from him followed, apparently at ten-minute intervals. The last one was short and to the point.

"I have to leave. Will call again tomorrow. Fourteen hundred your time. Be there."

Cursing, Duke realized that Charles had meant two p.m. London time, not East Coast time as he'd thought. He dialed quickly, waiting impatiently through the many clicks and buzzes that told him the call was going through.

Finally he heard the ringing of the phone on the other end. A loud click silenced the ring, then his shoulders slumped as the recorder announced that Charles was on vacation.

Quickly Duke dialed the head office. This time the wait was longer, as the special number was relayed through the code system. Royce's voice answered on the first ring. He sounded impatient, as if he'd been interrupted from something important.

"I just wondered if Charles was back yet," Duke said, hoping he wasn't in for a long lecture.

"No, he's not. Still looking for that bourbon?"

Duke winced at the testy note in his voice. "Do you have a number where I can get hold of him?"

The pause was significant. "If I knew that," Royce said quietly, "I'd call him myself. I told you, he's on some yacht cruise somewhere off Tahiti, or one of those islands. I won't be able to get in touch with him until he gets back.''

The warning bells in his head were louder now. Charles obviously had access to a phone. And the number at Duke's apartment. He must have talked to Royce at some point after Duke had left for England.

''Oh well, guess I'll have to make do with what I can get. When are you expecting him back, anyway?''

''In a week or two. How is everything there? Making any headway?''

''Slow, but improving. I'll let you know if anything breaks.''

''How is she?'' Royce asked, obviously still cautious in spite of the scrambling.

''Fine. Looking good. I'll be in touch.'' Royce would have to be satisfied with that, Duke thought, hanging up. He didn't know why he felt so reluctant to tell Royce about the photographer, but until he talked to Charles, he didn't think he wanted to tell Royce anything.

The thought bothered him and he paced around the room, trying to analyze his feelings. He had nothing to base them on, just a gut instinct. Once more he wondered if he could rely on that anymore. Or if he was making a big mistake by not reporting both the search in his apartment and the stranger who took his picture to the only man who could help him.

Carol's excuse of working with Win had been pure fabrication. She needed time to think, to sort out her conflicting feelings about Duke Winters. The thought of spending a quiet evening alone catching up on some chores seemed inviting for a change.

She dragged out the ironing board and set it up in the kitchen, then tuned her radio to her favorite station. She was humming to a well-known show tune when she heard the ring of her front doorbell.

Setting the iron on its rest, she flicked it off, then crossed the living room, wondering who her visitor might be. When she opened the door, Jasper Golding stood in the hallway, and the cold anger in his eyes chilled her.

"Good evening, Carol, permit me to come in?" Without waiting for her consent, he stepped past her, his bulky frame dwarfing the furniture in the room.

Feeling a twinge of nervousness, Carol closed the door and turned to face him. "Is something wrong?"

"Yes, dear lady, I'm afraid something is very wrong. You are not going to like what I have to say. Not at all."

Carol stared at him in growing dismay. She could tell by his expression he had something serious to discuss. Anxiously, she waited for him to speak.

Duke paced restlessly around his small apartment, feeling like a caged bear. He didn't like it. He didn't like it at all. Carol had denied there was anyone she was close to in the States. But she had to be protecting someone.

If only he could ask her outright. But of course, then he'd have to tell her who he was, and once she knew there was even less chance of her telling him. He was facing a brick wall, and he had no idea how to climb over it.

He slumped down on to the couch and spread his legs out in front of him. He was going about this all wrong. Instead of trying to find out who was the main man, he should be concentrating on who the connections were in London. And that meant thoroughly checking out everyone associated with Carol. Starting with her odd friend, Win, from upstairs. Leaning forward, he reached once more for the phone.

* * *

Carol watched Jasper's grim face, wondering what was coming. His eyes seemed to bore right through her as he stared down at her.

"You have to do something about that window cleaner," he announced at last. "He is becoming an unmitigated nuisance."

Surprised, Carol said hesitantly, "I'm not sure what you mean."

"He was snooping around," Jasper said in disgust, "outside your door. When I asked him what he was doing, he leaned up against the wall, folded his arms and . . . well, I cannot possibly repeat to a lady the words he employed, but it was to the effect that it was none of my business and I should leave immediately."

Carol almost smiled, well able to imagine what terms Gordon had used.

"None of my business!" Jasper said, rolling his expressive eyes up toward the ceiling. "What does he imagine I am paid for, if not to safeguard the tenants and their property? He talked as if I had no right to be in the hallway, when he was blatantly trespassing."

"He probably just wanted to see if I was home," Carol said reasonably. "He'd called earlier and I told him I was busy. He obviously didn't believe me."

"Well, I don't like it." Jasper shook his head with a loud grunt to emphasize his disapproval. "I can't be certain of course, but as I approached him, it appeared to me as if he were examining the lock on your door. When he saw me, he quickly rang the doorbell, as if he had just arrived. But I'd seen him come in several minutes earlier, in plenty of time to ring the bell and discover your absence."

Carol reached out and patted his thick arm. "I appreciate your concern, Jasper, I really do, but don't worry about

Gordon. He's harmless and I can handle him. He's just a little persistent, that's all. Once he realizes I'm not interested, he'll get tired of the chase and quit, you'll see.''

Jasper slowly shook his head. ''Well, I hope you are right, dear lady. But I think that young man could be a considerable problem. I caution you to take care. I won't always be around to protect you.''

The shrill ring of the phone in the kitchen made her jump. ''I'd better get that,'' she said, thankful for the interruption, ''but thanks for the warning. I'll keep it in mind.'' She hurried across the room to answer the phone, leaving Jasper to let himself out.

She had expected it to be Gordon again, and was all set to give him a piece of her mind. To hear Duke's gravelly voice instead took her off guard.

''I was hoping you'd be through with Win,'' he said, when she returned his greeting. ''How about joining me for a pizza and beer? I could order in or—''.

She jumped in before his voice could work its magic on her wavering convictions. ''I'm sorry, Duke, but I'm busy tonight.''

He paused, and she waited, her fingers tightening on the receiver. ''Okay,'' he said quietly. ''So how about tomorrow night?''

''I'm busy then, too.'' She hoped miserably that he'd accept defeat and hang up, but somehow knew that would be too much to expect.

''The next night then?''

''Sorry.''

She could hear the note of impatience in his voice when he said, ''All right, you tell me when you're free.''

''I'll call you.''

This time the pause was longer. ''Is this a brush-off?'' he asked finally.

She closed her eyes. "Duke—"

"Will you at least tell me why? Is it because I lost my temper with that jerk this afternoon? Because if so—"

"Why can't you just accept the fact that I don't want to see you again?" She could feel her stomach tying itself in knots. She couldn't take much more of this.

"Because," Duke said fiercely, "the look in your eyes this morning was telling me something else. I want to know what happened to change your mind."

She'd had enough, Carol decided. "I just did, that's all. You'll simply have to accept it. Goodbye, Duke." Her hand shook as she replaced the receiver. Trying to compose herself, she went back to the ironing board and took a firm grip on the iron. She'd done it. Now all she had to do was convince herself she didn't regret it.

She'd finished the ironing and was folding up the ironing board when her doorbell rang. Cursing, she shoved the board into the closet and crossed the room. Pausing in front of the door, she was tempted not to answer it, to pretend she wasn't there.

It was probably Gordon, which meant she had another bad scene to get through. Might as well do it all in one day, she thought, and dragged open the door.

Chapter 6

"I'm glad you opened the door," Duke said evenly. "I was prepared to pound on it all night." He didn't wait to be asked in, but stepped into the room before she had a chance to speak.

One look at his face and she knew she had a determined man on her hands. Her heart skipped a beat as he looked down at her and said quietly, "I don't like being dumped without an explanation and a chance to defend myself."

"And I don't like being hounded like this. I told you I was busy."

He looked around the room with stormy eyes. "Doing what?"

"It's none of your business."

"I'm making it my business. I'm not leaving until you tell me what the problem is."

Shaking with temper, Carol glared up at him. "The problem, I should think, is fairly obvious. You can't take no for an answer. You don't understand that I just might not want to pursue a relationship with you. You figure that if you're persistent, I'll come around and agree to whatever you want.

"Well, it doesn't work that way, Duke. That's exactly the kind of arrogance I despise. It doesn't matter to you how I feel, or what my wishes are, all you're concerned about is your damaged ego."

She paused for breath, and he said sharply, "My ego has nothing to do with it. I just don't get why you're blowing so hot and cold. I figure I'm entitled to an explanation."

Determined to stick to her guns, Carol stepped closer to him. "Let me put it more clearly, in case you don't get the point. I've had it up to here with domineering men. I was married to one." Despite her efforts to control it, her voice rose. "And if you imagine that I want to get involved with another Mack Everett, you are badly mistaken."

She saw his face blanch, and his eyes smoldered with a dangerous heat. "Damn it," he muttered, "I don't want you involved with another Mack Everett. I want you involved with me." Before she could fully comprehend his words, he reached for her arms and dragged her hard against his chest.

Looking up, she found his mouth poised perilously close to hers. "I'll leave," he said harshly, "if that's what you want. But first I'm going to prove something to you."

She pulled in a breath for a feeble protest. Before she could utter a sound, he smothered her mouth with his, taking the advantage she'd given him.

The shock of his tongue inside her mouth destroyed all her resistance. She couldn't think of a single reason why she wanted to fight him. The sensations he'd aroused the last time he'd kissed her were mild compared to the red-hot passion that now swept over her.

She raised her arms and slid them around his neck, stunned by the excitement roaring through her body. He wrapped his arms around her and increased the relentless demands of his mouth.

Clinging to him, she returned the fire of his kiss. How could he do this to her so quickly? she wondered, as her body ached with the craving that only he could arouse.

He wanted her, too. The knowledge sent her soaring, heady with the power that he'd handed her. Unable to stand it any longer, she plunged her hands inside his jacket and tugged at his shirt.

He lifted his mouth, and his voice sounded hoarse when he muttered, "Wait . . . are you—"

"I don't want to wait," she said fiercely. "You started this, now finish it."

His eyes widened as he stared down at her, then very slowly, he smiled. "Lady," he whispered, "you got a deal." His hands roamed over her body without restraint as she clung to him.

She tipped her hips forward, and a sharp thrill skimmed down her belly when she felt the hot length of his need. Some part of her mind warned her this was too fast, too soon. But the physical hunger she couldn't deny easily overpowered her reasoning. She felt his hand slide underneath her sweater. The brush of his fingers on her sensitive skin sent sparks down to her toes.

Raising her arms higher, she wound them around his neck, thrusting her breasts forward as he covered them with his hands. His fingers found her nipples and squeezed painfully.

She welcomed the pain—reveled in it. Her entire body was on fire, craving the feel of his touch on her bare skin. Fiercely his mouth sought hers again, and once more she was caught up on the ferocious tide of naked desire. It was as if another person had entered her body and guided it, telling her what to say, what to do, what to think.

She had never been this abandoned with Mack. Even in the early days, she had never lusted with this unreasoning need to satisfy the unbearable pressure that had built so swiftly.

She dug her hands under his shirt while he struggled to get his arms free from his jacket. The sheer pleasure of running her hands up his flat stomach to the soft fuzz on his chest took her breath away.

Duke lifted his chin at her touch. "Oh, God, Carol," he muttered, "you don't know what you're doing to me."

She smiled, enjoying the feeling of power it gave her to hear the raw emotion in his voice. She pressed closer to him, sliding her belly in a seductive move against his. "Tell me," she whispered.

"No." He looked down at her, and her pulse leapt at the fierce hunger in his eyes. "I'd rather show you."

She couldn't seem to get a deep breath. It didn't matter. All that mattered was the desperate need in his eyes, and her own powerful craving to satisfy it.

She raised her arms, and he slid her sweater up them and over her head. Emerging from the soft, warm folds, she met the full force of his mouth on hers again as he expertly unhooked her bra.

A shudder of sheer pleasure shook her body when his hands closed over her breasts once more. She found the buckle of his belt and dragged it open. Carefully she eased his zipper down and slipped her hand inside.

His sharp groan excited her, then she echoed it as he dipped his head and fastened his mouth on her taut nipple. The pleasure was so intense, she wondered how long she could bear it. Holding her breath, she tightened her fingers on him and closed her eyes.

He was breathing hard when he lifted his head. He spoke in a guttural whisper. "I want you. Now."

"I want you, too."

"Bedroom?"

"Yes." She tried to control the floating sensation as she led him to the bedroom door. Reaching inside, she felt for the light switch, but his fingers closed over hers.

"Leave it. I like the dark."

She blinked, taken aback by the unexpected request. Then his arms closed around her from behind, his fingers resuming their sweet torment on her breasts. She arched her back with a soft moan, and he turned her in his arms to cover her hungry mouth with his.

Propelled by his foot, the door closed, plunging them into darkness. And with the darkness came a subtle change in Duke's attitude. Now he was the impatient one, dragging the rest of her clothes off with a ferocity that excited her to fever pitch.

He pushed her back onto the bed, and she waited for him in the dark, hearing the rustling of his clothes as he tore them off.

Then his hands found her hips. Her gasp sounded loud in the quiet room as he stroked up her stomach, over her breasts to her shoulders. She obeyed the pressure and lay back, and the breath rushed out of her lungs as he lowered his hard, pulsating body onto her belly.

She was on fire again, writhing beneath him as he brushed his fingers up her thigh. Then he found her, and her voice rose on a pleading moan. His shoulders felt smooth beneath her hands and she dug into the sinewy muscles while her body shuddered with unbearable spasms of pleasure.

She wanted it to go on and on, and knew she couldn't bear it another second. Panting for breath, she clawed at his shoulders; her body arced as the tension became a desperate urgency. Then the release came with a rush and she collapsed, her chest heaving with exertion.

"Good," Duke whispered above her. "Now we take our time."

Where, Carol wondered, as the pressure built again, did he find the control? And how could it be so different with one man from another? How could she not have known that her body was capable of such intense, powerful sensations?

She thought she couldn't possibly experience any higher plateaus of pleasure, but when he finally drove himself into her, she passed beyond all coherent reasoning.

Over and over again he slammed into her, faster and faster, while her mind spun and whirled, taking her beyond the boundaries of control. Finally, with a convulsive shudder of his body, he emptied himself inside her, and was still.

Only later, after the tumult inside her had eased and she lay holding his sweat-slicked body in her arms, did she ask herself one final question.

How could she not have imagined the wonder, the incredible exultation of discovering the perfect partner, the ultimate mating of two people so perfectly attuned to each other's needs? Slowly, savoring every second and holding it close, she allowed herself to drift into a dreamless sleep.

She jolted awake in a still-dark room, her heart pounding with apprehension. She knew immediately what had disturbed her sleep. Duke was twisting and turning, as if trying to escape the clutches of an unseen monster.

She could hear him muttering feverishly but couldn't make out the words. She waited for long, tense seconds, hoping he would come out of it, but he seemed to be in the grip of some terrible nightmare.

His muttering grew louder, and alarmed now, she lifted up on one elbow. The lamp sat on his side of the bed, and she leaned across him in an effort to reach it. Then her outstretched hand froze as an ice-cold chill swept her body. She could hear him now, his muttered words clear in the silence of the room.

"No," he said fiercely, his voice rising. "No, not Whitewater. I won't do Whitewater again."

She wanted to scream. She couldn't even breathe. Pulling back her hand, she tried to clear her mind. She had heard the name Whitewater before. Too many times. Mack had spoken the name more than once. He would never tell her what it meant, but after his death she'd asked Royce.

At first, Royce had been reluctant to tell her. But when she'd insisted, he'd finally given in. Since the word was now obsolete, he'd told her, it didn't really matter anyway. Whitewater was the code name for Mack's secret missions.

Oh, God. Oh, God. She couldn't seem to stop the phrase from repeating over and over in her head. Slowly she pulled herself upright next to Duke's muttering, heaving body. As she did so, sweat trickled down between her shoulder blades. Her face was wet with it, yet she shivered, her skin icy cold.

A vision seared her mind, clear and horrifyingly familiar. Duke's dark head leaning out of the car, his thumb and forefinger in the A—OK signal. Mack's signal.

Other memories crowded in. His odd reaction when she'd accused Brandon Pierce of causing Mack's death. His strange behavior on the walkway that morning. Why would Duke Winters get so furious about someone taking his picture?

Her heart pounded so hard it shook her body. It couldn't be. Both men had died that night in the wreck. Burned beyond recognition, Royce had told her. She would never forget those words. Yet she couldn't ignore the facts that her mind screamed at her now.

But he looked so different. Of course he did, she thought, her heart plunging in terror. He'd been burned. They would have had to perform plastic surgery on him. She'd heard of it being done plenty of times before. They could change his whole features, until no one recognized him. No one, not even her.

Trying to control her panic, she dragged her fingers through her hair. No wonder he'd seemed so familiar. No wonder she'd been plagued by that feeling she'd known him before. But if she was right, why had he come back, pretending to be someone else? Why wouldn't he tell her who he was? What did he want from her that he had gone to all this trouble to hide his true identity?

It was all coming back to haunt her. The fear, the threats, the accidents, the terror of never knowing what the threat was or from where it would come. The sense of violence and danger that had permeated her marriage was hovering around her once more.

It was all happening again. She hadn't escaped it after all. All the horror and dread she had lived with for so long had followed her all the way to England. She had just made love to her supposedly dead husband.

Nausea gripped her, doubling her over. No, she thought fiercely. She wouldn't give in to it. Not this time. She was stronger now. This time she would fight.

Duke still lay muttering at her side, but his restless tossing had ceased. Think, she urged herself. If Mack had been burned and undergone surgery, he would have the scars. Her heart fluttered again as it occurred to her that that was the reason he'd wanted to make love in the dark. He hadn't wanted her to see the scars.

His facial scars could be covered by his hair. But there would have to be other scars. Ones that couldn't be hidden when he was naked. If she could see them then she'd know for sure. And she had to know.

Holding her breath, she inched forward, her hand outstretched toward the lamp. It was farther away than she'd realized. She shifted closer, and Duke's muttering stopped. She froze, certain that her thumping heart would waken him. He groaned quietly, then his breathing deepened, becoming slow and even.

She waited several seconds more before stretching out her hand again. Her naked breast brushed his chest, and she caught her breath as he groaned again. Then, to her intense dismay, his arms closed around her.

"Mmm," he murmured in her ear, "what a way to wake up."

For a moment the panic almost overwhelmed her, then she made herself relax. "Go back to sleep," she whispered. "It's early yet."

"What's the time?"

"I don't know." Her heart thudded against his chest. "I'll put the light on and take a look."

She tried to break free but he held her fast, his hand sliding down to cup her buttocks. "Doesn't matter. I'd better get going anyway. Don't want Jasper Golding breathing down my neck for seducing one of his tenants."

She managed a nervous laugh. "I seem to remember doing some of the seducing."

He wriggled his body beneath her. "Yeah, I remember that. How about a repeat performance?"

Closing her eyes, she willed herself to stay calm. "How about giving a lady a rest?"

"Ah-ha. Too much for you, huh?"

"Something like that. Maybe I'm out of practice."

"Yeah?" His lips found her neck and traced a path up to her chin. "Well, I reckon I can remedy that."

The immediate response of her body horrified her. To what depths had she plunged, that she could forget this man could be the husband she'd feared and despised? The man she thought she'd buried?

She felt his hand on the back of her head, pulling her toward him. Telling herself that she had to go along with it for now, she let his mouth find hers, and returned his kiss.

Gently, he set her on her side and slid away from her. "I'll just grab my clothes and dress in the bathroom. Then you can go back to sleep. I'll call you later."

She wanted to insist that he stay while she put on the light. But she'd lost her nerve, and she could only lie there helplessly as he slipped out of the door and closed it quietly behind him.

She waited until she heard the thud of her front door close before slipping out of bed. Switching on the light, she saw it was almost five. It would be midnight in Washington. Quickly she crossed the room and reached in the closet for her robe. Dragging the warm fabric around her shivering body, she thrust her feet into slippers.

Somewhere, she thought, as she hurried into the living room, she had Royce's number. Only in an emergency, he'd told her. Well, she thought grimly as she hunted through a desk drawer, this was an emergency.

She found the scrap of paper taped inside the lid of a screwdriver kit, where she'd hidden it on Royce's request. Trying to find the buttons with her trembling fingers, she dialed the number and waited.

The operator's voice answered. "Which route to Alaska would you prefer?"

Feeling silly, Carol read out the first answer written on the paper. "North, through the San Juans."

"Which month?"

"September."

"It can be rough waters in September."

"I'm a good sailor."

"Hold on."

She waited, feeling a pulse throbbing in her throat, as the line clicked, then hummed, then clicked again.

"Westcott."

Carol's palm felt sticky as she pressed the receiver to her ear. "Royce? It's Carol."

"What's happened?"

Hearing the alarm in his voice, she tried to reassure him. "Nothing. At least I hope it's nothing."

"What do you mean? What do you mean, Carol? Why did you call me then?"

She took a deep breath. Now that she was wide awake and facing the situation, she was beginning to think she had to be crazy to believe what she believed. She wished she hadn't called. She wished she could hang up. But now that she had called him, she had to tell him something.

And she might as well go for broke. "Royce, I want to know where Mack is."

The pause on the end of the line went on and on. Carol could hear the dull drone of a jetliner passing overhead on its way to Heathrow. Or maybe from. The thought brought a pang of homesickness so bad she closed her eyes. She would give anything to be back in New York, she thought desperately.

"I don't understand what you're asking, Carol." Royce said in her ear. "You know as well as I do that Mack's ashes are in St. Martin's Memorial Gardens."

"No, I don't know that," Carol said unsteadily. "I know the urn is there. How do I know Mack's ashes are in it?"

Royce's voice came clearly over the line, vibrating with shock. "Good God, Carol, are you doubting my eyes? Do you know what it did to me to see those two men after the wreck? I identified the bodies, Carol. There was no mistake. No mistake at all. Mack is dead, Carol. Your husband is dead."

She refused to cry. Blinking back the tears she thanked Royce, apologized for disturbing him, and hung up. She was going out of her mind. She had to be crazy. How could she have imagined for one single minute that Duke Winters, the man with whom she was rapidly falling in love, could possibly be the cold, relentless man who had ignored the threats to her life in order to pursue what he considered was his duty?

Wandering into the kitchen, she tied her robe closer around her. Yet surely she couldn't have imagined that muttered word in the silent bedroom? Whitewater. The word had been burned on her brain ever since she'd first heard Mack utter it.

She filled the coffeemaker with water and measured coffee into the filter. Maybe that was the reason she'd thought she heard Duke say it. After all, she hadn't been fully awake. She could have been mistaken.

Yet she still couldn't shake the feeling that Duke Winters was not who he seemed to be. At the first opportunity, she would question Jim Bedford and find out just where he'd found his new mechanic.

And, just to satisfy any last lingering doubts, at the first opportunity, she'd get a look at Duke's body to see if he had any scars. Even if she had to get naked with him again to do it.

Duke was just about to step into the shower when he heard the phone ringing in his living room. His nerves sharpened. It was a little after five-thirty in the morning. Maybe Charles had decided to call early.

Hurrying across the room to the phone, Duke rehearsed the hundred-and-one questions he was going to ask Charles. When he heard Royce on the line instead, his first reaction was sheer frustration.

Then his jaw tensed when Royce said bluntly, "She's beginning to suspect."

He didn't need it spelled out for him. He let out his breath in an explosive curse. "How do you know?"

"She called. Five minutes ago. She thought you were her husband. I think I managed to convince her both men are dead, but it will be only a matter of time before she arrives at the obvious conclusion."

That shook him. "What did you tell her?"

"That she was crazy. That I was there, and if anyone should know the facts, I should."

"Did she buy that?"

"I don't know. I honestly don't know."

"All right. I'll take care of it."

"I warned you this would happen."

"I said I'd take care of it."

"Give it up, Duke. You've got a new life now. Get on with it and enjoy it. Put all this behind you. It's over."

"It's not over for me. Not until I nail the bastard who did this to us."

Royce sighed. "You always were a stubborn man. I just hope you know what you're doing."

"So do I." Duke hung up, his nerves raw. Carol had thought he was Mack! He couldn't believe it. Surely she should know....

He strode back to the bathroom in his bare feet and turned on the faucet. No, of course she didn't know. How could she? He didn't look like either of them. But they were enough alike in height and build, and with the gestures they'd unconsciously copied from each other over the long period of their close relationship, it wasn't hard to see where she would make the mistake.

He stuck his head under the rush of water, hoping it would clear his mind. All he could seem to think about was her lying naked and hungry beneath him, waiting for him, ready for him, and oh, so eager to enjoy the passion that had driven the both of them wild.

The water cascaded down his body, soothing and stimulating at the same time. It had been so good. So damn good. How could she have thought...? He cut off the question, unwilling to believe that it could have been that good for her and Mack. He wanted it to have been special for her, as it had been for him. Because it would be the one and only time.

He shut off the water and climbed out of the shower, the ache already beginning in his gut. He would have to tell her. If Royce hadn't succeeded in convincing her that Mack was dead, there was no way he could let her go on believing Duke Winters could be her husband. He would have to tell her the truth.

And when he did, Duke thought, pulling on a clean shirt, she would hate him for what he'd done. Not that he could blame her. She had made no secret of how she felt about Brandon Pierce. To discover that the man with whom she'd made such passionate love was the same man she'd despised, the man she blamed for her problems with her marriage, would just about destroy her.

If only he'd had more time. Maybe if she'd had time to fall in love with the person he was now, she would realize that Brandon Pierce no longer existed, that he was a changed man, so different to the man she knew as her husband's partner.

Duke grabbed his jacket from its hanger. Jim Bedford had found his replacement, but he had a couple of things he needed to pick up from there. He could use the walk, he thought, letting himself out of the front door. It would help clear his mind, and prepare him for what was bound to be an uncomfortable meeting with Carol.

Not only was he going to tell her who he was, but now he would have to send her back to the States for her own safety. He would ask for a complete list of everyone she had connections with, and go from there. But if he had to put her on a plane himself, he was going to make sure she was out of it. And knowing Carol, she wouldn't like that at all.

Carol parked her car in the underground city garage, then climbed the stairs to the ground floor. Stepping out into the street, she glanced up at the clouds scudding across a pale blue sky. At least the weather looked as if it might hold.

The early morning crowds surged past her, and she fell into step behind a smartly dressed woman carrying a briefcase and the inevitable umbrella. The moving mass of humanity paused at the curb as the lights changed, and Carol halted, her mind reliving the moment she heard Duke muttering in his sleep.

Now that she'd had time to think about it, in daylight with people all around her, her fears seemed ludicrous. How could she have imagined for one minute that Duke Winters was Mack come back to life? She had to be crazy. Her nerves must be really bad to let her mind get so paranoid.

The lights changed again and she moved forward in the crush. She was actually smiling at her own foolishness when someone grabbed her roughly by the arm. Carol's heartbeat accelerated in panic. A man looked down at her, a grin splitting his mouth.

Her heart stopped altogether when she saw the white scar, standing out vividly on his cheek in the sunlight.

"Hallo dahlin'," he said pleasantly, "sorry to spoil your morning, but I'll have to insist you come with me."

Carol halted, nearly tripping up the stout man behind her. "Let me go—" Her eyes widened when she felt the hard round barrel of a gun in her side.

"It's got a silencer," the man said, his grin revealing a missing front tooth. "One tiny sound from you and it's all over. No one would even notice in this crowd. I doubt if you'd even fall down at first. They'd just carry you along with them to the next lights."

She bit back the scream, while the full realization of the situation hit her. It had finally caught up with her. All the horror, imagined or otherwise, now confronted her, accumulated in the deadly pressure of the gun in her side and the man who held it.

She tried to think rationally. She could scream, but he was right. One bullet in her side and he could be gone, long before anyone realized what was happening.

Even now, although she struggled to be free of him, people pushed and shoved past her, intent on getting to work on time, heedless of the panic-stricken woman who was merely a nuisance and getting in their way.

"Let's go. And remember, not a sound." The man began moving with the crowd again, forcing her along, the gun now concealed by his raincoat.

She sent a desperate glance around, trying to find some way of letting someone know what was happening. Even though she knew it was doubtful anyone would help her. No one would be stupid enough to fight a man with a gun. Even if they did, she could very likely end up dead anyway.

They had almost reached the next curb when a well-built young man suddenly shoved forward, obviously impatient with the slow pace of the people in front of him. He badly jostled the man holding her as he pushed his way through the crowd, and Carol felt the grip on her arm slacken.

She didn't stop to think. Putting her head down, she plunged into the crowd and ploughed through the gaps. It was a desperate move and she knew, a fruitless one. With her fragile high heels she could hardly outrun him. Any second he could be on her, jamming the gun into her side, maybe this time firing a deadly bullet into her heart.

The thought gave her momentum, and she clawed her way past a couple of women, both of whom yelled something at her as she struggled by. She was past caring. Her life depended on her actions in the next few seconds.

Ahead of her she saw a stream of people moving down the stairs of the Underground station. Maybe if she went down with them he wouldn't realize it and would go on past, expecting her to still be somewhere in front of him.

She didn't have time to think. Swerving to the right, she dove into the swarming bodies. The impatient crowd half carried, half pushed her down the stairs.

Risking a backward glance over her shoulder, her heart stilled in terror. She could just see the head and shoulders of the photographer, framed against the sky at the top of the stairs. The murderous look on his face chilled her blood.

She jerked her head around, a new fear beginning to paralyze her breathing. Ahead of her the stairs plunged down into an inferno of lights...and noise...and people...and suffocating darkness. She couldn't go down there. She couldn't.

She tried to stop the onward rush of her feet, but the crowd pushed into her from behind, forcing her on. And somewhere behind her, *he* was waiting for the opportunity to grab her. Her choices had become extremely limited.

Somehow she reached the platform, just as a train burst from the tunnel with a deafening roar, charging at her like a ravenous monster bent on swallowing her up. She could feel her limbs locking and knew her face glistened with perspiration.

She couldn't breathe. She couldn't move. She would just have to wait there for him to come and get her. Anything was better than the awful blind panic that already threatened to blot out her senses. The air thickened around her, potent with the smell of nicotine, sweat and sickly sweet perfume.

The train halted with an earsplitting screech. The doors slid open, spitting out the commuters in a frenzy of impatience. People behind her surged forward. She struggled, vaguely hearing an impatient male voice behind her.

"Come on, luv. I ain't got all day." A hefty shove between her shoulder blades sent her stumbling against the door. Hands from inside the carriage reached for her, hauling her in as the doors slid together behind her.

The train jerked and she spun around, just in time to catch the furious glare of the photographer, trapped by the arm of a hefty-looking guard.

"They ought to put more trains on in the mornings," the young woman who had grabbed her remarked. "There's never enough room for everybody, and here we are, jammed up together like sardines." She smiled at Carol. "You were lucky to make it. If the guard hadn't pushed you, you'd still be standing on the platform."

Carol gulped and made a feeble attempt to thank her.

The woman frowned. "Are you all right, dear? You look a bit sickly. Here, hang on to this pole." She took hold of Carol's hand and guided it across the chest of an impeccable business suit. The man's face above it appeared not to notice.

Carol clutched at the smooth, cool steel, wrapping her fingers around it. If she could just make it to the next station. If she could just find the strength to get out. If she could just stay conscious long enough to...

The train jerked to a stop. The doors opened, letting in a rush of cool air. "Thank you," Carol managed to gasp, before the human tide swept her off the train and up the stairs to glorious fresh air.

She didn't wait for the strength to seep back into her legs. He would guess she would get off at the next stop. Any minute now he could charge up the stairs behind her.

A bus honked loudly, followed by a screech of brakes and the sound of someone swearing. Looking over, Carol saw a taxi driver with his head stuck out of the window, waving his arm at the offending vehicle, which towered over him.

Seeing the For Hire sign lit up, Carol leapt across the space at the edge of the curb. The startled driver twisted his head as she tugged the door open and jumped inside.

"'Ere watchit, mate," he said, frowning at her, "you could get clobbered pullin' a stunt like that."

Carol gasped out a quick apology and the address of her office.

Shrugging, the cab driver turned back and pulled into the street, narrowly missing a delivery van coming the other way.

Carol closed her eyes and sank back against the worn leather. No matter what happened now, nothing could be as bad as the last few minutes. Gradually the strength flowed back into her body as she let her mind go over the terrifying events.

Where had he come from? Had he followed her from her apartment? What did he want from her? And the most important question of all. *What did Duke know about all this*

It seemed fairly obvious that he knew something. It explained why he chased the man on the walkway. Either Duke recognized the man as some kind of threat or...

Carol opened her eyes wide. Why hadn't she thought of that before? What she had thought was Duke's excessive fit of temper at the man's rudeness could have been a desperate attempt to get back the film from the camera.

If so, why was Duke so anxious to destroy his picture? And if so, why was the photographer so anxious to take it? And what could the strange man with the scarred face possibly want with her?

Chapter 7

Carol sat forward, all her fears and doubts surging back. She should call the police. After all, she'd been threatened with a gun, attacked in broad daylight on a city street.

But reporting her suspicions could take hours. Hours of taking down descriptions, going through mug shots, avoiding all the wrong questions that could lead to her past connections to the agency.

No. She needed to talk to Duke first. And as soon as possible. No more playing guessing games. She would call him and insist that he tell her the truth.

The cab pulled up outside her building, and she scrutinized the area carefully before climbing out. Trying to ignore the prickling feeling down her spine, she hurried up the steps and through the doors. It wasn't until she was safely inside her office that she finally breathed a sigh of relief.

Picking up the phone, she dialed the number of the garage. Jim Bedford answered. "Sorry," he said, when she asked for Duke, "you just missed him. He left about ten minutes ago."

Carol closed her eyes in frustration. "Do you know when he'll be back?"

"He's not coming back, as far as I know. He quit."

Her heart skipped. "When?"

"Three days ago. Said he'd decided to go back to America."

"I see. Thank you." Carol put down the phone. Three days ago. Why hadn't he said anything about it? Once more her heart began to pump heavily as she dialed the number he'd given her for his apartment.

He answered on the second ring, and momentarily confused, she'd begun to speak before she realized it was a recording. She waited with mounting impatience for the beep to sound, then said tersely. "Duke. I have to talk to you. Please meet me in the Coachman, it's a pub a block south of my office, at noon. I'll buy you lunch."

She hung up, then sat staring at the phone, deep in thought, until a light tap on her door disturbed her. She lifted her head as Anna came into the office, carrying a sheaf of papers. Her bright yellow scarf added a splash of color to the somber room, and Carol relaxed.

"You always look so fresh and bright," she said, taking the papers Anna handed her. "Don't you ever have a down day?"

"Not often." Anna flashed her white teeth in a grin. "You were late this morning. Did your mechanic keep you from getting your beauty sleep last night?"

Carol felt the warmth on her cheeks. Anna had an uncanny way of hitting too close to the truth. "Sorry to disappoint you, but it had nothing to do with my mechanic. Now, since you've given me all this extra work, perhaps you'd better let me get on with it."

"Okay," Anna said cheerfully. "I can take a hint. But you'd better be careful, Carol. Not enough sleep will put bags under your eyes." Laughing, she left and closed the door behind her.

Carol groaned. So far, with everything else that had happened, she'd managed to keep the memories of last night buried. Now they surfaced to torment her, despite her efforts to ignore them.

She hardly recognized herself as the woman who had acted with such abandon. And now she was faced with a possibility so intolerable she couldn't let herself think about it.

And she wouldn't, she decided firmly, drawing the papers toward her. She would concentrate on work instead, until she'd had a chance to confront Duke Winters and demand the truth.

And she would do exactly that over lunch at the Coachman. Because if what he had to tell her was something she didn't want to hear, she preferred that it be in a public place. Otherwise, she wasn't at all sure what her reaction might be.

Once again Duke's hopes were dashed after he'd found the light flashing on his recorder and played back the message. He'd hoped it was Charles, although Charles had said two p.m.

He listened gravely to Carol's message and glanced at his watch. He'd heard the strain in her voice and could guess what she wanted. He didn't want to talk to her yet. Not until he'd had a chance to talk to Charles. It took him a while to look up the number of her office then, when someone answered, it was with a British accent.

"Carol has left the office," the polite female voice said. "She has errands to run and then a luncheon appointment. I don't expect her back until after one."

Duke thanked her and hung up. There was nothing for it. He'd have to face the music. He'd still have time to get back for the call from Charles. And by then he hoped to have convinced Carol to go back home. Then he could concentrate on finishing this thing on his own, with Charles's help.

When he entered the pub an hour later, he saw Carol right away. She sat at the bar, one hip perched on a stool, laughing at something the barman had said to her. She'd tied her hair back again and wore a light gray business suit with a hot pink blouse.

He wasn't prepared for the way his heart turned over at the sight of her. He'd never allowed himself to experience emotions in the old days. He wished he didn't have to now. He'd had no idea of the pain that could come from loving someone, when there was no hope of them loving you back.

For a moment he stood transfixed as the reality of his true feelings sank in. Then someone nudged him with an elbow, reminding him that he was blocking the doorway.

When, he asked himself as he threaded his way through the crowd toward her, had he fallen in love with her? Last night, when all his fantasies had unexpectedly become realities, and he'd finally known what it was to make love to the right woman?

Or had it been all those years ago, when he'd looked into her eyes on that warm summer evening in the park? Had he always carried this raw hunger for her somewhere in the recesses of his mind, only to acknowledge it when he'd finally made love to her?

It didn't matter, he decided. Whenever it was, it didn't diminish the power of it to hurt him. That thought intensified when he reached her side and she looked up at him.

For one very brief moment, he saw a flicker of warmth in her eyes. Then it was gone, hidden by a curtain of mistrust. "Hi," she said. "You're early."

"So are you. I was hoping to have a beer before lunch."
Now that he really looked at her, he saw the tension in her
jaw, the nervous tap of her fingernail on the side of her
wineglass. Guilt tugged at him in a shaft of pain. He
hadn't wanted to hurt her. Damn it, he hadn't wanted to
hurt himself. But then he hadn't known he was in love with
her until now.

"You have time," Carol said, looking at her watch. "I
don't have to be back until one."

"That's okay, I'll order at the table."

She nodded and slipped off the stool, her raincoat over
her arm. He took it from her and followed her as she led him
around the end of the bar and through a narrow passage.

"Watch your head," she ordered sharply, and he ducked,
barely missing the low beam that had supported the doorway for centuries.

He stepped down into the cozy dining room, feeling as if
he'd just grown several inches. Just above his head, thick
black beams marched across the low ceiling in uneven rows.
Below them, on a wide ledge bordering all four walls, an
assortment of tankards and mugs crowded together, looking as if one sneeze would send them toppling over the edge.

The room smelled of brandy and cigar smoke and looked
as if it had been there since the beginning of time. Divided
into booths, it managed to be secluded in spite of its limi-
tations.

The waitress, dressed as a medieval wench, showed them
into an end booth. Duke sat down facing Carol, with his
back to a leaded pane window that overlooked a cobbled
courtyard behind him.

Only one other booth was occupied, on the other side of
the room, by a young couple who only had eyes for each
other. Duke felt a twist of envy before looking back at
Carol.

"Interesting place," he said, picking up the oversized menu.

"It's very old. I love the atmosphere. Most people prefer to eat in the bar, so it's usually quieter in here. And the food is very good."

She avoided his gaze, staring down at the menu as if she'd never seen it before. She waited until the waitress had left with their order before saying in a low voice, "I was attacked this morning."

The shock of her words chilled him. For a moment he wondered if he'd misunderstood. "Attacked?"

"Yes. It was the man who took your picture on the Tower Bridge walkway."

His reflexes jerked, as if pulled by invisible strings. "Where?"

"About a block from my office. It was the man who tried to take your picture on the walkway."

"Are you all right?" His mind raced with possibilities. Good God. If they'd—

"I'm fine . . . now. But it was terrifying at the time. I . . ."

He saw her throat working and ached to reach for her, to take her in his arms and hold her. He steeled himself to stay where he was. "What happened?"

He listened while she told him, shivers running down his spine when she described how the man had stuck a gun in her side and threatened to shoot.

"I got away," she said, her voice low and unsteady, "but I had to go down into the subway to do it. I thought . . . I didn't . . ."

She gulped, and he covered her hand with his in a quick reassuring gesture. Remembering what she'd told him about her claustrophobia, he could well imagine how tough that must have been for her.

"Did he say what he wanted?" His fists opened and closed, itching to fit them around the jerk's neck.

"Only that he wanted me to go with him."

"He gave no clue as to why, or if there was anyone else involved?"

Her blue eyes, dark as a summer night, stared into his with a pleading misery that bore right into his heart. "Duke," she said quietly, "I know something strange is going on. I believe that it's connected to Mack in some way, and I believe you know what it is. I have to know the truth. No matter what it is."

His pulse leapt. *Connected to Mack.* Then she'd apparently believed Royce when he'd assured her that her husband was dead. She didn't suspect him of being Mack after all. Possibly she had not considered he could be Brandon Pierce. Royce must have done a good job of convincing her.

His mind raced ahead, concocting a believable story. If only he could buy some more time. It was the one thing he needed. Time to track down who was at the bottom of all this, and if he was tied up with the wreck.

More importantly, he needed time to try to convince Carol that the Brandon Pierce she once knew no longer existed. That he was a changed man. That he could be the kind of man she could possibly love.

It would mean more lies for the time being, but when he got back to the States he could pursue the relationship and eventually, he would tell her the truth. Once she knew him as he was now, and learned to trust him, just maybe they might have a chance of building something lasting between them.

"All right," he said carefully, keeping his voice low, "I'll tell you what I can. I work for the U.S. government. We're investigating the death of your husband and his partner, Brandon Pierce. We know very little about the events of the night they were killed, except that someone shot out the tires, causing the car to crash.

"So far the investigation has turned up nothing and the agency is determined to find out who was responsible for the wreck. I'm here on special assignment to investigate the case."

It was as close to the truth as he could hope to get. Now all he could do was hope Carol accepted it. Long enough to give him the time he so desperately needed. Holding his breath, he waited for her to speak.

Carol sat for several seconds, trying to absorb what he'd just told her. It would explain a lot of things. The code, the signal, the sense of familiarity. "But it's been over a year. Why now? And why here?"

"We have a new lead that led us here. That's why I contacted you. I was hoping you could help me with that."

"I don't understand. Why didn't you say something? Why all the pretense?"

He looked down at his hands, and she had the uncomfortable feeling he was avoiding her gaze. Then he looked back at her, and his eyes seemed as direct as ever. "The agency thought you might not be willing to talk to me if you knew why I was here."

Her nerves, already raw, splintered into anger. "You have a damn nerve, Mr. Winters. Don't you think you carried your investigation a little too far? Was it really necessary to seduce me to find out what you wanted to know?"

She saw him glance over at the other couple. Leaning toward her, he said quietly. "That had absolutely nothing to do with my job. I arranged our meeting, yes. It was necessary. But I never intended for it to go that far. You are a beautiful, desirable woman, Carol. And very seductive. I found that impossible to resist. Not too chivalrous of me, I have to admit, but I don't remember you putting up too much resistance."

"Damn you. And why the hell would you think I had anything to do with all this?"

"I never believed that you did. But you know as well as I do that in cases like this, we have to consider every possibility."

Mack was always so good at putting on an act, she thought, striving to get her thoughts untangled. Yet, surely, she would recognize her own husband? Even if his looks had been changed, his mannerisms, his walk, the way he held himself, all that would remain the same.

True, Duke reminded her of Mack, yet there were subtle differences. And about one thing she was absolutely sure. Never, in seven years of marriage, had Mack aroused the passionate response in her that this man had managed to do.

The full realization of that last thought hit her. She jutted her jaw at him. "So what's the verdict?"

"Carol." He reached for her hand and she snatched it out of the way. He sighed, then said quietly, "I'm sure you had nothing to do with it."

"Really. And just how long have you been so certain of this?"

Wariness crept into his eyes. "A couple of days or so."

"Before you made love to me?"

"Yes."

Her fierce whisper sounded harsh as she leaned forward. "Then why didn't you tell me who you were? Were you afraid I wouldn't sleep with you?"

His face was so close to her now that she could feel his breath warm her cheek when he muttered, "Damn it, Carol, I wasn't thinking about anything except how much I wanted you. I couldn't tell you because I had orders not to. We felt it would be safer for you if you didn't know."

She felt a chill brush her shoulders. "Safer?" This time she didn't pull away when he reached for her hand.

"Carol, we believe you might have information that you're not aware of. Something or someone you're acquainted with, who is connected to this case. If we're right, that someone must be aware that you have this knowledge. They won't want you passing it on to a government agent. They'll do what they have to in order to prevent that. If you didn't know who I was, you couldn't tell anyone."

She moistened her lips with her tongue. "The man with the camera? Is that why he wanted your picture?"

"It's very possible he's involved, yes. He probably wanted to identify me as an agent before grabbing you. Now tell me, and think hard, have you ever seen this man before? Anywhere? Maybe in an elevator, on the street, in your apartment building, your office building . . . think."

"I don't have to think. I am positive I've never seen him before."

Duke nodded. "Well, he could have been tailing you without you noticing him."

"I still don't understand why."

"We'll find that out when we catch up with him."

"Well, I can't imagine what he wants. I don't know any more about that night than you do. Probably a lot less."

She sat back as the waitress arrived with their order. Looking down at the steaming bowl of soup in front of her, she tried to sort out her chaotic thoughts. Something was still at odds, but she couldn't pin it down.

The waitress left, and once again Duke leaned forward. "You might not think you do, but there could be something you've forgotten, something that didn't seem significant at the time, that might be able to throw some light on all this."

She swallowed a spoonful of the soup, trying to dispel the persistent chill that settled in her stomach. "Like what?"

"I don't know. Something Mack said, something you said to someone—"

Her spoon clattered against the china bowl. "You think I'm responsible."

He looked unhappy. "Not intentionally. But Carol, you have to admit, besides Royce and Charles, you were the only person who knew exactly where your husband would be that night."

"I didn't tell anyone," she said sharply. "I might have had problems with my marriage, but I would never have betrayed my husband's confidence, intentionally or otherwise. I am intelligent enough to understand the importance of secrecy. I was married to him for seven years."

He held up his hands in a gesture of defeat. "We can talk about this later. Let's eat."

She finished the soup, even though she barely tasted it. She couldn't believe they actually suspected her of blabbing to someone about Mack's whereabouts. Feeling angrier by the minute, she waited until the waitress had cleared their plates, then leaned forward again. "Do the local police know why you're here?"

Duke shook his head. "U.S. Government privileged information. You know what your husband did for a living. If I bring in the local police it could be politically embarrassing for the U.S. I can't risk upsetting diplomatic relations that way. It's a touchy subject, you know that. I have to deal with this as best I can on my own."

She could well understand that. "So where do we go from here?"

"I can tell you where you go. Back to the States."

"No way." She saw the determination in his eyes and braced herself.

"Look, after what happened this morning, it's obvious that someone suspects who I am. They'll have to stop you from telling me what you know. It's no longer safe for you to be here. I'm putting you on a plane this afternoon."

"You don't have that authority."

"Maybe not, but—"

"What about my job? My rights as a citizen? My freedom of choice?"

"Carol, you don't understand. If what we believe is correct, this man is only a very small part of it. There is possibly an entire organization behind this. Your husband played big time. We could be up against a formidable force."

"I'm not leaving. And unless you show me a warrant for my arrest, you can forget about putting me on a plane. I have a stake in this, too. If this man can lead you to the people responsible for Mack's death, I have as much right, if not more than you do, to know who they are. I can't leave until this is over now."

His eyes glinted with frustration. "You're putting me in an impossible situation. I can't guarantee to protect you—"

"I'm not asking for any guarantees." She leaned forward to emphasize her point. "If I leave, it's possible he'll follow me back to the States. You have a much better chance of catching up with him here in London, right?"

Duke's eyebrows slowly rose. "You're setting yourself up as bait?"

"I figure I'm a target already. I'd much rather stay here and see this through than live with the fear of someone stalking me for the rest of my life. What guarantees do I have for protection back home?"

"Not much," Duke admitted. "Not unless you go under The Federal Witness Protection Program."

"And give up my family, my friends, my job? No thanks. I'll take my chances here."

"I'll agree on one condition." Duke balled up his napkin and dropped it on the table. "I want to move into your apartment."

The thrill of excitement caught Carol unawares. Angry with herself she said coolly, "I don't think that's a good idea. Jasper would throw us both out."

His hiss of frustration almost made her smile. She wouldn't let him near her again. For one thing, no matter how convincing his story sounded, she wasn't totally assured that he was who he said he was. For another thing, even if he were telling the truth, she wasn't about to get involved with a government agent. She'd had all she could take of danger and excitement in her life.

"All right," Duke said, "in that case, will you at least have a friend move in with you? Or better still, move in with them? At least until this business is taken care of."

She looked at him, mulling it over in her mind. "I could probably move in with Win," she said at last.

His shoulders relaxed visibly. "That will help. I'll get Jasper Golding to keep an eye on things, too."

The waitress approached with the bill and Carol looked up at her. "I'll take that," she said, stretching out her hand. She glanced at it, then dug in her purse for her wallet. "How are you proposing to do that without explaining why?"

"I'll think of something. In the meantime, there's something I want you to do for me. I want you to try to remember everything that happened in the days leading up to the wreck. Any detail, no matter how small, that might help us figure out how the information got passed on."

"I told you—"

"I know what you told me. But if there's the slightest chance of pinning this down, we have to try it. Okay?"

He had a point. Still unconvinced that she could think of anything that would help, she nodded. "Okay. I'll try."

"Just promise me one thing. You won't take any chances."

She looked up, her pulse leaping at the look of concern in his eyes. "Like what?"

"Like being alone with someone you're not absolutely sure about."

Like him, came the unbidden thought. "I thought you were satisfied it wasn't someone I knew?"

"I didn't say that." He slid along the bench and stood up. "This man isn't working alone. It's entirely possible that he has an accomplice. Maybe more than one. And it could very well be someone you know."

For some reason, a vision of Gordon popped into her mind. She remembered him standing on the top step, staring after Duke when he'd given her that signal. Jasper telling her that Gordon had been snooping around.

It was on the tip of her tongue to tell him, but she dismissed it. She had nothing to go on except her own fanciful imagination. And she didn't need Duke's insistence on following her around to ensure her safety. In fact, the less she saw of him the better. She didn't need the constant reminder of how easily he could destroy her defenses.

"I'll call Win this evening," she said, standing up to pull on her raincoat.

"I'd rather you called her now, from here. I want this settled."

She would have liked to argue but knew by the set of his jaw that he wasn't going to give in on this one. "All right. But she won't thank me for disturbing her writing time."

She stopped in front of the public phone, which was mounted on the wall by the front door. Duke stood close by her elbow in the narrow space, shielding her from the flow of customers in and out of the door.

"She's not there," Carol said, after listening for a minute or two. "Her recorder's on. She's probably immersed in her writing and doesn't want to be disturbed. I'll have to call her later."

She hung up, aware of Duke's body pressed against her as someone struggled by them. "Not much room in these old places," he remarked, when she looked up at him.

Something in his eyes quickened her heartbeat, and she stepped into the street, thankful to be out of the smoky atmosphere of the pub.

"I'll meet you back at your apartment," he said, as they waited at the curb for the lights to change.

"No." Aware that she'd spoken sharply, she softened her voice. "I'll be fine."

She was startled when he grabbed her arm and pulled her into the doorway. "Look, Carol, I know this has all been a shock for you, and I can understand how you feel—"

Her anger materialized unexpectedly. "Oh, you can? Then tell me, Duke, how does it feel to know you've been used—"

He ducked his head without warning, smothering the rest of her sentence with his mouth hot on hers. She struggled, but he held her trapped against the wall with his body, and the pressure of his growing need against her stomach wiped out all her resistance.

She sagged against him, her mouth as hungry as his, until he pulled his mouth from hers. Faintly surprised that no one passing by paid attention to them, Carol drew in a shaky breath.

"Now tell me you don't feel what's going on between us," Duke said harshly. He rubbed his lower body hard against her. "Does this feel like I'm using you? Doesn't it tell you what you do to me?"

"I don't think this is the place—"

"All right. Then we'll continue this conversation tonight. I'll meet you at the garage and stay with you until you are moved in with Win. And I'll also have a little chat with Jasper while I'm there. And I'm not going to argue about it, so don't even try."

She didn't want to argue. No matter what her head told her, her heart and her body had taken a stand. She knew how fragile her defenses were. She knew that if she allowed herself to be alone with him again she would not have the willpower to prevent the inevitable. He only had to touch her and she melted like sun-warmed snow.

She knew all that. And yet, as she stared into his dark, intense gaze, she heard herself saying, "I hope you like beef stew for dinner."

Duke let himself into his apartment and flung his jacket onto a chair. It missed and fell to the floor, but he left it there and crossed the room to the kitchen. Almost two. If Charles was going to call, it should be any minute now.

He needed something to do while he waited, so he washed up the dishes that were piled in the sink, dried them and put them away in the cupboard. As he closed the doors, the phone rang, setting his nerves on edge once more.

He crossed to it swiftly and snatched up the receiver. This time his pulse leapt as Charles's voice said softly, "Duke?"

"Yeah. Finally."

"Is it safe to talk?"

"I think so. I had a break-in a couple of nights ago but I checked it all out pretty thoroughly. I didn't find any bugs."

"Well, if you think—"

"Charles." He tried to curb his impatience. "At this point I'm willing to take a risk. Just tell me what's so damn urgent."

"All right." His breath echoed eerily on the line. "I know why you're in London. And you could be on the wrong track."

"What are you talking about?"

Charles swore. "Duke, if anyone can hear this—"

"I'll take full responsibility. Now spit it out."

"Okay, okay. The day after the accident I was in Royce's office. You were still unconscious and he was at the hospital. Anyway, a fax came through on his machine. Since I have security clearance I ran it through the decoder in case it was important."

Duke tightened his fingers on the phone. The back of his neck had begun to prickle. "And?"

"It was a memo from the research office. It said that the woman Royce had made enquiries about had been located. She had returned to her own country in Central America where a group of rebels had slit her throat. Apparently she had died in some primitive jungle village."

"So, what's that got to do with me?"

"It finished with a final comment. It was therefore impossible to question her about her connection to the wreck that had killed Pierce and Everett."

His throat felt dry. So now he knew. Was that the end of it? Was he going to be denied the satisfaction of seeing Mack's killer rot in jail? He should be happy, he thought, that the person who had taken away his identity had been dealt what she deserved. But he wanted more.

It left so many unanswered questions. Number one, had she been working alone or for someone else? And why hadn't Royce told him about this? And where did the guy with the camera fit into it?

"Did Royce ever follow it up?" he asked, his pulse quickening once more.

"That's the strange part about it," Charles said. "I asked him about the memo. I asked him why the woman was a suspect. He jumped all over me for reading it and told me to forget I ever saw it. It was a mistake, he said, and meant nothing."

Once again Duke's neck began itching. "A mistake? Whose mistake? The research department? Or Royce's?"

"I don't know. I might not have given it another thought, except that for some reason, Royce seemed to be preventing me from talking to you. I had a hell of a job to get into the hospital, and then when I did and you finally woke up, I was hauled out of there before I could talk to you."

"Yeah," Duke said slowly. "I seem to remember that."

"And I've been sent on overseas assignments ever since. Royce has absolutely refused to give me your number, giving me some rigmarole about security. That's why I had to come back here to get it."

"You're not on vacation then?"

"Vacation?" Charles gave a dry laugh. "You know how I feel about vacations. I'm supposed to be in South Africa. But through a chance meeting with a colleague I found out you were in England. I guessed why you were there. You thought Carol could help you find the killers, right?"

"Perhaps," Duke said, hating what he was saying. "Someone leaked that information and I didn't have a whole lot of choices."

Charles cleared his throat. "Look, I'm not throwing out accusations or anything like that. But there's something else about that memo. When I mentioned it to Royce again, he became very defensive. He told me he had no idea what I was talking about. He denied he'd ever received it."

Now Duke knew why his neck was bothering him. "Are you trying to tell me that Royce was the leak? But that doesn't make sense. Why the hell would he do that?"

"Maybe," Charles said quietly, "he didn't do it intentionally."

"God." He'd said exactly the same thing about Carol. His mind spun with the implications Charles had raised.

"Look," Charles said, his voice quickening, "I've got to go. I'm taking a chance as it is. I flew back here to warn you. If Royce was behind this, he's not going to want you to find that out. He'll stop you, Duke, anyway he has to. I didn't want him getting Carol in the cross fire. She's had enough grief."

"Yeah," Duke said grimly. "I know."

"I could be wrong about all this, of course, but there's something very odd about this entire situation. He's done his best to make sure you and I never had a chance to talk, and this thing with the memo is at the bottom of it."

"I take it he didn't give you my phone number, then?"

Charles hesitated, then said quietly, "No, I broke into his office and searched his desk."

Duke's mouth twitched. "You might be the only person in the world who could have done that and managed to get away with it."

"That's the good thing about being the chief's assistant. You know all the security traps."

"Charles," Duke said, thinking rapidly, "I need you to do something for me. I've been getting some flack from a Brit over here. Run it through the computer files. See if you can dig up anything on him." He gave a hurried but concise description of the photographer.

"A scar like that should be easy to trace. You think he's connected with this?" Charles sounded worried.

"I don't know. It could be something else altogether. But it's a little too much of a coincidence, don't you think?"

"I don't know what to think." He paused. "I'll try to check all this out, if I can. Be careful, Duke. I hate to think Royce is involved, but if he is, you know what you're up against."

He certainly did, Duke thought, hanging up the phone. And he agreed with Charles, something didn't smell right. But Royce? Somehow he couldn't believe that. There had to be an explanation somewhere.

Chapter 8

Duke's mind still buzzed with possibilities as he walked to meet Carol later that afternoon. Although the rain had kept off, the clouds had dominated the sky all day. Now that darkness had fallen, they gathered ominously overhead. A chill wind blew the last of the dead leaves along the sidewalk, making them dance in the pale light from the street lamps.

He stuck his hands in his pockets and thought about waiting inside the garage. Changing his mind, he decided to wait in the warm foyer of the apartment building. He could watch the street from the doors and would see her drive by. While she parked her car, he could walk down to meet her.

He felt chilled by the time he reached the steps of the building. Hoping he wouldn't have to wait too long for Carol, he ran up them and pushed the door open. He saw the two men facing each other immediately. One was Jasper Golding, who stood with his beefy arms folded across his chest, his face an inscrutable mask.

Duke recognized the man standing with his back to the door. It was the redheaded punk who'd been manhandling Carol.

"It's a free country," Gordon was saying, his voice low and threatening. "I'm going up to see her and you're not going to stop me, so you'd better not try it."

Duke tensed as he saw Gordon's hand stray to the back pocket of his jeans. Guessing he carried a knife there, Duke stepped forward. "He might not want to stop you," he said quietly, "but I sure will."

Without taking his eyes from Jasper's face, Gordon half turned his body. "What're you doing 'ere?" he said nastily.

Duke strolled over to take up a stance next to Jasper and arranged a pleasant smile on his face. "I was just about to ask you the same thing."

"Yeah, well, it ain't any of your business, so p—"

"I think it is my business. If you've come to see Ms. Everett, you're out of luck. She and I have . . ." he paused for effect " . . . an understanding."

Gordon lifted his chin in a gesture of belligerence. "What's that mean?"

"It means, my friend, that Carol Everett is spoken for. Off limits. She and I are an item. A couple. A—"

Gordon asked an impertinent and offensive question. Duke longed to squeeze his jugular. Instead he nodded. "You got it."

"I don't believe you." Gordon stepped forward, but Jasper intervened.

"Believe it, dear fellow. I caught sight of this gentleman myself, leaving the building in the wee hours of the morning."

Gordon scowled. "So what. There's plenty more fish in the sea. Always did think she was a stuck-up b—"

With a great deal of satisfaction, Duke grabbed the man's greasy collar and escorted him none too gently through the door. "Beat it," he muttered, as he shoved him down the steps. "And don't let me see you hanging around here again, or you'll have more trouble than you can handle."

Gordon muttered something unintelligible and slunk off.

"That," Jasper remarked when Duke returned, "is the last we'll see of that unpleasant young man."

Duke grinned. "I hope you're right. Thanks for the backup."

Jasper closed one eyelid. "It was entirely my pleasure. Howevah, I would suggest that you leave the building at a more reasonable hour in future. We have a reputation to protect here. Not to mention my position."

"Sorry." Duke tried to look repentant. "I guess I was worried about leaving Ms. Everett at night."

"Ah-ha," Jasper drawled, in obvious disbelief.

"As a matter of fact," Duke went on, "I was wondering if you'd keep an extra careful eye on her for me over the next few nights. I don't trust that jerk." He nudged his head at the door. "He looks like bad news to me. I think I'm going to suggest that Carol move in with her friend, Win, for a day or two. Just in case."

Jasper's chest swelled. "You can trust me, dear chap. I won't let him, or anyone else, near Ms. Petrov's apartment. You can count on that."

Duke held out his hand, feeling a little better. "Thanks, Jasper. You're all right."

Jasper beamed. "And you, my dear fellow, are also...ah...all right." He pumped Duke's arm, then glanced beyond him. "Oh, there's Ms. Everett now, just driving past the door."

Duke hurried across the foyer, calling out his thanks.

"Not at all," Jasper boomed, as the doors closed with a soft thud.

Hurrying down the street, Duke silently thanked Gordon for giving him the perfect excuse to enlist Jasper's help. The man had come in useful for something, at least.

He reached the garage just as Carol stepped outside. She smiled when she saw him, starting the sparks flying in his belly again.

"I thought you might have given up," she said, as he took her arm. "I got stuck in traffic."

"There's something you should know about me," Duke said, glancing around to make sure Gordon wasn't still skulking in some dark corner. "I don't give up easily. Besides, beef stew is high on my list of foods I can't live without."

"What a coincidence."

"Yeah. Life is full of coincidences." His mind suddenly jerked back, as if tugged by an invisible cord. He and Charles had talked a lot about coincidences. It had occurred to him at the time that there was more than one, but he couldn't put his finger on it. Something that Charles had said that had nudged his memory. What the hell was it?

"Are you all right?"

Looking down into Carol's anxious face, he smiled. The cold light from the street lamp made her look pale, and he felt a tug of compassion. This had to be a tremendous strain on her nerves, he thought, wishing he hadn't had to put her through it all.

Then they moved into the shadows and her eyes seemed dark and inviting. Unable to resist, he pulled her to a halt and gently kissed her mouth. Excitement stirred in him as she responded immediately.

"I missed you," he whispered.

She laughed, a soft sound that warmed his insides like fine brandy. "It's only been a few hours."

"I know. That's what surprises me. I'm beginning to get real interested in you, Carol Everett."

She dropped her gaze, and he felt the ripple of tension in her arm. "You don't know me," she said, tugging him forward again.

"I know you enough." If only she knew just how well he knew her. "I know what pleases you. I know how to make you hungry for more."

She shot him a look he couldn't decipher. Somewhere between awareness and mistrust. He didn't like that look. He thought he'd eased her misgivings about him. He thought he'd set her mind at rest. Apparently he hadn't.

Did she still nurse the possibility that he could be Mack? He hated that thought. He mounted the steps behind her, more determined than ever to erase that prospect once and for all from her mind. And he knew just how he wanted to do it.

He followed her into the living room, his arms already aching to hold her. Cautioning himself not to rush it, he asked lightly, "Is there anything I can do to help?"

"Yes, you can pour me a glass of wine. The stew's already made, it just has to be heated up."

He walked into the kitchen with her, enjoying the quiet intimacy of the domestic scene. Inwardly he laughed at himself. Who would have believed that Brandon Pierce, the mean, ruthless mercenary, could be happy and content puttering around like an old married man? Mack would roll over laughing in his grave.

The thought sobered him instantly. That's what this was all about, now. That's why he was there, in that kitchen, with Carol. Not because of the investigation. Not because he thought she had anything to do with it anymore.

It was simply a very real need to separate her memories of Mack and whatever she'd had with him, from the wild frenzy of pleasure that he, Duke Winters, shared with her.

He wanted her to know, beyond a shadow of a doubt, that the man who could bring her writhing and moaning to the height of passion was not her dead husband. Nor was he, in the emotional sense, the partner who was supposed to have died with him—did in fact die with him in a way.

"Are you going to open it or stare at it all night?"

He jerked his head up and met Carol's laughing gaze. Something curled inside him—something hot, demanding and impossible to resist. Very slowly, he put down the corkscrew he'd been holding for the past few minutes.

He saw her expression change. Her lips parted, and the tip of her tongue moistened her lips. "Duke..."

He heard the warning in her voice but chose to ignore it. He knew by the heat in her eyes that she wanted it as much as he did. Even so, he made himself give her the option. Holding out his hand, he said softly, "Come here."

She stared at him for several intolerable seconds, while his heart pounded painfully against his ribs. Then, with a long sigh, she took two steps toward him.

She'd taken off her jacket earlier, and the pink blouse clung to her generous figure, sleek and silky. She stood looking up at him, her eyes already soft and warm with expectation.

He reached for the top button of her blouse and eased it undone. Then the next one. And the next. The back of his fingers brushed the soft, smooth curve of her breast. He heard her intake of breath, and excitement exploded in his belly.

His fingers shook as he finished unbuttoning her blouse, then pulled it free from her skirt. It slipped easily from her shoulders and settled in a soft heap on the floor.

He could smell her perfume, subtle, exotic and devastating. He'd once spent a memorable night in Maui sleeping alone on the beach. The tropical night scents had tormented his mind with unfulfilled yearning. That's how he felt now, looking down at her flushed face and the swift rise and fall of her partly bared breasts.

"If you want to stop me," he said, his voice raw with his need, "you'd better do it now."

A smile curved her lips. "If I'd wanted to stop you, I wouldn't have invited you to dinner."

"Good. Because I think it's already too late." He grasped her hand and pulled it down to his belt. "See for yourself."

He couldn't believe the tearing hunger he felt for her as she unzipped him. He ached with it, in a deep, intense agony of need that had to be satisfied. And he wanted so very badly to give her pleasure, to know that he had aroused the same powerful sensations in her that ravaged his own body.

He wanted her to feel it again, too. He wanted her to share in the same delirious climb to release that had stunned him the last time he'd made love with her. He wanted that for her more than he wanted it for himself. And the knowledge filled him with a sense of wonder, that she could have summoned this awareness in him, revealing a part of himself he had never known was there.

She touched him and, unable to stand it any longer, he lifted her in his arms and carried her to the bedroom. Kicking the door shut behind him, he wished with all his heart he could have switched on the light.

Determined to make it last, he took her in his arms, his hand stroking her hair. "You feel so good," he whispered, his lips close to her ear.

"So do you."

She wriggled against him, pressing closer, and a shaft of hot pleasure shot through his belly. He didn't know why it should be so different with her. He only knew it was, and that each time he held her like this, it would only get better.

He felt her hand on his hip, traveling slowly over the curve to his thigh. Before she could explore farther, he drew it back to his mouth and kissed her fingers. Then her arm, then her shoulder. He felt her shiver of pleasure as he drew his mouth down to her breast.

"I love to touch you this way," he murmured. His tongue teased her and her sharp gasp tightened his body. His body began to take over, urging him on, banishing all coherent thought. His need took over, and all he could think about was her warm, writhing body under his lips, the silky smooth skin that smelled of exotic flowers and the mysterious musky fragrance of a woman ready for him.

"Oh, God," she whispered, as he buried his fingers inside her. How he longed to see her face while she thrashed beneath him, making the soft little noises in her throat that drove him wild. How he ached to see the curve of her body as he stroked her with his tongue, the look in her eyes when he drove himself into her.

Unable to hold back any longer, he took her hard and fast. The arch of her body beneath him told him she was close, and he heard his own growl of intense pleasure as they strained together. Then his final lunge took him over the top. He shuddered with the force of his release.

Lying beside her in the dark, he had to content himself with listening to her rapid breathing, the silky touch of her hair across his chest, the cool, velvet feel of her skin as he ran his hand over her hip.

He felt her lips move over his chest, and his body stirred again. He wrapped his arms around her and hugged her tight. "You are an incredible woman," he whispered against her forehead.

His skin shivered as her hand roamed down his stomach. "You make me feel incredible," she said softly.

He caught her wandering hand and brought it back to his chest. "That's an understatement of the way you make me feel."

"How do I make you feel?"

"I don't know if I can describe it. It's like I've had a part of me buried somewhere deep inside, kind of like buried treasure trapped on the bottom of the ocean. Now, after all this time, it's finally been lifted to the surface and opened. I can finally see it and its magnificence takes my breath away."

"Wow." Carol breathed against his skin. "For someone who doesn't know how to describe it, you did an incredible job."

He laughed a little self-consciously, embarrassed by the unfamiliar thoughts he'd expressed. "You're bringing out a whole new side of me."

He thought he felt her tense, then she said softly, "I'm glad." Her hand slipped from his grasp and began to roam again. Once more he caught it and held it fast. Although the scars had healed over, the skin had a different texture, and he knew she would be able to detect them. At a time like this, the last thing he wanted was to deal with awkward questions.

She was quiet for a moment or two, then she asked, "How did you become an agent for the government?"

He decided to tell her the truth. He knew it was unlikely Mack had told her. They were both so careful not to talk about each other. "I was heading for a prison sentence," he said quietly. "I was offered an alternative, and took it."

She was quiet for so long he was sure he'd made a mistake in telling her. "What did you do?" she asked at last.

"I tried to stop a guy from hitting on his wife. I had to get rough. He ended up in hospital and I ended up in front of the judge's bench. Things might not have gone so badly for me if I'd said I was sorry. But I couldn't lie. The guy had it coming. I told the judge I'd do the same thing again if the need arose. He slapped a sentence on me, said I was dangerous."

"Then what happened?"

"I'd been sitting in the cell for three or four hours when they said someone wanted to see me. I'd never seen the guy before, but he said he could offer me an alternative to doing time, if I was interested. I was interested. I had nothing to lose, no ties, no real home. It seemed like a good deal to me."

"What did they want you to do?"

He lifted her hand to his lips. "That, my sweet, is privileged information. But I will tell you that I enjoyed it so much, I stayed with the agency."

"What about your family? How did they feel about you doing a dangerous job?"

His laugh held no humor. "Let me tell you about my family. When my parents got married I was already well on the way. They were too young, too inexperienced and resented the hassle of having to take care of someone. Neither one of them missed an opportunity to let me know that. Then my mother got pregnant again and my father couldn't take the pressure. He left."

She stirred in his arms. "I'm sorry."

"Yeah," he said softly, "we were all sorry. Mom didn't like to be lonely, so there were always plenty of men around. Trouble was, none of them wanted to be a father to two kids."

He paused, his mind heavy with the bitter memories. "I got to hand it to her," he said at last. "She really knew how to wind them around her little finger. She'd act like she couldn't hold a screwdriver and get them to do all her repairs around the house free of charge.

"She'd have a problem with her car and the same day she'd bring someone home who could fix it. She'd give them all the sob story of how her kids were hungry and had no shoes, and take the money they handed her and when their backs were turned, she'd be down at the local booze joint stocking up on her supplies."

"That's terrible," Carol said, lifting her head.

"Yeah, I know." He ran a finger over her shoulder, smiling as the shiver vibrated through her body. "The trouble was, she taught my little brother to do the same thing—use the promise of his love to get what he wanted, play on people's emotions and manipulate them."

His sigh shook his body. "She tried it on me. She'd try to get me to do things by saying she wouldn't love me anymore if I didn't do it. I got wise to her, though. I didn't need her love. I didn't need anyone's love. The more I looked around, the more I realized just how many women used it to get what they wanted."

Carol made a shocked sound and raised herself off him. His skin felt cold with the loss of her touch. "That's a bit harsh," she said. "You can't judge everyone by your mother."

"I know that now." He reached for her and pulled her close. "But I'd never met anyone like you. If I had, my life might have been very different."

He aimed a kiss at her face, then let her go. "That stew is beginning to smell good," he said, sliding out of bed. "I'm getting hungry, so how about feeding me so I can get my strength back?"

"Sure. Hold on, I'll put the light on."

He scrabbled through the clothes on the floor and headed out the door, just as she switched on the light. Slipping into the bathroom, he closed the door behind him and leaned against it.

He couldn't play hide-and-seek with her forever. And it was becoming very apparent that they couldn't be alone together for long without heading for the bedroom. He would have to tell her. And soon. He prayed it wouldn't be too soon.

Carol lay in the empty bedroom for several minutes, trying to come to terms with what she'd heard. It couldn't be Mack. No one could have told that story with such conviction if they'd been lying. Mack had been an orphan. He'd never known his parents.

She would know, she told herself. Surely she would know if she were making love to her husband. There was just no way he could be Mack. So why, she asked herself as she crossed to the closet for a change of clothes, couldn't she rid herself of the persistent, niggling uneasiness in the pit of her stomach that just wouldn't go away?

All through dinner she wrestled with the problem, while Duke did his best to lighten her mood. She tried to respond to his gentle teasing, but in the end even he fell silent.

She accepted his offer to help with the dishes, then after they'd put away the last dish, she glanced at her watch. "I'd better get my things together if I'm going up to Win's tonight."

"I'll help."

She would rather he left so she could be alone with her turbulent thoughts, but she knew he would insist on staying until she moved upstairs.

He followed her into the bedroom, and she avoided looking at the rumpled bed. Just the sight of it created sparks of tormenting excitement. "There's not much you can do," she said, hoping he'd at least leave her alone to pack. "I can handle this."

"I know. I just wanted to get you in the bedroom again."

If only he wouldn't look at her like that, she thought desperately. If only her entire body didn't respond to him like wildfire leaping through a tinder-dry forest.

He reached out a hand and she backed away. "I'm not going to get anything done if you touch me." She'd said it lightly, hoping he'd take the hint.

Instead, his gaze roamed hungrily over her body, setting her on fire wherever it touched. "I know," he said, and grinned, turning her heart over.

He stepped forward and drew her, unresisting, into his arms. "I want to stay the night," he whispered, and brushed her lips with a feather-light touch that sent shivers cascading down her back.

"No. Jasper would—"

"Jasper won't know." Again he drew his lips across hers. "Please?"

"Duke—"

"Just this one night. Then you can move in with Win tomorrow."

She opened her mouth for one last protest, but never got the chance to utter it. Helplessly she gave herself up to the fire consuming her as his mouth moved relentlessly on hers. Whoever this man was, she thought, as once more her clothes fell to the floor, no one had ever had the power to destroy her the way he did. No one.

Then his hands claimed her and she stopped thinking altogether.

Once more Duke slipped from the room before it was light, after extracting a promise from Carol that she would call Win that morning. Carol barely had time to clear the sleep from her mind before he was gone. She lifted her head to look at the clock. It was a little after five.

He was leaving early, he'd told her, to avoid bumping into Jasper. She might have accepted that, if it hadn't been for his insistence on making love in the dark. And still she couldn't rid herself of the strange feeling that somewhere, somehow, she'd known him before.

The possible answer came from deep in her subconscious mind, stunning her like a blow to the head. Why hadn't she thought of it before? If she had been willing to believe her husband could have survived the accident, then why hadn't it occurred to her that his partner could have also survived?

She pushed herself upright, shock waves vibrating through her body. Brandon Pierce? No, she couldn't believe that. Maybe that's why she'd refused to consider it before. She didn't want to believe that.

Preposterous as the idea seemed, she had to consider it now. But why would he have contacted her after all this time? And more importantly, if he was Brandon, why couldn't he tell her who he was?

She was tempted to call Royce again but decided against it. The chances were he would lie to her, anyway. She could never fully trust anything that Royce had told her, knowing what Mack had done for a living.

She slipped out of bed, her mind a torment of whirling thoughts. No matter how feasible the idea was, she just couldn't equate the man who could arouse such intense emotion in her with the merciless, hard-bitten reprobate who had controlled her husband.

Only minutes ago she had made passionate love with a sensitive, seductive man who knew how to give pleasure to a woman as well as take it. Each time she was with him it seemed to get better. They were becoming attuned to each other, sensitive to each other's needs and preferences.

He was considerate, persistent without pressuring. He made her feel safe, secure in the knowledge that he was willing to protect her, and very capable of doing so. Yet there was a gentle patience in the way he touched her. That didn't sound like Brandon Pierce.

They had nothing in common. Nothing at all. Except for the fact they were both connected to the agency.

Turning on the shower faucet, she wished fervently that she could be sure. And then what? she asked herself. What if he were exactly who he claimed to be? He was still an agent, working for the government.

He was still in the same line of work as Mack had been. There would still be the danger, the secrets, the fear of never knowing where he was or what he was doing. She couldn't deal with all that again. Not even for a man who could set her soul on fire.

Sitting alone in her kitchen later, she warmed her hands around a mug of hot coffee. It was impossible to think of Duke being Brandon Pierce. She could remember the first time she ever saw Brandon. It was at a Fourth of July picnic in the park. The sun had sunk low in the sky by the time Mack had arrived.

"The food is just about gone," she told him, when he tapped her on the arm. She tried not to sound put out by the fact he was late, as usual. She was too glad to see him to risk an argument.

She barely glanced at the tall, fair-haired man standing at his side until Mack said, "Carol, this is Brandon Pierce. He works with me, and he's been looking forward to meeting you."

Surprised, Carol glanced up at the bronzed face. Although she had known Mack for several weeks, up until then he'd never mentioned friends or co-workers. She was beginning to believe he was antisocial, a thought that bothered her a great deal.

Relieved to discover she was wrong about that, Carol smiled. "I'm very pleased to meet you, Brandon."

He nodded, and she felt a chill. His light gold eyes pierced her like twin laser beams, and something in their depths, something deep and intense that she couldn't understand, made her pulse quicken in a way that was wholly disturbing.

She was about to withdraw her hand when he grasped it in warm, firm fingers. "I've heard a great deal about you, Carol. Mack wasn't exaggerating."

She could see no emotion on his face whatsoever. It was like a mask, smooth and impersonal, hiding the person behind it so effectively, she had the odd sensation that she was looking at a robot.

"Thank you," she said awkwardly, and pulled her hand back. Mack interrupted at that moment with a hand on her shoulder, breaking the tension. "Lead the way to what's left of the supper, Angel. There are two hungry men here ready to eat."

She didn't see Brandon Pierce again until the wedding. When Mack announced that Brandon was to be best man, she wanted to know more about him. As usual, Mack lied.

"He works with me at the agency," he told her. "He's a courier, carries important documents back and forth between our foreign embassies."

"He must do as much traveling as you do." Carol thought about the inscrutable face. "Does he have a wife and family?"

Mack laughed. "Brandon? Not on your life."

"I didn't think so," Carol said slowly. "He doesn't seem to be a very happy man."

"He's a very dangerous man," Mack said, lifting her chin to drop a kiss on her mouth. "And don't you forget it. There isn't a woman alive who could get the better of Brandon Pierce."

He'd refused to elaborate when Carol had asked him to explain that. Somehow she hadn't really needed an explanation. Somehow she'd known exactly what Mack had meant.

Carol shivered and put down the coffee mug. No, Duke Winters couldn't possibly be that hard-eyed man with the relentless expression. She had to be crazy to think so.

She got up and stepped over to the sink to rinse out her mug. It was all this secrecy, the lies and strange incidents again. It brought back all the feelings of helplessness that had been so much a part of her life.

It didn't seem possible that the agency suspected her of betraying Mack. Yet Duke was right, whoever shot at the car that night had known exactly when and where it would be.

She had been too shocked at the time to consider that question. Then later, when she'd struggled to put her life back together, she'd refused to think about what had happened. Until now.

Standing in the bedroom, she stared at the row of dresses in her closet without seeing them. How had they known? Who would have been careless enough to leak that kind of information? Only two people were supposed to know, besides Mack, Brandon and herself. And that was Royce and his assistant, Charles.

She had met both men very briefly, for the first time, at Mack's funeral. Afterward, she had managed a few brief moments alone with Royce, closeted behind the darkened windows of his car. She had wanted to know why someone had wanted her husband and his partner dead.

"Your husband was engaged in dangerous work," Royce had said that damp, gray morning. "He knew the risks he was taking. He was a brave man, Carol. A brave man. He gave his life working for the security and peace of the country he loved."

"He was a hired killer," Carol said quietly.

Royce's dark eyebrows rose. "He did what was necessary. Only what was necessary, Carol. You don't understand."

"Oh, I understand. What I need to know is why. Why it's necessary to hire civilians to do a job that surely should be done by the military, in a responsible and ethical manner."

"Look, Carol, I understand how you feel but you must know I can't discuss this with you."

"I know that you all hide behind that bureaucratic doubletalk." Carol did her best to control her anger. "I was married to my husband for three years before I knew what he did for a living. And now I'm a widow, without knowing the reasons why."

"I'm sorry, Carol," Royce said, actually looking it. "I don't have the answers. But I'm glad we had a chance to talk. There's something I have to discuss with you."

She looked at him, waiting, wondering if he was merely trying to change the subject.

"I think it might be best if you sell the house and move somewhere else. Out of state preferably."

She frowned. "I really don't see what that has to do with you."

Royce looked uncomfortable. "I'm just concerned about your safety, Carol. I don't think you'll have any more trouble, now that Mack is dead, but—"

"Trouble?" Her heart began pounding again, as it had so many times over the past few years.

"Yes, I mean the threats. I know Mack wasn't worried about them, but even so—"

"Mack *knew* about them?"

Royce's eyebrows shot up and down. "Well, of course. He told me not to be concerned, that they were bluffing and that he'd take care of you. But I think, under the circumstances, it might be better if you had a new address. Just in case, Carol. Just in case."

She'd managed to get herself out of the car without falling apart. Somehow she'd controlled her rage until she was alone, in the empty house where so many of her dreams had been destroyed. Mack had laughed at her stories of phone threats, knowing all the time they were real. His wife's life had been in danger and he'd ignored it all, intent on doing the work that meant more to him than life itself.

The doorbell rang, startling Carol back to the present. Throwing the dress she'd been holding on to the bed, she grabbed her robe and hurried out to answer it.

She couldn't stop the thrill that coursed through her when she saw Duke's lean frame in the doorway. His eyes skimmed over her, starting the fires all over again. "I wanted to walk you to your car," he said, stepping into the room without waiting for an invitation. "Have you called Win yet?"

"Not yet, it's too early. I'll call from the office." She frowned up at him. "Is all this really necessary?"

"Until I catch up with our photographer friend, yes, it is necessary. Unless you've changed your mind and will fly back to the U.S.?"

She tightened her mouth. "Not a chance. Besides, you don't know if I'll be any safer back there."

"True. But I still don't like it."

"Neither do I. I especially don't like being under suspicion for the death of my husband."

He looked at her, wariness hovering in his dark eyes. "I thought we'd settled all that yesterday."

"Your agency thinks I know something about the night Mack died. Something I'm not telling, isn't that it? Isn't that why you're here?"

"Look, Carol—"

"No, you look. All I know is that my husband and his partner died under mysterious circumstances. Then you turn up a year later, pretending to be a mechanic and arrange a way of meeting me. Then, out of the blue, someone attempts to kidnap me. The same someone who went to a great deal of trouble to take a picture of you. Then you tell me you're an agent working for the government, and you couldn't tell me before who you were."

He looked down at her steadily, and she could see the calm acceptance settle over his face. "So what are you saying, Carol?"

She wanted to demand that he tell her the truth. The words hovered on her tongue, yet she couldn't bring herself to do it. Maybe she didn't want to know who he really was. Maybe she didn't want it to matter. Or just maybe she was afraid that if he convinced her that he was who he claimed to be, she wouldn't be able to control the way she felt about him. And that, she knew, would be a disaster.

Chapter 9

Aware of Duke's tense expression as he waited for her answer, Carol said carefully, "I'm saying that I find this all very confusing, and it's very difficult to think under these circumstances. I just can't remember much at all about what happened a year ago."

His shoulders relaxed, and a fleeting look of relief crossed his face. Then he smiled. "You're right. Maybe if we talk about the events that led up to that night, you'll be able to remember something significant."

"It's possible." And maybe, she added silently, she could satisfy herself one way or another about who he was.

"So how about tonight?"

"Well, don't forget I'm moving in with Win tonight."

"It would make things a lot simpler if you let me move into your place here."

"Maybe," she said lightly, "but something tells me we wouldn't get any serious talking done. This way you'll have to make the most of the time we have alone."

"I'm always willing to do that."

His grin threatened to start the fires again and she looked at her watch. "I have to get dressed. It's getting late."

"Need any help?"

Her pulse skipped as she looked back at him over her shoulder. "I think I can manage on my own. I do have a job waiting for me."

"Pity," he murmured, his hot gaze moving over her.

She hurried into the bedroom and shut the door behind her, before temptation got the better of her again.

Duke spent a restless morning waiting around his apartment, half hoping to get some news from Charles. He knew it was too soon, but there didn't seem to be much else he could do at this point. Looking for one man with a camera in the midst of a crowded city was like looking for the proverbial needle.

Yet he hated the idea of just sitting in wait, hoping that something would break. In the end he decided that he would wait until the end of the week. If by that time nothing had happened, he would fly back to Washington and question Royce himself. Maybe then he'd get some answers. And maybe not.

Charles was right, Duke thought, staring up at the street level from his apartment window. If Royce had something to hide, he certainly wasn't going to reveal it to the one man who'd had the most to lose from what had happened. Except for Mack, that was.

But then Mack was dead, and Brandon Pierce was still very much alive. And getting more frustrated by the minute. Duke pulled away from the window and wandered into the kitchen to make some coffee.

A lot of that frustration was because of Carol, he knew that. On the one hand he very much wanted to tell her who he was and get it out in the open where they could deal with it. On the other, he was afraid to do that, in case she refused to have any more to do with him.

She was mad enough when she thought he was an agent putting the make on her. What would she do if she knew he was Brandon Pierce? Probably run a knife through his heart, Duke thought gloomily.

He couldn't take the risk of losing her trust now. Not when she could be in danger. Even more danger than he'd thought, if Royce was behind all this. He wouldn't stop at silencing Duke; he'd have to silence Carol, too.

Duke's blood ran cold at the thought. He had to keep Carol's trust if he was going to protect her. Somehow he had to persuade her to fly back to the States with him at the end of the week. Although, if his suspicions were correct she wouldn't be safe anywhere. Neither would he.

He waited until eleven-thirty, then put in a call to Carol's office. She answered right away, her pleasant voice warming his heart.

"How about dinner tonight?" he asked, coming straight to the point. "I know a great little restaurant in Soho, if you like Italian."

"I love Italian, but I'll have to take a rain check. I have a few chores to take care of before I move in with Win."

His disappointment was intense. "Lunch then?"

"Sorry. I have a lunch meeting with Anna and some prospective clients. She wants me to help with the presentation. It's too much of a strain on her voice if she talks for too long."

He was losing his appetite, fast. "I'll meet you at the garage then and walk you home."

He knew by the length of her pause what was coming. "Duke, not tonight, okay? I...kind of want to be alone for a little while. I'll be fine. I'll be careful, I promise. I'll call

Jasper and have him meet me in the foyer if it makes you feel better, okay?"

He had to agree to that, though the ache in the pit of his stomach was a good indication of how much he resented it. "So how about if I call you at Win's tonight? Just to make sure you're settled in okay, all right?"

She sighed. "Sure, Duke, that's fine. I have to go now, Anna's waiting. I'll talk to you this evening."

He let her go, hating the feeling of helplessness that rushed over him. He'd sensed her uneasiness that morning when he'd left her. Now it came through loud and clear. Something had changed since last night. Something was bothering her, and he was very much afraid he knew what it was.

He walked to his favorite pub for lunch, his mind churning over the events of the past two days. Uppermost in his mind was his conversation with Charles. He still couldn't bring himself to believe that Royce had been responsible for the shooting. Intentionally or otherwise.

He'd known Royce for fifteen years. He was a dedicated agency man, and both Brandon and Mack would have bet their lives on his integrity. Maybe they did, Duke thought, as he reached the doors of the pub. Maybe they had bet their lives that night, and lost.

He pushed open the doors, to be greeted by a babble of noise and warm, smoky air reeking of beer. As he stepped inside, a fleeting thought flashed through his mind, too fast for him to catch it.

It was the same sensation he got when he'd been trying to remember a name and it would suddenly pop into his mind hours later. A small piece of knowledge that just needed a prod to come to the surface when he least expected it.

He fought his way to the bar and ordered his beer, then waited, still trying to force the thought back into his mind.

For some reason, he felt it was desperately important. Important enough to bother him for the rest of the afternoon.

The long day finally came to a close and Carol sat behind the wheel of her car, feeling more weary than she ever remembered. The depression weighing her down had nothing to do with the day's work. She'd felt it intensifying as each hour passed, and although she tried not to think about Duke, somehow his image played constantly on her mind.

She sat now, in the grumbling, throbbing jungle of cars and towering red buses, and wished she hadn't been quite so adamant about not returning to the States. The cool, quiet peace of New England seemed very inviting, and a pang of homesickness brought an unexpected mistiness to her eyes.

Even New York seemed preferable right now. Just to see the Empire State building soaring above her, or hear the familiar accents of the cabbies yelling at each other, or the smell of a hot dog stand. Even the coffee smelled different in New York.

Carol stepped on the gas as the bus in front of her lurched forward. *I'm beginning to get real interested in you, Carol Everett.* His voice whispered the words in her mind, potent, insistent, impossible to ignore. Damn him, she thought, slamming on the brake again as the bus screeched to a halt.

Part of her was relieved she wouldn't have to deal with him that night. Another part of her ached to be with him again. She couldn't listen to that part, she reminded herself. She'd been that route before and bitterly regretted it.

Even so, she was more than a little disappointed that he hadn't ignored her wishes when she walked down the street to her building, half expecting him to pop his head out of a doorway any minute.

She'd forgotten all about calling Jasper, as she'd promsed. The foyer was empty when she walked in, and she hurried over to the stairs.

She'd feel better, she decided, once she was moved in with Win, though again she felt a sharp pang when she remembered Duke's invitation for dinner. She'd be glad, she told herself, when all this was over and he was out of her life. He brought back too many bad memories, and she'd fought too hard to escape them to want a constant reminder of the hell she'd been through.

She reached the door of her apartment and fit the key in the lock. She heard the soft sound behind her, but before she could turn an arm snaked around her face, and a rough-skinned palm slammed over her mouth.

"Get the door open fast," Gordon's voice said softly in her ear.

The smell of raw alcohol on his breath made her gag. Then she froze as she felt the cold blade of a knife press tightly against her taut throat.

"Don't make any sudden moves," Gordon muttered, "or you'll be spilling blood down that nice clean frock."

Her fingers shook so badly she couldn't turn the key. With a muttered threat Gordon took his hand from her mouth, slapped her fingers away and twisted the key himself.

He needn't have warned her not to make a sound. Her throat was paralyzed with fear. She felt a sharp shove between her shoulder blades and stumbled forward into the room. Grabbing onto a chair to steady herself, she turned to face him.

He stood just inside the door, breathing hard, his gray eyes glittering with a strange kind of excitement.

"What do you want?" Carol demanded, mustering as much authority in her voice as she could manage.

"You, darlin'." Gordon twisted the knife to catch tl light and grinned. "You've been stringing me along. I' 'ere for what's coming to me."

Carol's stomach gave a sickening lurch. "You'd bett leave," she said sharply. "I'm expecting a friend any mi ute."

"Oh yeah?" Gordon took a step forward. "Well, y ain't gunna be opening no door for him, are you, lu You're gunna be real busy with me."

"Gordon, listen to me—"

"Shut up. I done enough listening. I had to listen to yo boyfriend the other night, telling me all about you a him."

Carol gave a start of surprise.

Gordon laughed. "Didn't tell you about that, did h Well, you'll have plenty to tell him when I'm done wi you." His grin vanished. "Take your clothes off."

Carol curled her fingers into her palms. "Gordon—"

"Either you do it or I do it for you. So get a move on.'

She lifted a chin. "Then you will have to do it. Becau I'm damned if I'm going to undress for you." She hoped sl sounded more forceful than she felt. She was in for a figl maybe for her life, but there was no way she was going submit to this disgusting lout.

"Be my greatest pleasure, darlin'." The repulsive grin sp across his face again. Fingering the knife with his thumb a forefinger, he stepped forward.

Carol braced herself.

A second later the door slammed open. It crashed again the wall with a deafening crack. Jasper stood there, breat ing fire, his shoulders bunching as he let out a roar a charged forward.

Carol screamed out, "He's got a knife!"

Jasper appeared not to hear her as he hurled himself into the room.

Gordon whipped around and brandished the knife. His hand snaked out and Jasper let out a muffled oath.

Carol felt sick when she saw the bright red line appear just above Jasper's elbow. Without waiting to see more, she rushed to the kitchen and grabbed the phone. Seconds later she was gasping out her address to the calm voice of the dispatcher.

"Hurry," she begged into the phone. "He'll kill him."

"Hold on," the dispatcher said, "don't hang up."

The noise from the living room almost deafened her. Animal-like grunts and groans accompanied the solid thump of bodies. It seemed to go on forever.

Carol winced as the crack of splintering wood was immediately followed by the shattering sound of broken glass. Then silence. Shocking and terrifying in the contrast.

"Oh, God," she whispered.

"Are you all right?" The urgent voice of the dispatcher repeated the question twice before Carol could answer.

"I don't know." She had to go and look. She couldn't just stay there, cowering by the phone, not knowing what had happened. Any minute she expected Gordon to appear, the evil grin contorting his face.

"Can you hold on?" she said, still whispering.

The woman's voice sounded perfectly calm. "Be careful. I'll hold on until I hear from you again."

Carol let the phone dangle from the wall and drew in a shaky breath. Then very slowly, she leaned forward to look into the room.

A broken chair lay close to one wall. Gordon lay sprawled underneath it, face down and motionless. A few feet away the knife glinted on the carpet. Carol's relief quickly turned to fear when she saw the bloodstains on it.

Moving into the room, she saw Jasper sitting on the floor, his back propped against the wall. With a cry of concern, she rushed forward and fell to her knees.

She felt a little better when she saw his weak smile. "I kept my promise," he said weakly. "He can't hurt you now."

Her eyes filled with tears as she patted his blood-soaked arm. "Hold on, Jasper, help's coming."

He nodded, then his eyes closed and his chin dropped to his chest.

Carol scrambled to her feet as the first faint blare of the police sirens sounded in the distance. She hurried back to the phone and spoke into it. "I'm fine, and the police are almost here. Thanks for holding on."

"Don't mention it. Is everything secure there?"

Carol swallowed. "Everything's secure." She hung up and turned, blinking in disbelief as Duke materialized in front of her. Without a second thought she went into his arms.

The next half hour went by in a blur of confusion. The police arrived, followed closely by the ambulance. Jasper regained consciousness enough to explain, with Carol's help, what had happened, relieving Duke of answering any awkward questions.

A concerned Win arrived on the scene, having heard the commotion, and Carol promised to go up to her apartment later, after she'd cleaned up the place and collected her things. "I called to see if you'd checked in with Jasper," Duke explained, when they were finally alone. "When he said he hadn't heard from you I told him to check on you, then called Win. When she said she hadn't heard either, I got a cab over here."

Seated on the couch with him, Carol was grateful for the comfort of his arms. "I thought he was going to kill Jasper," she said with a shudder.

Duke tightened his hold on her. "I tell you, when I stood n the doorway and saw Jasper sitting there covered in lood…" He left the rest of the sentence unsaid, but his lips ound her forehead and planted a kiss there.

"He was wonderful," Carol said shakily. "I hate to think vhat might have happened if he hadn't arrived when he id."

"Well, that settles it. You're going back to the States."

"No!" She surprised herself with the vehemence of that vord. "Gordon had nothing to do with Mack's death," she aid more quietly. "He was drunk. And he was just trying o salvage his wounded pride."

"It will be a while before he tries that again." Duke sat up nd turned her to face him, his hands on her upper arms. 'But that's not the problem. I was counting on Jasper to vatch out for you. Now he'll be out of action for at least a veek or two."

"I'll be fine," Carol insisted.

"You're being stubborn."

"And you're being arbitrary."

"I'm concerned for your safety. Very concerned."

She recognized the gleam in his eye and hardened her resolve. "I'll move in with Win tonight. I promise you, I'll be ine."

"I want to stay with you."

It cost her a great deal to shake her head. "No. I don't hink that's a good idea."

"Then come back to my place and stay there."

"I promised Win," Carol said, pulling out of his grasp. 'Now I'm going to make some coffee, then I have to clean p this place."

She stood up, but he caught her hand. "Will you at least t me help?"

She smiled. "I was afraid you weren't going to offer."

He stood up and pulled her into his arms. His expression looked serious as he gazed down at her. "Carol, when all this is over, you and I have some talking to do. There are lot of things I want to explain."

Her heart skipped. She was glad now she'd held fast to her convictions. She pulled away from him, before he could tempt her with his kiss. "I'll make the coffee," she said, and walked determinedly into the kitchen.

He didn't follow her, and she was glad. She needed time to collect her thoughts. She couldn't think straight when he was close. And she didn't want to think about what it was he wanted to explain. She was very much afraid that she wouldn't like it.

Realizing she hadn't eaten, she opened the freezer and looked inside. There didn't seem to be a whole lot of choice. "How hungry are you?" she asked, poking her head around the corner to look at Duke.

"I'm always ready for food." He raised his eyebrows at her. "What've you got?"

"Frozen meat loaf, which will take a while to defrost and heat up. It's either that or an omelet."

"I'll vote for the omelet then. Need any help?"

"Yes, you can open a bottle of wine for me."

She'd ended up eating dinner with him after all, she thought, as she folded the puffy omelet in the pan. It made her uneasy that somehow, Duke Winters always got his way in the end.

"This might be a good time to have our discussion," Duke said, as they sat down to enjoy their meal. "That's if you're up to it."

"I'm up to it." She took a slow sip of her wine and put down the glass. "I'd like to get to the bottom of this as much as you do."

"All right, then." Duke took a mouthful of the omelet and murmured his approval. "Now, how about starting, say, about a month before Mack died. Anything and everything you can remember. Who you met, who you talked to, anything that could help pin this down."

She finished her mouthful, reluctant now to start talking. She had worked so hard to bury the memories, it wasn't easy to dig them all up again. "I don't know how much I can remember," she said, when she couldn't stall any longer. "It was over a year ago, that's a long time to remember details."

A look of concern brushed across his face. "If this is too painful for you—"

She stopped him with a quick shake of her head. "No, it's all right. It's just that... I've tried to forget so much, it might take a while to get it back."

"Take your time. We have the rest of the evening. Win's not expecting you for a while, is she?"

"No." Carol broke off a piece of her roll. "I guess I should start with the day Mack came back from his last assignment. That was the day I told him I wanted a divorce."

Duke's voice sounded strained when he said, "How did he take it?"

"Very badly. At first, I wasn't sure he'd heard me. He was distracted, on edge as he always was when coming back from a mission. As if he was sorry it was over." She shivered as the chill slid down her spine. "I could never understand how he could be that way after he... after what he'd done."

"Did he ever talk about it? The missions, I mean?"

"No. Never. I always knew when he would be leaving, and when he was expected back. But I never knew where he went, or any of the details of the mission. If he hadn't talked in his sleep—"

She broke off, remembering the whispered word in the middle of the night. *Whitewater.* Duke's glance at her face seemed to bore right into her mind.

Recovering herself, she said quietly, "If he hadn't talked in his sleep, I would never have known what he really did for a living. At first I couldn't make sense of the words he kept muttering.

"When I did I couldn't believe what I'd heard was for real. But when I confronted him about it, he admitted the truth. I was..." She shook her head at the memory, unable to find a strong enough word to describe the horror she'd felt.

"I'm sorry." He laid down his fork for a moment to cover her hand with his.

Shrugging, she said, "Anyway, as I said, this particular night he arrived home on schedule. I was on edge, too. I'd waited all week to tell him I intended to leave him. I dreaded it. I finally blurted it out as he was pouring himself a drink."

She paused, seeing again Mack's face when she hit him with the news. "He looked at me as if he didn't believe me at first, then swallowed his drink in one gulp. Then he asked me how long I'd been planning that dramatic scene."

"In his usual sarcastic way," Duke commented dryly.

She looked at him sharply. "Then you did know him?"

His dark eyes never flickered as he looked at her. "Of course. Didn't I tell you that? We bumped into each other a lot at the agency."

Her heart pounded with the rapid beat of a military tattoo. His direct gaze held steady, and she fought to control the wild flutters of suspicion. Why hadn't he mentioned that before? Or was it simply that she hadn't asked?

Unnerved, she took a gulp of her wine. Struggling to keep her tone even, she said, "Anyway, we argued long into the night. It didn't matter what I said, he shouted me down, in sisting that I was overreacting to everything. He said there weren't any problems between us that couldn't be fixed. I kept repeating that I wanted a divorce, and finally, he gave up. He left the house in the middle of the night. I didn't hear him come back.''

''But he did come back.''

''Oh, yes, he came back.'' She sighed. ''Things were difficult. I wanted to move out, I told him I wanted to go back to New York to live. He argued against that. He said he was going on another mission in a couple of weeks. He didn't know how long he would be away, he told me, but he hoped it would be long enough to give me time to get my head together.''

Duke put down his fork on his cleaned plate. ''All right. Now, think hard. Between then and the night Mack left, can you remember who you might have talked to?''

Carol frowned, forcing her mind back. ''My mother. Probably my neighbor. We sometimes went to the movies together. A checker at the grocery store, the mailman . . .''

She shook her head helplessly. ''Any number of people, I guess. But I swear, I told no one that Mack was leaving on a mission. I didn't even mention we were getting a divorce. Not even to my mother. I was going to tell her after I'd talked to the lawyer.''

Twisting the stem of her glass between her fingers she said quietly, ''Of course, I don't know who Mack told. I'm quite sure he told Brandon Pierce. He told him everything.''

Duke reached for the bottle of wine to refill her glass. ''They must have been very close.''

''They were.'' She tried hard to keep the bitterness out of her voice. ''Mack told me once that Brandon was the only person on earth he could trust. When I asked him if that meant he didn't trust me, he said that if a man was smart he'd never trust a woman. Whereas a man's friendship was a bond that couldn't be broken."

"You resented that?"

She looked up, but his gaze concentrated on the wine bottle as he poured some into his own glass. "I resented the fact that Brandon only had to lift his finger and Mack came running. I lost count of the meals I cooked for him, only to have him call and say he couldn't make it home because Brandon needed him for something."

She made a sharp sound of disgust. "It was Brandon said this and Brandon did that until I was sick of the name. It was like living with a ghost, unseen but always there. I think Brandon resented Mack being married to me, and did everything he could to sabotage our relationship."

"Damn." Duke lowered the bottle and began mopping at the growing stain spreading around his glass. "Sorry. Guess I wasn't paying attention."

Carol frowned at him. "Did you know Brandon, too?"

"Yes, I did." He kept his gaze on the table, mopping vigorously.

"What did you think of him?" She waited, holding her breath as Duke carefully folded up the napkin.

"I didn't know either one of them well enough to pass an opinion," he said, finally looking up at her. "But I'm a little surprised by what you've told me."

She let out her breath slowly. "You are? Why?"

"I got the impression they were both very independent men," Duke said, his dark gaze intent on her face. "I wouldn't have thought either one of them would have appreciated that kind of constricted relationship."

She smiled. "That just goes to show how little we really know about the people we meet."

"I guess it does," Duke murmured.

He changed the subject then, apparently having given up on her remembering anything significant. But the conversation stayed with Carol long after he'd seen her safely into Win's apartment.

"He's a nice man," Win said, after Duke had thanked her for helping Carol and then left. "He reminds me of someone."

Carol lifted her head sharply. "He does?"

"Yes." Win put down the blankets and pillow she'd brought for Carol's makeshift bed. "Someone I used to know a long time ago. We were in love, but I wasn't ready to get married. Now I know what a mistake I made."

That would explain Win's odd reaction after she'd first seen Duke, Carol realized. "I'm sorry," she said softly.

"So am I." Win smiled. "Don't make the same mistake I did, Carol. If you love him, it's worth taking a chance."

Carol agreed. That was the big problem, she thought as she settled herself on Win's couch for the night. No matter how confused she was by everything that had happened, no matter how strong were her doubts, no matter how much she warned herself about falling for a man who lived constantly on the edge of danger, she couldn't ignore the way she responded at his slightest touch. And that was something she didn't seem able to do anything about.

Duke had a restless night, disturbed by dreams he couldn't remember clearly when he finally awoke to find he'd overslept. He lay still for a moment, his mind going over the conversation he'd had with Carol the night before.

He hadn't learned anything new after all. Yet somewhere deep in his mind, the thought persisted that he was missing something somewhere. If only he could grasp it, he thought as he rolled out of bed, maybe it would give him the lead he so badly needed.

He finally gave up and after a quick shower, gave Carol a call at the office. "How about lunch?" he asked, as soon as she answered his greeting.

"Sorry. Got another meeting."

His spirits sank. It was beginning to sound depressingly like an excuse. "Anna again?"

"No, the big chiefs. Vice president is visiting from New York."

He felt a little better. "Dinner, then? You still have that rain check."

He waited through the brief pause, then relaxed when she said, "All right, I'd like that."

"Okay, we'll take your car. I'll be there at seven. Are you all settled in with Win?"

"Yes, everything is fine."

"Good. I have to wait for a phone call, but it gives me a couple of hours to kill. I thought I'd look in on Jasper this afternoon."

"Oh, that's sweet of you. Take him some chocolate—it's his favorite food."

He could hear the smile in her voice. His spirits rose considerably. "Will do. See you at seven."

Carol put down the phone, still smiling.

Seated opposite her, Anna said, "Your favorite mechanic, I take it?"

Her mind still on the conversation with Duke, Carol said absently, "He's not a mechanic anymore."

"Oh? Then what is he?"

The interest in Anna's voice alerted her. Furious with herself, Carol said carelessly. "Oh, he quit. I guess he got tired of London. I imagine he'll be going back to the States soon."

"Ah."

There was a wealth of curiosity in that one word. In order to forestall any more questions, Carol said hurriedly, "He's going to spend the afternoon with Jasper." It seemed natural then to launch into an explanation of how Jasper landed up in the hospital. By the time she was through, Anna appeared to have forgotten all about Duke quitting his job.

Carol was surprised when Anna said, as she was getting up to leave, "Oh, I nearly forgot. I have this big presentation to do this afternoon. If you're free I could really use your help."

Frowning, Carol looked at the calendar. "When did this come up? I thought you had nothing until next week?"

"I didn't. But I got a call late last night asking me if I could bring it forward. It's a big account, so I couldn't refuse. The tenants in one of those huge blocks of flats in Greenwich are interested in the direct sales products."

Anna cleared her throat. "You know how I always have problems making myself heard to a large group of people. If we could put this across it could mean a big increase in sales in that area."

"All right." Carol flipped the page of her appointment book. "What time? I'll be free by two."

"That will be perfect."

"Just as long as I'm back before five."

Anna paused at the door, her smile brightening her face. "I'll make sure of it. Can't have you late for your hot date tonight." Laughing, she disappeared, leaving Carol grimacing behind her.

At the hospital that afternoon Duke found Jasper sitting upright in bed, his upper body and arms encased in bandages.

His usual grin spread across his face when he saw Duke. "Come on in, my man. Sit yourself down. I'm dying to talk to a human being instead of these automatic robots in white uniforms."

Duke dropped a pile of magazines and a bar of chocolate on the bed. "Have you been driving them crazy, Jasper?"

"Who, me? I have been the soul of decorum, dear fellow." He lifted his bandaged arms. "Not that I have a choice."

Duke unwrapped the chocolate bar and broke off a piece. "If I put this in your fingers can you get it in your mouth?"

Jasper nodded vigorously. "I can get chocolate in my mouth with my toes. It happens to be my favorite form of sustenance."

"I know." Duke fit the candy into Jasper's fingers. "Carol told me."

"Ah." Jasper chewed on the chocolate with a look of bliss on his face. "She's a dear, sweet lady," he said, after he'd swallowed.

"She is indeed." Duke broke off another piece of chocolate.

"You're going to marry her?"

"I'd like to." Duke paused in the act of handing Jasper his candy. He couldn't believe what he'd just said. Yet the more he thought about it, the more sure he became. Yes, he wanted to spend the rest of his life with Carol. If she'd have him. The knowledge started a sizzling excitement spreading through his body.

Jasper cleared his throat loudly, his eyes fixed on the chocolate.

"Sorry," Duke muttered, coming back to earth. He had a big obstacle to overcome before he could ask her the vital question. And he didn't have the faintest idea how he was going to manage it. Judging from the way she'd been holding him off lately, he wasn't at all sure he'd get the opportunity to explain.

He fed Jasper the rest of the chocolate, listening once more to the details of the fight the night before. "I want to thank you, my friend," he said, when Jasper paused for breath. "If there's anything I can do for you, just name it. Things could have turned out real ugly for Carol if you hadn't charged in and taken care of that punk."

"My reward was seeing that lovely lady's smile, and knowing that she was all right," Jasper assured him.

Duke looked up as a nurse tapped his arm. "I'm sorry, sir, but you'll have to leave. Mr. Golding has to go to X ray."

"But I just got here." He looked back at Jasper. "I'll wait till you get back."

"It could be an hour or more," the nurse said, glancing impatiently at her watch.

"Oh, don't worry, dear chap," Jasper said, "I'm sure you've got better things to do than sit around a hospital room."

Duke stood, brushing crumbs from his jeans. "In that case, I'll come back tomorrow afternoon, and bring you some more chocolate."

Jasper beamed. "I'll look forward to it."

"Thanks again, Jasper," Duke said, wishing he could shake the wounded man's hand. "I'm just sorry you had to get hurt in the process."

"No problem, dear fellow. I'll heal. It could have been worse. I could have had my throat cut."

"Yeah," Duke said slowly. "I'm sure glad you didn't."

"Not half as glad as I am," Jasper said, smiling.

Duke didn't answer him. Something had rung a bell again, deep inside his subconscious mind. And with it came the certainty that whatever it was, it would give him the answers he needed.

Chapter 10

Carol was late leaving her last meeting and found Anna pacing impatiently up and down in her office when she returned. "I'm sorry," she said, glancing at the clock. "It took longer than I'd expected."

To her surprise, Anna's usual sunny disposition had changed to irritation. "We'll have to hurry," she said sharply. "The traffic will be getting bad now and will slow us down."

"So what time is the appointment?" Carol asked, as they hurried down the street to the parking area.

"Two-thirty. It's almost that now."

"Well, I'm sure they'll all wait. Did you call and let them know we'd be late?"

"No—yes—I did."

Carol glanced at her friend. "Is everything all right? You seem a little tense."

"I just hate being late, that's all." Anna's accent sounded stronger than ever.

Carol led the way to her car, wondering what had happened to change Anna's mood. Her companion didn't speak until they were lining up with the rest of the traffic to cross Tower Bridge.

Tourists thronged around the entrance to the Tower, and above their heads the Union Jack flag billowed in a stiff breeze. Apparently making an effort to relax, Anna said casually, "How was your trip to the Tower the other day?"

"Great." Carol kept her eyes on the road as the car in front crept forward. "Have you ever been there?"

"Yes, I have. I enjoyed it very much."

Relieved that the woman seemed to have recovered her good humor, Carol smiled. "So did I. The crown jewels are breathtaking."

"They are, yes."

The traffic flow resumed, and Carol headed the car across the bridge. She'd checked the map earlier to find the best route to Greenwich, and she turned left onto the Old Kent Road.

"It's amazing the amount of construction along the river here," Carol said, as the road cut back toward the docks. "Are the apartment blocks new where we're going?"

"Yes." Anna seemed preoccupied, staring out of the window at the river. "Actually, they're close to the water's edge. If you looked out of the camera windows on the walkway last week, you probably saw them from the bridge."

Carol frowned. She had told no one about the visit to the walkway. After the incident with the photographer, she'd kept quiet about that part of the trip. All she remembered telling Anna was that she planned on going to the Tower. But she hadn't known then that she was going up to the walkway. She hadn't known then that there *was* a walkway. So how had Anna known she was up there?

Only one person, besides Duke, could have told her. The man with the camera. Carol's mouth felt dry. What, she thought frantically, did Anna have to do with the photographer?

Her palms felt sticky on the wheel. Could Anna possibly be connected with Mack's death? But that was impossible. She'd never met the woman until she came to London. If Mack had known Anna in the States, surely she would have heard of her?

Even as she thought it, Carol knew the question was ridiculous. Just how much had she known of Mack's secret life? Very little.

A teenager on a bike cut in front of her, and with a muttered curse, Carol stamped on the brake. A squeal of tires behind her accompanied the loud blare of a horn.

"Take it easy," Anna said at her side. "We're not in that much of a hurry. We want to get there in one piece."

"I thought you hated to be late." She'd spoken sharply, and bit her lip when she saw Anna's quick glance. She had to be careful. She needed time to think.

Anna couldn't be connected with Mack. She lived in London. *For how long?* Now that she thought about it, Anna had come to work for the company shortly after Carol had arrived. Why? To find out if the investigation was still going on? But she could have found that out in the U.S. And why wait until now?

It didn't make sense. None of it made sense. Carol barely scraped through the next light before it changed. She needed to talk to Duke. Maybe he could make sense of it. She glanced at her watch. Two-thirty. Duke would still be at the hospital. She would have to wait until she had dinner with him that night.

The cars ahead of her slowed, then came to a screeching halt. "I hope we're not going to sit in traffic all afternoon," Anna said, craning her neck in an effort to see up ahead.

She still couldn't believe it, Carol thought, glancing at Anna's profile. It just wasn't possible that this friendly, laughing woman with the expressive eyes could be involved in a cold-blooded killing. There had to be another explanation.

The thought gave her no comfort. If the photographer hadn't told Anna about her being on the bridge, then Duke must have. Was it possible Anna was another agent, working for the government?

She felt confused, and more than a little frightened. She didn't know what was going on. She didn't even know who she could trust anymore. She only had Duke's word that he was working for the government. And she had suspected right from the start that he was keeping something back from her.

The ache hit her below the ribs. Not Duke. Surely he couldn't be on the other side. Please, she prayed silently, not Duke. She couldn't bear that.

She could see the tall masts of the replica of the *Cutty Sark* peeking above the rooftops. They were almost there. The traffic crawled, but drew ever closer to the historic buildings.

They passed the pier, where the boats waited to take the passengers back to the inner city. "We should park in the car park," Anna said, as they approached the open area near the *Cutty Sark*. "Some of the flats are still under construction and the parking is limited. We can walk from here, it's not far."

Carol's fingers curled on the wheel. She had to know. She had to call Royce and find out if he had sent Duke to London. And Anna, too. If not, she'd know they were the enemy. She would call as soon as she got back to her apartment.

Pulling into a space, she cut the engine. Ahead of her she saw a sign announcing the Greenwich tunnel. She hadn't heard of it before, probably because it wasn't open to vehicles. Like the other tunnels, it ran underneath the Thames, coming up the other side. Chills attacked her spine when she thought about being under all that water.

She caught sight of a ladies bathroom, close by the entrance to the tunnel. "I'd better pay a visit to the bathroom, before we go," she told Anna. "I won't be a minute."

She was afraid Anna would insist on going with her, but the petite woman merely nodded her head. "I'll wait for you here," she said, settling back in the seat.

With a rush of relief, Carol opened the door and stepped out. She needed a few minutes alone, a breathing space to get her composure back before doing the presentation. A line of women stood waiting near the door, and she joined them, praying they would hurry before Anna got impatient.

At last she was inside the building. Somehow, she told herself, she would have to put all this turmoil out of her mind for the next hour or two. She couldn't afford to let Anna know she suspected her. Not until she found out more from Royce. Not until she knew for sure whether or not she could trust Duke.

Finally she could delay no longer. She reached the door and looked out. She could see her car quite clearly, with Anna sitting inside. She could also see the profile of the man leaning over to talk to her. It was the photographer.

Duke sat on the top deck of the bus, swaying from side to side, his forehead creased in concentration. Jasper's final comments about getting his throat cut still buzzed in his head. It reminded him of something Charles had said.

He frowned in concentration, trying to remember the exact words. *She had returned to her own country in Central America where a group of rebels had slit her throat. Apparently she had died in some primitive jungle village.*

He didn't know why that statement bothered him. But he had the distinct impression that it had something to do with the elusive thought that still tormented him.

It was there, right on the edge of his mind. Something Carol had said. The bus lurched around the corner and slowed for the next stop. Duke slid out of his seat and swung himself down the narrow curving staircase, holding onto the rail to keep his balance.

Walking swiftly down the street, he tried to chase the memory again. She'd been talking about the different people she knew. Jasper, Gordon, Win... What was it she'd said that seemed so significant now?

He unlocked the door of his apartment and stepped inside. The light on his answering machine flashed like a beacon across the room. In two strides he reached the phone and hit the button. A throaty whisper answered him.

"Duke? This is Anna, Carol's friend. She asked me to call. She's on her way to Greenwich. She has something very important to show you. She said you'd understand. She'll wait for you on the top floor of the Empress Court flats, just east of the Greenwich pier. She said to tell you it was urgent."

The tape hummed, then clicked off. The noise of the traffic outside invaded the small room while he stared at the phone for several moments. Piece by piece, it all fell into place.

Swearing, he picked up the handset and dialed. "Carol Everett, please," he said, when a female voice answered.

"Ms. Everett is out of the office for the afternoon. Can I ake a message?"

"When did she leave?"

"About twenty minutes ago, but—"

"Never mind." He slammed down the phone and headed or the door.

Carol stared at the two heads so close together. The man alked urgently, waving his hands. Anna paid close atten-on, a frown creasing her forehead.

She could no longer deny that Anna and the photogra-her were working together, Carol thought, wishing she ould hear what they were saying. Had Anna hired the man take that picture of Duke? Why? She already knew what e looked like. Had she also hired him to kidnap Carol off e street? That made even less sense.

More to the point was the question of why he was here ow. Anna must have arranged to meet him. Carol stepped ack, her heart pounding. The presentation had been un-xpectedly "brought forward," Anna had told her. Had nna lured her there to hand her over to the photogra-her? Why? What did he want from her?

Whatever it was, he wasn't going to get it, Carol thought rimly. As scared as she was, she was happy about one ing. Apparently it wasn't Duke who had told Anna about e walkway. Somehow she had never been quite able to elieve that anyway.

Very carefully, she edged forward so she could look out f the door without being seen. The disfigured man had raightened and was glancing at his watch. Then, as she atched, he strolled across the parking lot and disappeared ound the side of a building.

Carol looked back at the car. He was probably waiting for r to walk past him with Anna, then he could grab her.

Well, she wasn't going to be walking anywhere. She was going back to the car to give Anna some excuse, and then she was going to drive back to the office.

Wrapping both her arms around her stomach she walked toward the car, terrified that at any minute she would feel a hand on her shoulder. Or worse, a gun in her back.

Duke was right, she thought, as she saw Anna climb out of the car. She should have gone back to the States. Just let her get out of this mess and she would. On the first plane out.

She didn't have to fake the expression of pain on her face. Her stomach felt as if it were tied up in knots. "I've got a terrible bout of cramps," she said, as Anna looked at her, her dark eyes apparently full of concern. "I'm afraid the presentation will have to wait. I have to go back to the office."

Anna's eyes narrowed. "I have some aspirin—"

"No," Carol shook her head. "Thanks, but aspirin won't do it. I have to take special medication for it and it's back at the office. I didn't think to bring it with me. Stupid, I know, but I wasn't expecting an attack this afternoon."

"But the customers—"

"I'll call and explain," Carol said, walking around to the car door. "I'm sure they won't mind rescheduling it."

"Then I'll do it," Anna said, a look of frustration distorting her face. "You can sit with a hot cup of tea—"

"I'm going back to the office," Carol said firmly. "I'm sorry Anna, but I'm extremely uncomfortable." She yanked open the door and climbed into the car.

After a moment's hesitation, Anna climbed in beside her. Breathing easier, Carol started the engine and began backing the car out. Next to her, Anna opened her purse.

"I'm sorry, Carol," she said, her voice deadly calm. "I didn't want to do it this way, but you leave me no choice."

For the second time in the space of two days, Carol felt a
gun pressed into her side. Her hands jerked on the wheel,
throwing the car sideways. She straightened it, narrowly
missing the car next to her as Anna grabbed the dashboard.

"Careful," Anna murmured. "I wouldn't want this to go
off too soon."

"Why?" Carol muttered through her teeth. "What do
you want from me?"

"I don't want anything from you," Anna said. "It's your
boyfriend I want."

Her foot trembling on the brake, Carol stared at the small
woman. "Boyfriend?"

"The good-looking mechanic."

"I don't understand."

Anna smiled. "All in good time, Carol. You'll find out
what this is all about when he gets here."

The cold chills streamed down her back. "Why would he
come here?"

"Because I left a message on his machine asking him to
meet you here, that's why. And when he does, I intend to
take care of him."

Carol's breath stilled at the malice in Anna's eyes. She had
no doubt what the other woman had in mind.

"You told me he was spending the afternoon at the hospital," Anna went on. "Visiting hours are over at four. By
the time he gets home, hears the message and fights the rush-
hour traffic to get here, it will be dark. The workers will
have left the construction site long before then. It will be
nice and private for your reunion."

Carol thought of the photographer waiting around a corner somewhere, ready to pounce. Duke wouldn't stand a
chance. She had to warn him. Somehow she had to get away
and warn him.

Without giving herself time to think again, she slammed her foot down on the accelerator. The car shot forward straight into the wall in front of her.

Prepared for the jolt, she'd braced her hands on the wheel, and apart from wrenching her shoulders, she was unhurt. The impact had jerked Anna forward, cracking her head on the dashboard. She was still conscious, though dazed, the gun still grasped firmly in her hand.

She had no time to worry about the chances she took, Carol decided. She flung open the door and scrambled out, expecting to feel a bullet in her back any minute. Precious seconds ticked by while she tried to decide in which direction to go.

A boat or a cab would take too long to find. Anna was recovering fast and would be behind her any second. She had only one clear option, one safe avenue of escape. The Greenwich tunnel. Trying not to think about what lay ahead, Carol sprinted for the entrance.

The iron staircase wound down to the darkness below, looking for all the world like the steps to a dungeon. Carol closed her eyes briefly as panic washed over her, then she grasped the handrail. Led by two harassed-looking women, hordes of children streamed down beside her, all chattering excitedly.

Fighting the waves of nausea, Carol plunged down after them. At the bottom of the steps the tunnel stretched ahead of her, sloping down in the middle and rising again at the other end. It seemed interminably long.

Her gaze flicked up to the curved roof, and her mouth went dry. The entire width of the river Thames rested on that roof. Even as she thought it, a drop of moisture fell on her face and terror surged through her, freezing her limbs.

She couldn't do it. She had to go back. She couldn't breathe. The roof was closing in on her, suffocating her, everything was getting dark and shadowy. She knew she was going to faint and sat down on the bottom step, her head spinning dizzily.

I'm beginning to get real interested in you, Carol Everett. His voice seemed to be whispering to her from a long way off. Duke. If she didn't warn him, he would walk right into a trap. He would hear Anna's message and would come without hesitation. She knew that. She had to stop him. And the only way she could do that was to go on.

Children clattered down behind her, giving her curious stares as they passed her. She got unsteadily to her feet and grasped the rail. She couldn't think about what was overhead. All that mattered was to get to the other end of the tunnel and freedom.

She conjured up a mental picture of Duke's face, his dark eyes intent and hungry, his mouth curved in the smile that always made her tingle with excitement. Barring everything else from her mind, she slowly walked forward.

Ahead of her the kids' voices echoed eerily down the tunnel. She quickened her step, her eyes on the upward slope that would tell her she was past the halfway mark.

One of the boys discovered that the louder he yelled, the louder the echo came back to him. Before long a dozen or so children were screaming at the tops of their voices.

The sound filled the tunnel with earsplitting noise, despite the halfhearted attempts of the adults to stop it. Carol's heart began to race and she clamped her hands over her ears. She couldn't escape it. The shrill tumult of noise stabbed at her ears, her head, her back; her entire body seemed to vibrate with it.

She started to run, the panic catching up with her as she raced headlong for the end of the tunnel. She stumbled and almost fell. A uniformed soldier coming toward her caught her arm to steady her.

Beyond reasoning now, Carol snatched her arm from his grasp and tore past him, desperate to get into the open air before the darkness overtook her.

Then she was on the bottom step and surging upward, stumbling past the slower visitors, heedless of the surprised looks directed at her.

The sun shone weakly in a pale sky as she burst from the entrance, her lungs heaving, her face wet with perspiration. People flowed back and forth across the busy main street.

She wanted so desperately to ask for someone's help. But no one could help her. She had to handle this on her own. Glancing down at her watch she saw it was after three. What if Duke left the hospital early? He could reach home and be on his way to Greenwich before she could get there to warn him.

Glancing around she saw a public phone booth across the street. As the lights changed, she darted across the road, barely making it to the other side before the traffic began to move.

Luckily no one was in the phone booth. But she'd left her purse in the car. She had no change to make the call. Holding the receiver to her ear she punched the button for the operator. "I have to make an emergency call," she explained to the terse voice. "I don't have any money."

"I can't put your call through without money," the operator said firmly. "Unless you want me to reverse the charges."

"What?" Realizing she meant a collect call, Carol said quickly, "All right, yes. Reverse the charge."

The phone rang twice, and Carol's pulse leapt as the line clicked open. Then her spirits plummeted as Duke's recorded voice informed her he wasn't home. At least she could leave a message on his answering machine and tell him to ignore Anna's message.

"Your party isn't at home," the operator reported, cutting off the line.

"I *know*," Carol said, her voice rising in frustration. "But I want to leave a message."

"You have to pay to leave a message."

"I want to reverse the charges."

"I'm sorry, madam, but I can't do that without the party's permission."

"You don't understand." Carol made an effort to lower her voice. "This is a matter of life and death."

"In that case," the operator said, sounding unconcerned, "I advise you to contact the emergency services. I can put you through to them free of charge."

"No...thank you." Carol heard the line click as the operator ended the call. She dropped the receiver in place, wishing she could scream like the kids in the tunnel. There had to be something she could do. Maybe someone would take pity on her and give her the ten pence to put in the phone.

She hated to beg, Carol thought, pushing the door open, but she was desperate enough to try anything. A man waited outside the booth, and she stuck out her head. "Excuse me, but..."

The words died in her throat. He stood there with an unpleasant grin on his face, a patch of dark red burning beneath the scar on his cheek. "Hello, dahlin'," he said, taking hold of her arm. "Anna's been worried about you."

Carol darted a helpless look around her. Even if she could attract someone's attention, it wouldn't do her much good. Not with a gun stuck in her side.

"Come on," the photographer said, giving her arm a tug. "She's waiting for you."

Carol dug in her heels. "I'm not going through that tunnel again," she said, desperation adding conviction to her voice. "I can't. You'll have to shoot me first."

"Nah, I don't think you want me to do that." He poked her side with the gun, making her wince. "Puts a nasty hole in you, it does. You wouldn't like that, dahlin'."

"Quit calling me that," Carol said loudly, tugging at her arm.

A woman pushing a pram looked curiously at her as she passed by.

"Now look 'ere," the photographer said, his voice warning her. "Anna's on the corner with your car. We're going to walk down to it, and get inside, nice and casual like. Either that, or you end up dead right here on the street. Take your choice."

She didn't have much of a choice. But as long as she was alive, she had a chance of breaking free again to warn Duke. Whether she lived or died, he would obey that message. And she wouldn't be much help to him dead.

She let the photographer lead her along the street to where Anna waited with the car. He pushed her roughly into the back beside Anna, then climbed in behind the wheel.

"Did she get through?" Anna said, leveling her gun at Carol's ribs.

"Nah. She ain't got no money, has she? I told you she wouldn't get through. Don't worry, your friend will turn up and then you can—"

"Shut your mouth, Ned," Anna said in a vicious whisper.

Carol looked at her, shocked by the change in the woman she'd considered a friend. This was a side of Anna she would never have guessed at. Hiding behind that ready smile and teasing manner lived a tough, malicious woman. A dangerous woman. Carol stared out of the window as the car crawled along. Anna must have figured out that Duke was an agent. Something must have happened to put Duke on her trail, so Anna would have to take care of him, as she put it.

Why hadn't Duke said anything if he'd suspected Anna? That one was easy, Carol thought ruefully. She simply wouldn't have believed him and might have tipped off Anna. But now Anna knew, and Duke was in terrible danger, and she was the only one who could warn him.

Carol's stomach turned as she saw where the car was heading. The Blackwall Tunnel. At least she didn't have to walk through, she thought, closing her eyes as the car sped into the entrance. She tried not to think about it as the tires swished all around her, sounding loud in the confined area. Even so, she was bathed in sweat by the time the darkness lightened in front of her eyelids.

Cautiously, she opened her eyes. They were on the other side. The shadows were already darkening by the time Ned had the car parked again, in the same spot Carol had left it before.

She winced when she got out and saw the damaged hood. The front bumper had buckled and protruded well into the engine compartment. It was a miracle the car still ran.

"Let's go," Anna said, as Ned cut the engine.

"Can I take my purse?" Carol asked, and grabbed it when Ned threw it at her. It gave her a small measure of comfort; if she got away again, at least she'd have money to use a phone. The thought depressed her. She knew what her chances were of breaking free again.

She obeyed Anna's command to get out of the car, looking around hopefully in case there was some way she could attract someone's attention. But by now the tourists had left, anxious to get wherever they were going before the evening rush hour started in force.

There was nothing she could do but go meekly along with Anna and Ned, and watch for a chance to make a break for it. Her spirits sank lower when she saw where Anna led her.

The huge block of apartments, still under construction, loomed like a massive prison above her head, the walls stark and gray in the fading light. They appeared to be deserted. Carol could see no sign of workmen when she glanced around.

"No good you looking for help," Ned said, as they reached the opening in the wall that would eventually be a doorway. "They all knock off around four in the winter."

Anna pushed her through the opening, and Carol shivered as the damp cold settled over her. Her thin jacket and skirt were no protection from the cool evening wind across the river.

Sawdust and shavings covered the bare floorboards inside the building. The windows had no glass as yet and the walls were unfinished, with bright orange insulation nestled between the beams.

Above Carol's head, a partially finished ceiling covered half the cross beams. Wiring protruded from a gaping hole, waiting for the fitting that would bring light and warmth to the room. She found it hard to imagine that desolate room ever being warm.

"Upstairs," Anna ordered, nudging her toward a partially constructed stairway. "Stay close to the wall if you don't want to fall off."

Carol didn't need the warning. The stairway had no railing on the open side and dropped off abruptly at the edge of the steps. She crept up, keeping one shoulder pressed against the wall until she reached the landing at the top.

She barely had time to catch her breath before Anna urged her up the next flight. Her knees trembled by the time they reached the third floor. Anna's shove from behind sent her sprawling into the empty room.

The area looked like a vast warehouse without the connecting walls that would eventually separate it into individual rooms. Rows of beams crisscrossed in a forest of posts, reminding Carol of the pilings of a large dock. Windows were spaced at intervals around the walls, all without glass or frames.

The ceilings hadn't been finished, and the rafters overhead leapt from post to post in a well of darkness below the roof. Dust swirled like chalk as Anna led her over to an upturned crate and pushed her down on it.

Ned tied her wrists behind her and fastened them to a beam with rope that had been left in a corner. He had just finished when a faint scuffling sound came from above their heads.

"What was that?" Ned said sharply, peering up at the rafters.

"Probably rats," Anna said, without looking up. "I saw some in here the other day."

Carol shivered. How long had Anna had this planned? All the time she'd been smiling and teasing in that friendly way, she'd been plotting to lure her there and murder both her and Duke. Her stomach knotted as she finally acknowledged the fear uppermost in her mind. It was obvious they couldn't let her go. They would have to get rid of her, too.

She heard the scuffling again and curled her fingers into her palms. She remembered the day Duke had told her about his fear of rats. It was the day they'd gone to the Tower.

It seemed a long time ago, now. That was before all the craziness had started up again. She'd been relaxed with him then, walking hand in hand, chatting about everyday topics, watching his smile and feeling the warmth of it.

What she wouldn't give to have that back again. Before all the suspicions, before the growing sense of fear and danger had come between them.

"You might as well settle down," Anna said, sweeping some shavings off the window frame so that she could sit on it. "It will be at least an hour before Duke gets here."

And she wasn't about to sit there and wait for him to walk into the trap, Carol thought grimly. If she could work the rope loose she might be able to make a grab for Anna's gun while Ned was preoccupied with Duke's arrival.

Ned had wandered over to the other window and was staring into the darkening shadows outside. Probably waiting for Duke, Carol thought, switching her gaze back to Anna.

The petite woman sat swinging one foot, apparently deep in thought as she stared at the floor. If it wasn't for the gun held loosely in her hand, Carol thought, she'd look like a little girl in her short navy blue skirt and thick white sweater-jacket.

"You'd better get on with it," Anna said suddenly, looking over at Ned. "There won't be anyone around now."

He nodded and hurried across the floor, his footsteps echoing up into the rafters overhead. Carol watched him leave, a feeling of dread creeping over her. He must have gone to meet Duke.

She twisted her wrists back and forth, testing the tautness of the rope. Now that she was alone with Anna, this was her chance to do something, if she could only get her hands free. Using as little movement as possible, she started to work at the rope.

"I'm sorry you had to get caught up in this," Anna said, looking across at her.

Carol relaxed her hands. She didn't answer, hoping Anna would give up having a conversation and look away again.

Her hopes were dashed when Anna added, "You made a very big mistake when you married Mack."

Shock made her forget about keeping silent. "You knew Mack?"

The darkness closing in made it difficult to see Anna's expression. But Carol couldn't mistake the bitterness in the other woman's voice when she said, "Yes, I knew him."

She was afraid to ask. Yet she had to know. Although she was dreadfully afraid she already knew the answers. "Where did you meet him? And what does all this have to do with Mack?"

Anna sat for a long time in silence. Carol couldn't tell whether she was watching her or not, but it was so dark now that she knew the other woman wouldn't be able to see clearly anyway. Very carefully, she started twisting at the rope again.

Part of her prayed that Anna wouldn't want to talk, so she wouldn't be watching her. A larger part of her demanded to know the truth. It was obvious now that Anna, somehow, had the answers she so desperately needed.

She jumped when Anna slid off the window frame and picked up her large purse from the floor. She opened it and pulled out two long sticks. It wasn't until Carol heard the scrape of a match that she realized they were candles.

The flames flickered violently in the draft as Anna lit them, then settled down to wavering back and forth, sending shadows leaping over the walls.

"I met him in my country," Anna said. "He was in Central America on assignment. Only I didn't know that at the time." She settled herself on the window frame again and leaned her back against the frame. "I thought he was in love with me," she said, her voice fading to a whisper.

Carol stared at her. "When was this?"

"Almost two years ago."

She'd been married to him for five years then. Why hadn't she known? Again she scoffed at the question. She had never really known her husband.

"He was the most exciting man I'd ever met," Anna said in her hushed voice. "I had never known a man like him. I was desperately in love with him from the moment he first kissed me."

Her sigh trembled in the quiet shadows. "When he made love to me I knew I would die for him. I didn't know how close I would come to doing just that."

Carol caught her breath. "What happened?" She had felt no pain at the thought of Mack making love to this woman. Only a very real anger with herself for being such a fool.

"Your husband," Anna said harshly, "was very good at playing a part. He convinced me he was in love with me. So much so, that in a very short time I trusted him enough to tell him where my brother and his companions had their hideout. Which was why he'd seduced me, of course—for the information."

Carol began twisting her hands again, aware of Anna's ragged breathing. The woman was becoming agitated, and with a gun in her hand, anything could happen.

"Apparently," Anna went on, "it would have been embarrassing for your country to arrest a group of rebels who were only trying to uphold their political beliefs in order to achieve a better world for their people.

"So, once Mack knew their location, he sent for his partner, Brandon Pierce. The two of them found my brother and his compatriots and slaughtered them, leaving their bodies to rot in the jungle like wild animals."

Carol closed her eyes. She had known what he'd done for a living. She hadn't allowed herself to think about the methods he'd used.

"Out of forty-three men," Anna whispered, "only two escaped. My brother was not one of them. When it was discovered how Mack had found the hideout, they came for me. I was to find Mack and his partner, and kill them both. If I failed, I, too, would lose my life."

"So you went to Washington to find them."

"Yes. I was happy to do what they asked. I wanted revenge for my brother's death, and I wanted Mack dead."

Now, Carol thought, the big question. For the moment all thought of getting free was forgotten, so absorbed was she in the story. "How did you know where they would be that night?" she asked, not really expecting an answer.

"Royce Westcott told me."

Carol's gasp echoed around the barren room. Above her head some creature scuffed along a beam, sending a tiny shower of dust down on her head. She barely noticed it. She was too shocked at what she'd heard to worry about rats right then.

"Royce?" Her voice resembled Anna's harsh whisper. "But why?"

"Oh, he didn't know he'd told me." Anna turned back and leaned against the wall. "I borrowed Mack's methods. It was easy. Royce was bored with his marriage and flattered by my attentions. In no time we were engaged in a hot and heavy affair.

"I was supposed to meet him at his office one night. When I got there I heard him on the phone, talking to his assistant, Charles. I waited outside the door and listened. He told me what I wanted to know." Anna shrugged. "He must have wondered why I never turned up that night."

"So then you were the one who shot out the tires?"

"Yes. It was easy. There was no one about. I took a high-powered rifle up on the overpass. I had a lot of time to practice in the jungle. It took only two bullets."

Carol squeezed back the tears. What a terrible waste of so many lives.

"I thought it was over," Anna said. "But soon after I arrived back in my country, my brother's friends came for me again. Apparently I had failed to kill both men. One of them survived. They cut my throat and left me for dead."

She wouldn't throw up, Carol told herself firmly. She started taking in long, slow breaths.

"By a miracle I survived." Anna slid off the window frame and turned to look out. "Some villagers found me and took care of me until I was well enough to leave. The rebels were waiting for me. They gave me one last chance to come back and finish the job. And this time if I fail, they will make sure I do not live."

"Who. . . ?" Her voice broke, and she swallowed.

Anna turned. "Your friend, Duke Winters, is not a mechanic, Carol. He was a mercenary. One of the men who killed my brother and his friends. He should have died in that wreck—"

She broke off as Ned clattered up the stairway. Carol's heart thumped, but Ned was alone.

"It's all taken care of," he said. "I'll set it when we go down. Once it's wired, a mouse could set it off."

Carol was barely listening to him. Her attention was all on Anna. "Who?" she demanded, as Anna turned back to face her. "Which one survived?"

Even before Anna spoke, she knew. Deep down she'd always known. It came as no real surprise when Anna said softly, "Duke Winters used to be called Brandon Pierce. And tonight he dies for the second time."

Chapter 11

Brandon Pierce. Carol swallowed hard. The man she'd hated almost as much as her husband. The man who had controlled and manipulated Mack. The man with whom she'd been stupid enough to fall in love.

The full realization of her feelings for him hit her like a cold shower. She couldn't possibly be in love with Brandon Pierce. She loved Duke Winters, who didn't exist. He was nothing more than a clever illusion, and she had been as gullible and as foolish as Anna had.

"I guess this is goodbye, Carol," Anna was saying. "It will be quick, I promise you."

Slowly, Carol realized what the words meant.

"Yeah, it will be quick all right." Ned's laugh held no humor. "I've set a charge that will blow the entire floor out of the building. The only way up here is on that staircase. Pierce only has to step on any one of the steps leading to the third floor and—" he threw up his hands "—boom! Up she goes."

"It won't be long to wait, Carol," Anna said, crossing to the stairway. "Brandon should be here within a half hour o so." She paused at the staircase. "No one will ever find you or Brandon. There will be nothing left of you." She turned and disappeared down the steps.

Grinning, Ned followed her, leaving Carol alone in the flickering candlelight. The footsteps clattered down the stairs, then faded into the night.

Desperately she tugged at the rope that held her. Maybe if she yelled someone would hear her, she thought, then knew that wouldn't work. Duke—Brandon would hear her and come rushing up the stairs.

Maybe if she heard him coming up she could shout ou and warn him about the bomb. But knowing Duke, he would be creeping silently up the steps. Whatever kind o message Anna had left, he would be on his guard.

The rope cut into her wrists as she struggled to free her self. She didn't want to die like this, she thought with a rush of panic. Sitting there, helpless, waiting for the man she'e thought she loved to put a violent end to her life.

She'd been through so much, and had finally begun to ge her life back together. Now it was about to end, in a horri ble way, with no one to mourn for her or even know wha happened to her.

What would her parents think? Would they spend the res of their lives thinking she had simply abandoned them? I was as if Mack had reached out from the grave to claim her She hadn't escaped from him after all.

Again something stirred above her head, showering mor debris down on her. Nervously she looked up, then her hear stopped beating altogether. Something moved in the shad ows above the rafters, something large.... The figure of man.

"Hold on, Carol," Duke said softly, "I'm coming down."

Her first reaction was indescribable joy that she wasn't about to die. She watched him swing from his hands, then drop to the floor.

"How did you..." Her voice trailed off as her relief got the better of her.

He moved swiftly, reaching behind her to untie her hands. "I got thrown out of the hospital, luckily. Jasper had to go down for X rays and didn't want me to wait."

He released her hands and stepped back. "Anna hadn't figured on me coming back quite so soon. I heard the message on the recorder and came right here. Took the boat—I remembered you said it would be faster than a cab. I figured it would give me a chance to get here first."

Carol winced as the blood rushed back into her hands. Rubbing them together, she stared at Duke's grim face. Even now, knowing what she knew, it was hard to believe that he was Brandon Pierce. He looked so different. He'd seemed so different.

She caught herself before the ache could begin. "How did you know it was a trap? Anna said she told you to meet me—"

"Her name isn't Anna. It's Maila. I talked to Charles. He told me a woman who had been a suspect in the shooting had had her throat cut and had apparently died in a Central American jungle. I knew then it was Maila. Mack had told me about her. Then I remembered what you'd said about Anna and her throat surgery. Actually, it was something Jasper said about getting his throat cut that finally triggered the memory.

"When I heard Maila whispering on the answering machine I put the two together. I figured out she must have survived. I knew it had to be someone who knew you, and the pieces all fit."

Carol nodded. "She told me. About the raid on her brother's hideout—" She shuddered. "How could you do something like that?" she whispered.

"Carol." Duke took her hands in his and began rubbing them. "Someone has to do it. Sometimes we have to do things we don't necessarily agree with, to get the job done. Just like a soldier going into battle. You're disciplined. You don't think about the ethics of it, you follow orders. We were heavily outnumbered. It was either them or us. Kill or be killed. That's the way it is."

He paused, staring down at her hands held in his. "No true soldier likes to kill a fellow human being, no matter how justified," he said at last. "Unfortunately, we live in a world where sometimes we have no choices. Sometimes we have to eliminate the evil in order to save the innocent."

"But you enjoyed the excitement and the danger. Just like Mack did."

"I wouldn't say enjoy is the word. I was willing to risk my life because of what I believed in. Mack lost his life for the same reason. Whatever kind of man Mack was, he was a damn good soldier."

"He would have been proud of you." She snatched her hands away from him. "He would have approved of the way you arranged to meet me. And how easily you maneuvered your way into my bed. How you must have laughed, knowing all the time how much I resented you. You must have really enjoyed the irony of it."

"No," Duke said quietly. "You won't believe this, but I wanted to tell you the truth right from the start. But if I had, you would have reacted exactly the way you're reacting now. And I would have lost any chance of finding out what you knew."

"But I didn't know anything. I had nothing to do with that night. It was Maila. She—"

"I know that now. I heard it all from up there." He jerked a thumb at the rafters. "I'm sorry, Carol, but I had to know. I've lost my entire identity, everything that made me who I am. I can never get that back. I wanted the person who'd done that to me. I wanted the person who killed my best friend."

"And you suspected me," Carol said bitterly. "For God's sake, Duke, how could you possibly believe that I—"

"I had nowhere else to go. You were my only lead."

"I thought you were Mack." Her voice broke, and she swallowed. "You used the same gestures, the same turn of phrase. I kept thinking I'd met you before, but it was Mack's memory that kept coming back."

"We spent a lot of time together. I guess a lot of it rubbed off. We unconsciously copied each other."

"Can you imagine what I went through, believing my husband wasn't dead after all?"

"You must have known I wasn't Mack when—"

She shot a murderous look at him. "When you made love to me? Yes, I knew. But I couldn't make myself believe it was you. It was the last thing I wanted to believe. Maybe that's why it took me so long to consider the possibility."

"Then you guessed."

"I said I considered it. I was never really sure."

"Why not?"

He was looking at her with a curiously intent look in his eyes. Darker than the cold, hard, golden eyes she remembered. More like Mack's eyes. He must have contacts in, she thought. Wondering why he seemed so anxious for her answer, she said curtly, "Probably because I didn't want to accept the fact that I'd been so incredibly blind and stupid."

She stood up and brushed the dust from her skirt. "You seduced me to get what you wanted. You did exactly what Mack did to Maila. You betrayed me the way he betrayed her. You used me."

"No." He took hold of her arms, resisting her efforts to shake him off. "We don't have time to discuss this now. But I want you to remember one thing. I made love to you because of the way I feel about you. I have never lied to you about that, Carol. I hope you can believe that."

She had no answer to that. She would have liked to believe him. But she'd believed too many lies already.

He dropped his hands. "This isn't finished yet. We have to get out of here, and then I have to take care of Maila and her friend."

Carol stared at him. "They'll be long gone by now."

He shook his head. "I don't think so. Maila has gone to too much trouble and has far too much at stake to take anything for granted. I'm betting she's still out there somewhere, waiting to see if her little plan works."

"What are you going to do?"

"Try to pick them up and take them back to my apartment. Then I'll call Royce to send me the papers so I can take them back to the States and let the agency take care of them."

She relaxed for a moment, relieved that he wasn't going to shoot them in cold blood. Even if they had planned her death, she couldn't bear the thought of Maila dying at the hands of this man. Or anyone else for that matter.

"They both have guns," she said, her heart skipping at the memory of the revolver in Maila's hand.

"So do I." He lifted his hand, and the candlelight fluttered along the gleaming barrel of a revolver.

"Can you disarm a bomb?" Her heart jumped at the thought.

"No. And I don't intend to try."

"Then what are we going to do? Ned said that was the only way up here."

"The only way up here on the inside. Which is the way he expected me to come. But I came up the fire escape at the back of the building. I have to admit, I had a few bad moments when I thought about rats running around loose up here."

She almost collapsed from relief. It was almost over. She was going to pick up her things, check into a hotel and book her flight back to the States.

Duke shoved the gun inside his jacket. "Are you ready?"

She gave him a brief nod. She couldn't wait to get out of there and put the entire nightmare behind her. She ignored the ache at the thought that she would never see Duke Winters again. He was already dead, as far as she was concerned. Just like Mack. Except this time it hurt a lot more. It hurt like hell.

Duke picked up one of the candles and, shielding it with his hand, moved slowly forward. Carol followed him across the floor to the far corner of the building. The square opening of the window frame looked out on a cloudless night.

Duke stood and signaled for her to go first. "Be as quiet as you can," he said softly. "I'd like to take them by surprise."

"Surely they won't be this close to the building if they're expecting an explosion?"

"No, I figure they're waiting in your car in the parking lot until they hear the bomb go off. But noise carries at night. I don't want to take any chances."

She stuck her head out and saw the landing of the fire escape just below her. The moon cast a pale light over the steps leading down, but she could see nothing but darkness below. She shuddered, thinking of Ned and Maila waiting down there for her.

Reminding herself of her own statement about them keeping their distance, she climbed out onto the landing. Gripping the cold metal of the handrail, she began the climb down.

Step-by-step she drew closer to the ground. Duke's feet descended just above her head, keeping pace with her as she moved steadily down.

After a minute or two she could see the ground below her, with stacks of building supplies lying along the bottom of the building. She tried not to think about the chance of someone hiding behind them.

Her foot touched solid earth and she began shivering as reaction set in. Stepping back, she waited for Duke to join her.

He thudded softly to the ground next to her. She watched him take the gun out and tuck it into the waistband of his jeans. Then he slipped off his jacket and draped it around her shoulders.

Before she could speak, he warned her with a finger against his lips. His face looked pale in the moonlight, and she felt her stomach quiver. She hadn't thought about how he was going to overpower both Ned and Maila. It seemed like an impossible task. She could only hope he knew what he was doing.

Once more she followed him as he stepped carefully over planks of wood and iron piping, one hand brushing along the wall. She kept her eyes glued to her feet in case she should trip over something and make a noise.

Then Duke halted, holding up a warning hand. They had reached the corner of the building. Cautiously, he leaned forward to look around it.

Carol waited, her heartbeat pounding in her ears.

Duke drew back and nudged his head at another building fifty yards away.

She nodded, holding her breath as they crept quietly across the open ground to the next building. She could hear traffic in the distance, and somewhere in the huddle of apartment buildings someone played a radio too loud. The dank, oily smell of the river drifted on the wind, and dust stirred in its wake.

Her entire body tingled with apprehension, and she tried not to think about two pairs of eyes watching her, a gun focused on her unprotected back. What if they weren't sitting in the car? What if they were watching the building for Duke to turn up? What if they could see them now, skulking along in the semidarkness?

She reached the shelter of the next building, and Duke pulled her close. "Okay?" he whispered close to her ear. She nodded, though she was far from okay. She longed to be back in the safe, warm security of her apartment in New York.

If she ever got out of this alive, she promised herself, she would never come to London again. It would always hold too many bad memories.

Three more times they crossed a wide open space between buildings. Each time, Carol's nerves tightened to the screaming point, as she waited for the deadly blast of a gun.

One by one they skirted the buildings, keeping as close to the walls as possible, pausing at each corner to make sure the coast was clear.

Finally they reached the last one. The solitary lamp in the parking lot threw a ghostly pool of light across the end of the building, illuminating a large patch of ground beyond. Duke once more edged his head out to take a look, then quickly withdrew it.

Carol signaled a question at him with her eyebrows ar
he nodded. Her breath caught and held. Motioning at h
to stay where she was, he crept back the way they'd com
slipped around the corner and disappeared.

She felt sick. She tried not to think about what wou
happen if Duke was injured, or killed. The thought of th
was just too terrible to contemplate.

She pressed herself against the wall, praying she wouldr
have to go out there to help him. She wasn't at all sure h
legs would carry her that far. Yet she knew that if he calle
she would go. Damn him, she would still risk her life f
him.

It seemed that no matter what happened, she couldn
change the way she felt about him. Right now she couldn
think about that. There were too many pitfalls ahead on th
road.

All she could do right now was stand with her bac
against the wall, with the night wind rustling the trees tha
bordered the parking lot, and pray like hell that he'd con
back to her.

Duke edged his way to the end of the building and poke
his head around the corner. He could see Carol's car sittin
all alone at the edge of the parking lot. The reflection fro
the lamp fell across the rear end of it, but the front was i
shadow. He couldn't tell if anyone sat inside or not.

Moving from doorway to doorway, he edged closer. Th
railings that bordered the parking lot gave him some pro
tection, but not a whole lot. And to get close enough to th
car to achieve anything, he would have to expose himself.

He drew almost level with the car, and as he did so, he sav
a shadow move inside. His stomach flipped. So they wer
there. Now he had to figure out how to take them both b
surprise.

Dropping himself flat onto the ground, he pulled in a slow breath. His heart hammered against his ribs in a staccato of dread. He'd spent months promising himself that once this was over, once he took care of the person who'd shot out the car that night, he'd never touch a gun again.

He wasn't even sure he could shoot straight anymore. He didn't know if he could hold his hands steady enough to get a smooth shot off. He didn't know if he had the guts to shoot at another human being again.

Shoving the fears aside, he wriggled closer to the railing. Somewhere in the dark close-by something scrabbled in the weeds that grew along the edge. His skin crawled. If it was a rat—

The thought disintegrated as a sound shattered the silence of the night. The roar of the car engine sounded deafening, and he swore. Either they'd got tired of waiting, or they'd decided to take a closer look at the building where they'd left Carol.

He couldn't lose them now. He couldn't take the chance of them slipping away into the darkness. They would know before the night was out that the plan hadn't worked. They would disappear, to try again, another time, another place when he least expected it. And Carol would have to live with that constant fear.

The engine hummed, changing tune as the person behind the wheel put it in gear. Duke could feel sweat breaking out on his brow. If he made a rush for them, he would be exposed in the lamplight. They would have a clear target. He had only one option.

Propping himself up, he took careful aim at a tire and pressed the trigger. He heard one of them blow. Shifting his aim to the back tires, he emptied the gun. As he did so, he heard the door open on the far side of the car.

He leapt to his feet. From behind the car a flash lit the darkness, accompanied by a loud report. Before he could react, another shot sounded, then another. He felt something hit the ground at his elbow, and he froze.

He didn't have time to reload. A figure darted from the shadows behind the car, bent double and running fast. Maila.

Duke swore. He started to rise, but then a barrage of gunfire set him slithering backward until he reached the doorway of the building.

Lights had begun popping on all over the place. He prayed no one would get curious enough to investigate. He also prayed that if someone called the police, it would take them long enough to get there so he could take care of what he had to do.

Figuring that Ned had to be out of bullets, Duke decided to take a chance. Sending up a silent prayer, he hurtled out of the doorway and around the corner of the building.

He slammed straight into a soft body. For a moment he wondered frantically if it was Maila, then Carol's scared voice said, "What's happening?"

"He pinned me down. Maila took off." He snatched the round of bullets from his pocket and jammed them into the chamber. Carol uttered a muffled protest as he shoved her into a doorway. "Stay there," he ordered, "and don't come out until I tell you."

Her face looked as white as bleached flour as she huddled in a corner. He felt a desperate urge to grab her and reassure her, but somewhere out there Maila and Ned were waiting to mow them down, unless he could stop them first.

"I'll be back," he whispered, and left her alone. He edged slowly along the wall of the building, his gun leveled in front of him, every nerve strained to the breaking point.

From behind him he heard a soft scraping sound and whirled around, his finger on the trigger. A tabby cat slunk across the ground, its tail waving like a banner.

He relaxed and lowered his gun while he pulled in a long breath. He turned back and then froze. Silhouetted in the moonlight, Maila stood not ten paces away, both her hands wrapped around the gun she held steadily pointed at him.

"It's been a long time, Brandon," she said softly. "But I knew it would be worth the wait. Now drop the gun."

He saw her thumb on the safety and knew he hadn't long to act. Even if he could raise his own gun fast enough to get off a shot, he was doubtful he'd hit her. It was a sure bet he wouldn't avoid the bullet she'd put in him. It was worth a desperate gamble. It was all he had.

"You got it wrong, Maila," he said quietly. "Brandon Pierce died in the car wreck."

"Forget it, Brandon. I know you survived. I got access to the records from the hospital. Drop the gun. Now."

"How? They were supposed to be destroyed." She jerked her hands at him, and a cold acceptance washed over him as he relaxed his fingers, letting the gun fall. If this didn't work, he was a dead man.

Maila smiled. "They were. But not before I got copies of them. Thanks to modern technology and the computer, it wasn't that difficult."

"But the records were in the name of Duke Winters."

"Right. But the date you were brought into the hospital, your injuries, the location… No, Brandon. A little too much coincidence I'd say."

The safety clicked back and his nerves, already strung out, hummed like a live wire. "Did the records also tell you that my face was unrecognizable?"

"Yes. But there was only one burial. And it was Mack's."

"Wrong," Duke said softly. "That was all part of the cover. That was Brandon's remains in that casket. Not mine."

He thought he heard a soft sound behind him, but he ignored it. All his attention was on Maila's shocked face.

"I don't believe it," she whispered.

"It's true. Even Royce and Charles don't know the truth. I told them I was Brandon. I wanted out of my marriage. I figured it would be easier if Carol thought I was dead."

Maila's hands wavered. "Then why are you here?"

"To find you. I've never forgotten you, Maila. I've never forgotten how wonderful it was with you. I knew you were in London. I figured you'd be watching Carol, waiting to see if Brandon turned up. You wouldn't have recognized him if you'd seen him, would you, Maila? But you hoped that eventually he'd contact Carol."

"I still don't believe you." Her words carried little conviction and Duke silently prayed.

"If you kill me, you'll be killing your lover all over again. Give me the gun and—"

"No." The gun jerked in her hands, but she backed off a couple of steps. "I have to kill you," she whispered. "I will die if I don't."

"Not if I'm there to protect you." Duke began inching forward, a step at a time.

"You can't protect me from them," Maila said. "No one can do that."

"Maila," Duke said, putting all the emotion he could muster into his voice. "I love you. Give me the gun and let me prove I am Mack. Do you remember our last night together? Do you remember how good it was? Do you remember telling me all about your childhood? You cried in my arms that night, Maila. You cried for all the childhood friends who had died in the revolution."

"Oh, God. Oh, God." One hand over her mouth, Maila backed away.

"I am Mack. You must believe me. I love you. I have always loved you. And you love me. Can you look me in the face and shoot me in cold blood?"

She stared at him over her fingers, her eyes wild in the moonlight. Then, very slowly, she lowered the gun, while huge tears spilled from her eyes and splashed over her fingers.

For an instant he felt a pang of sympathy, then he remembered the last twelve months and hardened his heart.

"I'll die, anyway," Maila whispered brokenly. Before he could react, she dropped the gun and turned, racing for the corner of the building.

He snatched up his gun and took chase, but when he reached the corner, to his surprise he saw her running back to the building where she'd held Carol. For a moment he wondered if she had another car waiting there, but as he pounded after her he saw her reach the doorway. In that instant he knew what she intended.

Two buildings separated him from her when he skidded to a stop. "Wait, Maila," he yelled. "I'll help you, don't be a fool."

She ignored him and disappeared into the building.

For a moment or two he stood there, yelling her name over and over. Then he threw himself sideways behind the wall, his hands covering his ears.

Seconds later the roar of the explosion washed over him, while the vibration shuddered through the walls at his back. Dust and debris clattered all around him in a shower of noise, then silence descended, as still as death.

His stomach churned, but she was beyond his help now. In the distance he heard the faint blare of the police siren. Galvanized into action, he ran back to where he'd left Carol.

As he rounded the corner, his blood ran cold. Ned stoo
a few feet away, his gun aimed at Carol. Praying as he'
never prayed before, Duke lifted the gun, steadied it witl
both hands, and fired.

Ned groaned, doubled over, toppled to the ground, an
lay still.

Slowly Duke walked toward him, his gun trained on th
silent figure. Reaching him, he turned him over, then looke
up at Carol slumped against the wall.

"He'll live," he said, his heart going out to her. "I'll le
the cops take care of him. But you and I have to get out c
here, and fast. I don't need a lot of awkward questions fro
the police." He rose and moved toward her, holding out h
arms.

"Don't touch me," she said swiftly.

"Carol—"

"No. There's nothing you can possibly say that will mal
a difference. I heard what you said to Maila. I heard it a
Mack."

His heart sank. "You know I lied. I was trying to save n
life. And yours."

"Well, I'm sorry, but I've had it up to here with lies." Sl
dragged off his jacket and flung it at him. "I don't know
you're Mack or Brandon. But it really doesn't matter.
don't want to see either one again. Ever. So do me a fav
and stay out of my life." She started to walk away, taking
heart with her.

"Wait a minute," he said, hurrying after her. "How a
you going to get home?"

"I'll get a cab. Luckily I held onto my purse." She ke
walking, faster now that the sirens were drawing closer.

He followed her all the way down to the docks, until
saw her flag down a cab and climb inside. And he watch

er drive away, knowing that he'd lost her. He had never felt
o alone in his entire life.

"So," Royce said, folding his hands together on the desk
n front of him, "poor Maila forgot about the bomb. It was
n untimely end. Very untimely. But providence, I guess.
aves us prosecuting her."

Duke looked at him, wondering how he could ever have
orked for this man. "She didn't forget," he said evenly.
"She thought I was Mack. She couldn't bring herself to kill
e again, and she knew she wouldn't live long if she didn't.
t was her way of solving the problem."

He gained some satisfaction from Royce's shocked look.
"That was a bit drastic," Royce said, rubbing his forehead
ith his thumbs.

"It was the way Maila lived. She'd known violence all her
fe. To her it was a quick end, probably much preferable to
ying at the hands of her countrymen."

Royce sighed. "I thought she was already dead. I swear
, Duke, I really thought she was dead. I was convinced
Maila had died in the jungle. I had no real proof that she
as involved in the wreck, but when she disappeared right
fterward, I guessed I had a pretty good idea."

"Why didn't you tell me about the memo? You knew I
as going after Carol. You knew Carol had nothing to do
ith it. Yet you let me go chasing after her, putting her
hrough hell by dragging up the past all over again."

"I tried to stop you."

With an effort Duke curbed his temper. "You could have
opped me with one simple explanation."

Royce narrowed his eyes behind the thick glasses. "Could
? Even if you had known Maila was suspect, you would
ave done your utmost to find her."

"Not if I'd thought she was dead."

"Well, as it happened, it was just as well you did find her. Or you might have had a bullet in your back one dark night. She wasn't about to give up, from what I understand."

Duke let out his breath in an explosive sound. "Damn it, Royce, we almost killed Carol between us."

"Duke, I swear, if I'd had any idea that Maila was still alive, I would have warned you. But I thought she was dead. I had no proof she was involved, and I couldn't prove anything with her dead."

Royce held out his hands in a gesture of appeal. "For God's sake, look at it from my angle. If it had come out that I'd had an affair with her, I could have been charged with passing on information. I would have lost everything, and all for nothing."

"So you let me put Carol's life in danger."

"Not intentionally. No, not intentionally. I figured with Maila dead, it was all over and done with. I thought that once you realized Carol hadn't been involved, you'd give up and forget about it."

"Is that why you kept me from talking to Charles? So I'd give up and forget about it?" If he wasn't so damn mad at the guy he could feel sorry for him, Duke thought, watching the sheen of sweat form on Royce's brow.

"I couldn't let Charles tell you about the memo," Royce muttered. "I knew you'd keep digging until it all came out." He swiped at his forehead with the back of his hand.

"If he hadn't called to warn me, I would have walked right into Maila's trap."

"I know." He sighed heavily. "Thank God he had the sense to do that. I owe him a lot."

"I guess we all do," Duke said grimly.

"Look." Royce drummed his fingers on the desk. "If you're interested, I'd really like to have you back on the oster. Men like you are tough to find and I know the agency vould be happy—"

"Forget it," Duke said brusquely. "I've got plans."

"Want to tell me about them?"

"Yeah, I don't mind. I'm going to open up a garage, maybe tinker with a few cars myself now and again. It will give me an investment while I see a bit more of the world. t will be real nice to check out a few foreign countries vithout worrying about whether or not I'll get out alive."

Royce cleared his throat, looking embarrassed. "What bout Carol? Will you be seeing her again?"

Duke shook his head, his complacent expression hiding he heartache he felt at the sound of her name. "I guess she till hates my guts," he said quietly. "Some things never hange."

"Unless you change them, Duke. Unless you change hem."

Duke stared across the table at his former boss. Once in while, he thought, his pulse quickening, the bastard could ake a lot of sense.

The night air held just a hint of snow as Carol emerged om the Stamford train station. Thanksgiving was only a ouple of weeks away. The thought depressed her. She had ng ago given up on enjoying the holidays, but this year in articular loomed ahead like a black cloud. Why was it, she ondered, that problems seemed more intense around the hristmas season?

She approached her car in the parking garage, thankful least that she didn't have to deal with the frantic prepa-tions for the holidays in New York until Monday.

Moving back to Connecticut to live gave her a longer day ith the commute, but it was worth it to be out of the city on the weekends. Somehow the noise and bustle had lost its charm.

Car engines sprung to life all around her as she walked down the aisles to where she'd parked her car. The key felt stiff in the lock, and she wondered if it was frozen. It certainly felt cold enough.

She got the door open at last and climbed inside, shivering as the clammy chill wrapped around her shoulders. In spite of her quilted raincoat, she could feel the damp in her bones.

Anxious now to be home in her warm apartment, she turned the key in the ignition. Her heart sank when the starting motor turned sluggishly, then collapsed into silence.

It sounded like a dead battery. Pumping her foot up and down on the gas just to make sure, Carol glanced at her watch. It was after seven already. It could be hours before she could get someone out there. Her sagging spirits settled to the bottom of the pit.

She closed her eyes and tried the key again. Nothing. With a vicious swipe of her hand she cuffed the wheel and slumped back in the seat. She'd have to go back to the station and call a repairman. And a cab. Gathering up her purse, she pushed the door open.

The first thing she saw was a pair of leather boots, and above them, long legs encased in jeans. Her gaze traveled up, though she knew, long before she reached his face, who he was.

"Need some help?" Duke asked quietly.

Chapter 12

He was the very last person she wanted to see. She'd spent too many lonely nights struggling to put him out of her mind. Anger, swift and warming, filled her head, mercifully blotting out the shaft of sheer pleasure she'd felt at the sight of him. "I take it you're responsible for this?" She waved a hand at the hood of the car.

Without answering he leaned into the car, released the catch, then walked around the front of the hood to open it up.

Carol stood tapping her foot in exasperation while he studied the engine, a slight frown on his face.

A draught of cold air stole across the garage, stinging her face with its icy chill. Her voice reflected the sensation when she said, "Look, I'm freezing, tired and very hungry. I am not in the mood for games, so I'd appreciate it if you'd put back whatever you took out and let me get on home. Please."

He lifted his head, his expression inscrutable. "Keys," he said, holding out his hand.

Fighting back a retort, Carol gave them to him. She waited, hugging her coat closer around her, while Duke tried the ignition, without success.

"Did you turn on your interior light this morning?" he asked, his fingers reaching up over his head.

She thought for a moment. "Yes, I did. But—"

"Your battery's dead. I don't have a jumper cable with me."

She frowned at him. She was almost certain she'd turned off the light again. Almost. "What are you doing here, anyway?" she demanded.

"Meeting you off the train. I have something I want to discuss with you."

"I don't think there is anything you can say that could possibly interest me."

"You won't know that until you hear it."

She scowled at him. "Isn't this just a little bit too much of a coincidence?"

"It's important, Carol."

She didn't want to discuss anything with him. Nor did she want to stand around inside a freezing parking garage waiting for a repairman.

"I'll take you home in my car," Duke added, "and we can call a garage from there. I'll bring you back to pick up your car after we've had our discussion."

"How did you know where to find me?" She was stalling, knowing what her answer would be.

"Royce. He told me where you work and where you live. The rest was easy."

Carol turned away with a muttered curse. Would she never be free of the agency?

Duke climbed out of the car and handed her the keys. "My car's over there," he said, nodding his head at the black sedan at the far end of the garage.

A fresh gust of wind made up her mind for her. "All right," she said, starting toward the car, "but I don't listen well on an empty stomach. If you haven't already eaten, I have a chicken casserole in the fridge."

She couldn't believe she had actually invited him to dinner. Somehow her appetite seemed to have disappeared. The familiar fragrance of his cologne triggered memories she'd struggled too long to forget.

She gave him directions, then tried not to notice his hands on the wheel as he drove fast on the winding highway. The skin stretched smooth across his knuckles, and she felt a small quiver of remembered excitement at the image of his strong fingers caressing her naked skin.

In an effort to dispel the memories, she asked, "How have you been?"

He took the clichéd question seriously. "I'm doing okay. How about you?"

"Fine. Keeping busy at work. The holiday season is always an important one for us."

"Ah, yes. All those parties to get painted up for."

"Something like that. Are you still working for the agency?"

She didn't look at him, but kept her eyes firmly on the swishing beams of light ahead of her. Even so, she knew he'd glanced at her.

"No," he said, after a slight pause. "I'm in business for myself now."

"Oh?" She was almost afraid to ask.

She was surprised when he said, "I bought a garage. I should be opening up next week. It's in a good location, I think it'll do well. Word of mouth is always slow, but effective.''

''In Washington?''

''No, here in Connecticut. I always did like this neck of the woods. I live in Hartford.''

For some reason her heart had begun to pound. He lived less than two hours drive away. That was close. Much too close. ''What made you decide to leave the agency?''

''I'm not the man I was,'' Duke said dryly.

His words brought back all the doubts. She could hear his voice, husky and seductive in the cool, clear night air. *I love you,* he'd said. And he'd said it to Maila.

She shivered, unable to deal with the image of hungry flames and black smoke. She would have died with Duke in that inferno, if Maila had succeeded in her plan. Even so, the memory of the dark, expressive eyes and happy smile of the Maila she had known continued to haunt her nights.

She was glad when Duke parked the car in front of her condo. He followed her inside in silence, casting an appreciative eye around her comfortable living room.

After slipping out of her coat, she took his jacket from him and hung it in the closet. Looking back at him, she couldn't help thinking that her taste in French provincial furniture seemed a little fragile for the tall man seated on the blue-and-gray couch.

He stuck out his legs in front of him and leaned back carefully, as if afraid to soil the pastel fabric. The fingers of one hand drummed on the arm as he looked up at her. With a shock she realized he was nervous.

''Would you like a drink?'' she offered, deciding that she could use one. ''I have cognac, if you want to chase out the cold. Or would you prefer a beer?''

"I'll take the brandy." His gaze flicked across her face and away again, to rest intently on a Monet print on the wall behind her.

She poured a generous measure into each glass and carried them back to the elegant coffee table. "You'll find coasters in that drawer," she told him, and waited while he fished out a couple and laid them on the smooth, polished surface.

He took his glass from her and raised it in a salute. "To health and happiness."

She smiled, and dipped her lips into the burning liquid before setting the glass down. Her heart had begun pumping hard again. "All right," she said, not quite steadily, "what was it you wanted to discuss?" He looked up at her, his cool expression cutting her heart. "Aren't you going to sit down?"

"Is this going to take long?" She knew she sounded flippant. It was a way of covering up her sudden insecurity. She'd thought she'd come to terms with the way she felt about him. She'd thought she'd convinced herself that it was over. The ache in her heart warned her that she'd been wrong on both counts.

His eyes narrowed. "I'm keeping you from something?"

She sat down on the edge of the chair and reached for her glass again. It gave her something to do with her hands. "I just wondered if you were as hungry as I am."

He looked concerned. "I'm sorry. Go ahead and eat first. This can wait a while longer."

She shook her head. "I'd rather get this over with."

"Carol..." His voice trailed off as he shook his head, apparently at a loss for what to say next.

She was making it difficult for him. She couldn't seem to help it. Deciding to have it out with him, she blurted, "I'm sorry, but it's a little hard to know who I'm talking to here. I'm still not sure if you're Brandon or Mack."

A shadow crossed his face and then faded. "Neither," he said quietly. "They are dead. Both of them. I am Duke Winters. A different man in every way to either of them."

Her smile felt stiff, unnatural. "That's supposed to reassure me?"

He shrugged. "I don't know how to reassure you, other than tell you the truth. I want to start again. I want to start a new life."

He leaned forward and set his drink on the table, sloshing the liquid up the sides of the glass. When he looked up, she felt a jolt of hope at the anxiety in his eyes. "And I want to start it with you."

She remembered well that suffocating feeling. She'd felt it more than once when she'd been alone with him. But never more strongly than right now.

"I don't think—" she began slowly.

"Then don't. Don't think at all. Just listen, until I'm through, okay?"

She nodded, unable to think of any way past the slow flame burning behind his eyes.

"I have always wanted you, Carol, from the moment I first set eyes on you." He spread his fingers out, appearing to study the nails, but she knew he was looking back.

"I don't know what it was about you. I'd met beautiful women before, exciting, sexy, willing women before. But not one of them made my heart beat faster the way you did. I wanted so badly to take you in my arms, kiss you senseless and tell the world that I was claiming you for my own."

The hand holding her glass jerked, and she hastily raised it to her lips. She didn't want to hear this. She didn't want to be drawn into the fantasy again. Because that's all it was, a fantasy.

Duke sighed. "I couldn't of course. You belonged to Mack. My best friend. And you made it pretty obvious how you felt about him. But it didn't stop me wanting you."

His pause went on a little too long, and desperate to break the tension, Carol said quickly, "That was a long time ago."

"My feelings for you haven't changed. If anything, they're deeper and stronger now. What has changed is the man I am inside. I'm no longer a soldier of fortune living on the edge of the law. I'm an ordinary businessman, nothing else."

She had to smile. Whatever else he was, ordinary was not a term she would use to describe him.

He looked at her then, searing her with his intense gaze. "I want the chance to prove that to you, Carol. You owe me that chance. After everything we've been through together, you owe me."

She could feel herself drowning in the warmth of his words. She made one final attempt to save her sanity. Putting her glass down on the table, she made herself meet his eyes. "It wouldn't work between us, Duke. It couldn't. I would always wonder who you are. You were so alike, both of you so good at putting on an act, so smooth at lying. I never knew the man underneath. How can I believe what you're telling me?

"It would always be there, like a vicious little rat in a hole, just waiting for the opportunity to raise its ugly head and destroy whatever we had built between us."

"You can't just accept me as Duke, and forget the rest?"

She surged to her feet, unable to stay seated and fight the look in his eyes. "How can I?" She turned her back on him, struggling for the strength to resist him. It wouldn't work, she warned herself. It couldn't work. And the pain would be all the more intense for having tried and failed. "How could

I love you," she muttered, "knowing you could be the ma
who was once my husband?"

"What if I could convince you I wasn't Mack? Woul
that make a difference?"

She spun around, her heart accelerating when she saw hi
on his feet, a look of grim determination on his face.

"How—how do you intend to do that?"

He moved around the table and stepped toward her.

She wanted to back off, to run, to slam the door in h
face before he could tear her apart again, the way he did th
night he'd told Maila he loved her. Instead, she stood, sti
and unyielding, as he folded his arms around her and pulle
her closer.

"Did Mack ever make you feel like this?" He drew
gentle finger down the side of her cheek, then cupped he
chin and lowered his mouth to hers. His kiss was feathery
soft, brushing lightly across her tense lips until they sof
ened.

She kept her hands at her sides, fists balled, while h
tongue coaxed her mouth open. She tried to ignore the tin
shivers of excitement fanning out from deep inside.

Her tongue seemed to act of its own accord, sliding an
caressing against his in a slow, seductive duel until her ski
started to tingle.

He lifted his head, his eyes gleaming down at her. "Di
he do this?" He moved his hand down her arm until hi
thumb brushed her breast. "Or this?"

She could feel the strength draining from her as his han
traveled down her back until he could cup her buttocks
With a sharp movement he brought her hips up against his

"Or this?"

Heat spread rapidly through her body. He was hard an
more than ready for her. His fingers worked at the button
of her shirt, and she raised her hands to stop him. He ar

swered by covering her mouth with his, turning her faint protest into a helpless moan.

She allowed him to push the shirt from her shoulders and down her arms. Relaxing her hands, she let the garment fall to the floor. Her breath caught as he lowered his head to flick his tongue over the exposed curve of her breast.

"No—wait..."

"We've waited too long as it is. I don't want to waste any more time."

He slid his hands behind her back and unsnapped her bra. She was losing the game, and she knew it. With a groan she wound her arms around his neck and pulled his mouth down to her breast.

"That's better," he whispered against the tender skin, and she jerked her chin up.

She lost it all at once. In a frenzy of impatience she tore at his clothes, dragging them off him until he stood naked in front of her. She helped him shed the rest of hers, then wrapped her arms around his waist and pressed her lips to his chest.

Part of her mind registered that this was the first time she'd seen his naked body. She lowered her mouth down over his belly, enjoying his sharp indrawn breath. The salty taste of his skin as she caressed him with her tongue filled her with a burning excitement, heightened by the shudder that shook his body.

"God, that's incredible," he whispered, and closed his fingers in her hair.

She trembled from head to foot when she straightened and saw the blazing passion in his eyes.

"My turn," he whispered, and knelt in front of her.

Again and again she cried out, until he dragged her down on the soft carpet beside him. He pulled her on top of him, cushioning her as his mouth once more claimed hers in a fierce kiss that took her breath away.

Her mind spun in a crazy whirl of pleasure and pain. His teeth nipped her bottom lip, then he caressed it with his tongue. She felt his hands smoothing, stroking, and the pressure began building, pulsing inside her.

She wanted him as she'd never wanted anything in her life before. She knew he wasn't Mack. She had known it from the first moment he'd touched her.

She had refused to let herself be convinced of that. It had been a defense, a way of avoiding the fact that she'd fallen in love with Brandon Pierce. She knew that now. Just as she knew that it wasn't Brandon making love with her now. It was Duke. And she loved him so much she would die for him.

She felt his hands on her hips, lifting her onto him. The sensation jolted her, and she raised her chin sharply, echoing his groan.

Now she wanted to give back the pleasure. She straightened and began rocking, fighting to stay in control as his fingers roamed her breasts. Faster and faster, while his growls grew louder. His gaze locked with hers in a savage triumph of possession, then the desire spilled over, and she fought with him for release.

It came swiftly, in a tremendous rush of exquisite gratification. Panting, exhilarated, she lowered herself to his chest and relaxed.

For a little while he said nothing, and only the rise and fall of his chest beneath her ear indicated his spent passion. Finally he stirred, and wound his finger in her hair to pull it back from her face.

"Lady, you've been holding out on me."

She propped herself up on her elbows and grinned at him. "I have no idea what you mean."

"Oh? You mean I imagined that passionate tiger that just ade love to me?"

Wriggling her hips she said softly, "Does this feel like agination?"

He groaned and wrapped his arms around her to pull her outh down to his. "You'll make an old man of me," he hispered against her lips.

"Yeah. But what a way to go."

"I have one question, then we'll forget it, okay?"

For a moment she tensed, knowing what was coming. Okay."

"Are you convinced?"

For an answer she traced the outline of his mouth with her ngue, then fastened her lips to his. They were both reathless when she finally lifted her head.

"If that's a yes," Duke murmured, "I like it."

"That's a yes." She rolled off him and reached for his irt.

"We were never that much alike, you know." He sat up nd sorted through the pile of clothes for his jeans. "We ight have had similar looks and build, and I know we pied each other's gestures. That comes from years of a ry close association with each other. But we were very fferent in temperament."

Buttoning the shirt, she said carefully, "In what way?"

"Mack enjoyed his profession. I could see the excite-ent building in him whenever zero hour approached."

"I know." She smoothed her hair back with both hands. It would take him days to come down from a mission. e'd be moody and irritable, until he got another assign-ent. Then the cycle would start all over again."

A shudder rippled through her, chilling her. "I think it's ne I got dinner." She made a move to stand up, but he

grabbed her arm. The warmth in his eyes made her feel li
crying.

"I never believed in love," he said, stroking her arm wi
his thumb. "I didn't think I was capable of such deep em
tions. Until I met you. But you were in love with Mack. A
after you married him, I guess I gave up on myself again
turned my back on any kind of normal life, and I real
didn't care too much what happened to me."

"You never said anything. You never once gave me a
idea . . ."

"Would it have made a difference if I had?"

She looked down at her feet and wriggled her toes. "N
I guess not."

"Exactly. And I'd dealt with too much rejection in my li
to expose myself to more." He stood, pulling her up wi
him. "I've had a very long time to think about my lif
When you're lying flat on your back for months, there isn
much else to do. Even before the wreck I knew I didn't hav
the stomach for the job anymore. I knew there was no g
ing back to it. I intended to find the person responsibl
bring him to justice, then put the whole thing behind me.

"What would you have done if I had been the one r
sponsible?"

She saw his eyes harden for a moment. "I would ha
brought you in." His mouth curved in a rueful smile. "
guess I knew right from the start it couldn't be you. May
subconsciously, I was looking for an excuse to see y
again."

"And I think I knew all along, deep down, who yo
were."

"But you thought for a while I could be Mack."

"Not for long. You were right, Mack had never made m
feel the way you do. I just didn't want to think of you

Brandon. It was so hard to tell. Even Maila wasn't sure who
you were.''

"Maila must have known. She must have had the photo
that Ned took analyzed and compared, or else she couldn't
have been so sure who I was.''

She gave a start of surprise. "That's right, I'd forgotten
about that. Then why did she believe you could be Mack?''

"She was confused. In the stress of the moment it was
easy to throw her off balance, especially when I mentioned
her last night with Mack.''

"Yes," Carol said slowly, "I heard that. So how did you
know?''

Duke's smile seemed strained. "You said it yourself.
Mack told me everything. He told me about that last night
with Maila. I hate to say this, Carol, but I believed he did
love her, in his way.''

"As he never loved me. Maila was convinced he'd used
her. If he had loved her, she never knew it. But I don't understand. If he loved her, why did he fight so hard against
the divorce?''

"He knew he had no future with Maila. He had killed
Maila's brother. He knew she would find out. He knew that
before he went in. It didn't stop him, though.''

Carol shook her head. "I'll never be able to understand
what it was that drove him. I wonder if he ever really knew
what he wanted out of life.''

"He wanted a child. That's why he wanted to stay with
you. He chose you to give him a son.''

She felt a deep ache of regret. "Yes, I know that now.
Under the circumstances, I'm glad that we didn't have any.''
She hugged him closer, seeking comfort from his closeness.
His arms felt good wrapped around her, making her feel
safe and warm. For the first time in a very long time, she felt
secure, and content.

"It would have been easy to prove who I was," Duke said sounding just a little smug.

Her eyes narrowing in suspicion, she looked up at him "What do you mean?"

His smile teased her. "Wait a minute."

He let her go, and mystified, she watched him turn hi back on her, then dip his head into his palm. When h turned back, she caught her breath. His eyes were no longe the dark brown she'd become accustomed to. They wer light gold. The clear, intense eyes of Brandon Pierce.

"Contacts," she said, wondering how she could hav forgotten. "I thought about it once, then with everythin, that happened, it went out of my head." She frowned up a him. "Why didn't you do that earlier?"

"It was more fun my way."

"That was sneaky."

His smile faded. "I wanted the chance to make love t you. I wanted to prove to you that what you feel for me ha nothing to do with who I was then, but who I am now."

Once more he gathered her close, brushing her lips wit. his in a soft kiss. "I want the chance to show you that Duk Winters is a very different man from Brandon Pierce. Yes terday is gone, let's bury it where it belongs and look for ward to all our tomorrows together. I badly want thos tomorrows, Carol, but they'll mean nothing without you.'

She wanted them, too. He loved her, and that was enoug for her. Together they could make the tomorrows every thing he wanted them to be, and more.

"Kiss me," she said, and closed her eyes.

*   *   *   *   *

For all those readers who've been looking for something a little bit different, a little bit spooky, let Silhouette Books take you on a journey to the dark side of love with

SILHOUETTE Shadows™

If you like your romance mixed with a hint of danger, a taste of something eerie and wild, you'll love Shadows. This new line will send a shiver down your spine and make your heart beat faster. It's full of romance and more—and some of your favorite authors will be featured right from the start. Look for our four launch titles wherever books are sold, because you won't want to miss a single one.

THE LAST CAVALIER—Heather Graham Pozzessere
WHO IS DEBORAH?—Elise Title
STRANGER IN THE MIST—Lee Karr
SWAMP SECRETS—Carla Cassidy

After that, look for two books every month, and prepare to tremble with fear—and passion.

SILHOUETTE SHADOWS, coming your way in March.

 *Silhouette*®

SHAD1

INTIMATE MOMENTS®
Silhouette®

CONARD COUNTY

CONTINUES...

Come back to Conard County, Wyoming, where you'll
meet men and women whose lives are as dramatic as
the landscape around them. Join author Rachel Lee for
the third book in her fabulous series, MISS EMMALINE
AND THE ARCHANGEL (IM #482). Meet Emmaline Conard,
"Miss Emma," a woman who was cruelly tormented
years ago and now is being victimized again. But this
time sheriff's investigator Gage Dalton—the man they
call hell's own archangel—is there to protect her. But
who will protect Gage from his feelings for Emma? Look
for their story in March, only from Silhouette Intimate
Moments.

To order your copy of MISS EMMALINE AND THE ARCHANGEL, or the first two Conard County
titles, EXILE'S END (IM #449) and CHEROKEE THUNDER (IM #463), please send your name,
address, zip or postal code, along with a check or money order (do not send cash) for $3.39
for each book ordered, plus 75¢ postage and handling ($1.00 in Canada), payable to Silhouette
Books, to:

In the U.S.	In Canada
Silhouette Books	Silhouette Books
3010 Walden Avenue	P.O. Box 609
P.O. Box 1396	Fort Erie, Ontario
Buffalo, NY 14269-1396	L2A 5X3

Please specify book title(s) with your order.
Canadian residents add applicable federal and provincial taxes.

CON3

SPRING FANCY

Three bachelors, footloose
and fancy-free... until now!

Spring into romance with three
fabulous fancies by three of
Silhouette's hottest authors:

ANNETTE BROADRICK
LASS SMALL
KASEY MICHAELS

When spring fancy strikes, no man is immune!

Look for this exciting new short-story collection
in March at your favorite retail outlet.

Only from

Silhouette®

SF93

where passion lives.

AMERICAN HERO

It seems readers can't get enough of these men—and we don't blame them! When Silhouette Intimate Moments' best authors go all-out to create irresistible men, it's no wonder women everywhere are falling in love. And look what—and who!—we have in store for you early in 1993.

January brings NO RETREAT (IM #469), by Marilyn Pappano. Here's a military man who brings a whole new meaning to macho!

In February, look for IN A STRANGER'S EYES (IM #475), by Doreen Roberts. Who is he—and why does she feel she knows him?

In March, it's FIREBRAND (IM #481), by Paula Detmer Riggs. The flames of passion have never burned this hot before!

And in April, look for COLD, COLD HEART (IM #487), by Ann Williams. It takes a mother in distress and a missing child to thaw this guy, but once he melts...!

AMERICAN HEROES. YOU WON'T WANT TO MISS A SINGLE ONE—ONLY FROM

IMHER03N

INTIMATE MOMENTS® ™ Silhouette®

What a year for romance!

Silhouette has five fabulous romance collections coming your way in 1993. Written by popular Silhouette authors, each story is a sensuous tale of love and life—as only Silhouette can give you!

SPRING FANCY

Three bachelors are footloose and fancy-free...until now.
(March)

to Mother with Love

Heartwarming stories that celebrate the joy of motherhood.
(May)

SILHOUETTE SUMMER Sizzlers

Put some sizzle into your summer reading with three of Silhouette's hottest authors.
(June)

SILHOUETTE Shadows

Take a walk on the dark side of love—with tales just perfect for those misty autumn nights.
(October)

Silhouette Christmas Stories

Share in the joy of yuletide romance with four award-winning Silhouette authors.
(November)

 **Silhouette®**

A romance for all seasons—it's always time for romance with Silhouette!

PROM93

**Silhouette Books
is proud to present
our best authors,
their best books...
and the best in
your reading pleasure!**

Throughout 1993, look for exciting books
by these top names in contemporary
romance:

CATHERINE COULTER—
Aftershocks in February

FERN MICHAELS—
Whisper My Name in March

DIANA PALMER—
Heather's Song in March

ELIZABETH LOWELL—
Love Song for a Raven in April

SANDRA BROWN
(previously published under
the pseudonym Erin St. Claire)—
Led Astray in April

LINDA HOWARD—
All That Glitters in May

When it comes to passion,
we wrote the book.

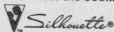

BOBT1R